night of
wenceslas

night of wenceslas

by LIONEL DAVIDSON

PERENNIAL LIBRARY
Harper & Row, Publishers
New York, Cambridge, Philadelphia, San Francisco
London, Mexico City, São Paulo, Sydney

To Vlasta

who kissed and told first

NIGHT OF WENCESLAS. Copyright © 1960 by Lionel Davidson. All rights
reserved. Printed in the United States of America. No part of this book may
be used or reproduced in any manner whatsoever without written permission
except in the case of brief quotations embodied in critical articles and
reviews. For information address Harper & Row, Publishers, Inc., 10 East
53rd Street, New York, N.Y. 10022.

First PERENNIAL LIBRARY edition published 1982.

ISBN: 0-06-080595-1

82 83 84 85 10 9 8 7 6 5 4 3 2 1

chapter 1

The Little Swine had his head well down in the books when I went in, so it was clear Miss Vosper had forestalled me after all. I had been popping up and down half the day to peer through the frosted glass of his door, and she wouldn't miss a thing like that.

He kept his head down religiously—usually he'd have a quick blink up to see who it was—and after a couple of minutes I shuffled my feet and coughed somewhat aggressively.

He looked up then, pretending his rather charming "tired" double-take and said, "Yes, Nicolas?" He kept his finger ostentatiously on the line.

"I'd like a word with you if you're not too busy." I'd promised myself I wouldn't say the last bit, and to salve my pride added loudly, "It's important."

"If it's important it won't wait," said the Little Swine humorously, and he carefully jotted down his last figure and pushed the ledger back an inch. "What can I do for you, Nicolas?"

"It's about money," I said, taking the seat he hadn't offered. I used to sit in it as a little boy waiting for my father. The Little Swine had been junior partner then. "I just can't manage on seven quid a week."

The Little Swine stared at me disbelievingly. "A young man with no responsibilities can't make seven pounds last seven days? What are you telling me, Nicolas? A postman with a family manages on very little more."

"Well, I can't. When I've paid for my digs and fares I've got about fifty bob left. I've got to buy clothes and—and entertainment, taking a girl out occasionally. . . ."

1

The Little Swine was shaking his head. "What new clothes, Nicolas? You got yourself a fine rig-out when you left the army. I myself buy a new suit only once in three years. It's the car, Nicolas. At the time I told you—a certain liability, unjustifiable extravagance. Do I have a car?"

He waited for me to speak, smiling, knowing in his swinish little way that he'd cobbled me, and when I didn't, said, "Nicolas, be a good boy and try just for once to follow my advice. You're a boy twenty-four—all right, a man then! When you've learned the business thoroughly you'll take up your full duties as a partner. This talk of jobs and rises is undignified in your position. You're getting spending money—a very handsome allowance— while you learn the business. Do you think you're worth even seven pounds a week to the business at the moment?"

He paused again with his hands outstretched and a whimsical smile on his face. I knew he'd tell me all this and Maura had told me what to reply, but for the life of me I couldn't sort the answers out. The Little Swine had known me all my life. His younger sister had been my nanny. He'd come into this room one day when I'd wet the chair. I even used to call him Uncle Karel—it still slipped out sometimes.

I said glumly, "All I know is I can't manage. I'm borrowing all the time and I'm in debt."

"Debts? Who are you in debt to?"

There was a bill for £7 16s. outstanding at the garage for the past four months.

"Various people," I said. "I even had to borrow a fiver from my mother a few weeks ago."

"You should not borrow from your mother," the Little Swine said reproachfully. "You know I would always lend you the money. It is too bad to worry her. How is the sweet lady?"

"She's all right." Maminka lived in Bournemouth, and I knew I had really borrowed the money from old Imre, who lived in the same private hotel; she would merely ask him for a loan until I had repaid it.

"It is so long since I have seen her," the Little Swine said sadly. "With business so hard to find I have not had a moment for years to go and pay her a visit. Is she still so beautiful?"

"Yes," I said truthfully. She was.

2

"And Mr. Gabriel? His lungs?" the Little Swine inquired delicately.

"Imre's all right." There was nothing wrong with Imre's lungs. He had been in love with my mother for years and his supposed enfeeblement gave him an excuse to live in Bournemouth, too. He ran a small stamp business from the hotel.

"I must go down to see them. I will try next month after the audit."

He looked as if he meant it, so I said hastily, "She lives in the past a great deal, you know." She had always treated the Little Swine in a very condescending manner (his first job had been sweeping the floor in her father's glassworks) and had got it into her head that he was merely superintending the business until I wished to take it over.

The Little Swine took the point, but he said, "And what a past! You would hardly remember Prague, of course, but your mother was the uncrowned queen, I assure you. An enchanting lady. It is no wonder she prefers to think of those days."

He sat there with a rather lingering smile on his face, no doubt well satisfied at the changes in their respective fortunes, until he recollected himself and drew the ledger back. "Well, Nicolas, we must not think of the past, but of the present and the future. There is a good one waiting for you as soon as you settle down and take an interest. Meanwhile, get rid of the car, my boy, and you will find you have money to spare."

He gave me a little nod, and automatically I stood up. I was outside his office before I realized I'd got nothing out of him. Nothing at all. No promises. No half promises. Nothing I could tax him with, even in my own mind. I didn't know what I was going to tell Maura.

My face must have been so glum that Miss Vosper, drawing her own conclusions, tried hard to suppress her hideous delight and began sticking stamps with her enormous gargoyle tongue.

"I've stamped all yours," she said with her unique leprous smile, "and checked the stamp book. It was only out ninepence this week."

"Right." The single word must have sounded so bitter that she turned her head to conceal a smile. The suppression seemed to release a gust of her special odor, and a cloud of it wafted toward me. I blew my nose hard.

"Is Mr. Nimek free now?" she asked, almost giggling.

"Yes."

She stood up with her notebook and paused over my desk for a moment so that I was almost choked and had to turn my head away. "He's been a thorough tartar all the week."

The idea of the Little Swine as a tartar was so singular that when she went I stared after her. Miss Vosper had been with him seventeen years; ample time to see him as he was. This new vision of him rivaled in lunacy only her demoniac hatred of me, the interloper, the young toff, the threat from the past.

My father had started this business, an Englishman who had worked for years in Prague where he had met and married my mother. He had set up the English end as a selling outlet for the Bohemian glassworks just before I was born, and had sent Karel Nimek, the Little Swine, over to look after it. The Germans took over the glassworks in 1938 and the London importing firm became the main business.

My father had died of cancer in 1941, having made over most of his shares to the Little Swine. He had not got much for them, for the main assets of the business consisted in a claim for compensation after the war. But he had left me thirty per cent, and had come to an agreement with the Little Swine that I was to be allowed to establish parity with him in our respective shareholdings when I left university and had received a grounding in the business. He had then bought my mother an annuity, settled a sum for my education, and had died confident the agreement would be honored.

Why he expected the Little Swine to honor so vague an undertaking I had never known. In effect he had put the Little Swine on his honor. A chancy thing to do. Since coming out of the army nearly a year before, I had been the general dogsbody of the office. My shares meant nothing, since he had never distributed any profits. Seven quid a week.

It was just on five—another hour to go before the office closed. I didn't think I could stand it a moment longer. I picked up my mac and the letters and walked out.

The liftman hated to come up two floors to take down-passengers, so I leaned on the bell till he did so. He came up white

4

and shaking and silent with rage and, cheered a little by this, I rode down and walked out into the street and as far as the Princess May before realizing I had forgotten to post the letters. I slipped them into my pocket and went into the saloon instead.

"Bitter?" Jack said.

I had been going to say Scotch, but thought better of it and nodded.

Jack pulled it. "What's up with you?" he said. "Lost your granny?"

I said, "Aa-ach," and took an enormous swallow of beer. "It's a bloody life," I said.

He stood leaning against the bar, amused. "Got the sack?"

"No such luck."

"Women?"

"No."

"Car broke down again?"

"It's the only thing that hasn't."

"Here," he said, "that reminds me." He groped in a cubbyhole behind the till and brought out the back of a cigarette packet with markings on it. "A customer wants to buy an old M.G. You thinking of selling?"

I started to say no, automatically, and changed my mind. "How much is he prepared to pay?"

"He'd go up to two hundred for what he wants."

"Cash?"

Jack scrutinized the card. "He didn't say. He looked as if he could afford it. You interested?"

"I might be. You'd better take my phone number in case he looks in again."

I wrote it for him on the cigarette packet and he returned it to the cubbyhole.

I couldn't afford another, so I left, feeling more dolorous than ever at the idea of giving up the car.

I thought about the car all the way home. I thought I might as well pick it up from the lockup in case the chap did want to come and see it over the weekend. This was not such a simple operation, for the rat-faced proprietor of the garage had been growing definitely old-fashioned toward me of recent weeks, demanding payment in full before I took the car out again.

I still had the key, however.

It was now just after six and the garage would be shut. I thought it was worth a try. My spirits rose a little when I saw the drive-in deserted, for the proprietor sometimes monkeyed around for half an hour at the front. They fell again when I turned into the alley and the lockups. His daughter, a solitary child of ten or eleven, was dancing about in some hopscotch squares. She ran off the moment she saw me.

I unlocked the door, pulled out the M.G. and was just relocking when Ratface appeared.

"Good evening," I said.

"Were you thinking of paying off your bill?"

"I'm afraid I've not brought very much money out with me."

"Well, you can just push that car back and give me the key. I'm not interested in promises or excuses. There's ten hours' work gone into that car in addition to the petrol feed, the carburetor and the gaskets. I don't mind letting you run on a bit with your lockup rent, but I've come to the end of my patience. Pay up or the car stays here."

Silently I reached for my wallet and scrutinized the contents. Six pounds ten in notes; payday. "I could let you have a couple on account," I said.

"I've told you. I want the lot."

"I'm very sorry, Mr. Rickett. I just haven't got it. I've been trying to get the money for you."

"Well, try a bit harder," he said. His face had gone pale with passion and his little pointed head was down dangerously as though he meant to savage me. "I don't want to be hard," he said after a moment, relaxing a little, and no doubt realizing that some was better than none. "You can take it if you pay half now and your word that I get the rest by the end of next week."

Half was nearly four pounds. That meant no rent for Mrs. Nolan. Or no lunches for me, and no dates with Maura. I suddenly remembered that I was supposed to be seeing her tonight. The thought momentarily distracted me so much that I gave him the four pounds. I made one last stand. "Would you mind shoving a couple of gallons in? I think I'm rather low."

He looked at me and something that could have been a smile

crossed his rat face. "Well, you're cool, I must say," he said. But he seemed so taken with the coolness that he actually unlocked the pump and let me have a gallon. "There's one," he said, "to get you off the premises."

He stood and watched me with the same smile on his face as I backed down the alley, and this tribute to my coolness, added to the pleasure of taking over the wheel, raised my spirits instantly. I backed into the road, pulled her round in two cool, snappy movements, and actually waved to him as I shot up the road. He did not return the wave.

This aged, red, strap-bound M.G. was my most important possession and if not, in fact, actually priceless, certainly represented to me more than it could possibly fetch. The week before I had bought it I had been unable to think of anything else. There were many things I should have thought of, like getting a flat and some furniture.

One of the troubles was that I had not known what I wanted to do. If the vague haven of the business had not been awaiting me for several years, maybe I would have exerted myself in some direction. As it was I was lazy, unable to project any alternative to Maminka's vision of the glorious future that awaited me.

Maminka's idea of the business was so grotesque that it embarrassed me to hear her talk about it. In my father's day, certainly, it had been a little more attractive—the office had occupied the whole floor, and somewhere in the East End there had been a large warehouse. Since then the Czech glass imports had dried up and the Little Swine had gone in for sidelines. He was now running a rudimentary two-room organization that suited him perfectly.

All through university and the army, on the infrequent trips I had made to see the Little Swine, the business had grown smaller and tattier, and his increasing joviality—"Well, Nicolas, we will soon be ordering your desk"—had depressed me more and more. In the event he hadn't even done that; I took over the desk of a clerk he sacked.

I had never known if this was all part of some deep-rooted scheme of the Little Swine's to make the future so unattractive

7

that I would opt out of it or if his affairs had not merely become with the years a more faithful expression of his personality; whatever it was, the prospect of settling in for life with him held no enchantment.

It was in this frame of mind that I first clapped eyes on the car, pointing her nose out of a secondhand lot. *£130. Nippy. Snip,* the whitewash said. I had £170. I was going to see a flat whose tenant wanted £120 for his furniture. I walked up to the corner and round it and stopped to light a cigarette, and then I walked slowly back.

A man in a dirty white coat nodded at me and smiled. "Saw you looking at her. Knew you'd be back. A beaut, ain't she? Cock your leg over and sit in her."

I cocked my leg over the low door and sat behind the wheel.

"Grab hold. Tight as a drum."

The steering was beautifully tight. (It did not, alas, remain so.)

"There," he said. "Buzz off to China if you want now." He walked away and left me with the car, and I sat there looking along the bonnet, and I was hooked. That tremulous moment before I was committed, when I knew I could afford the car or the flat but not both, was the most poignant of my life. I saw myself traveling light, sun-dappled roads, sea glitter, free, free as a bird; no young man of affairs with a valise, as Maminka saw me; no young chair-wetter to be schooled in a little, dreary, bloody business; quite a new vision I had never seen before; another, pleasanter, very agreeable identity.

"She's taxed to the end of the year," the man said, coming back. "Souped up, of course. Take a decko if you like." He opened up the bonnet. A lethal-looking supercharger winked in the sun. "Goes like a bomb and steady as a train."

I walked back to Paddington in a trance, without looking at the flat, and took the train to Bournemouth and leaned out the window, seeing the car all the way.

I bought it a week later, sick with relief at finding it still there.

In terms of hard cash it might not have been the keenest bargain of my life; in all other terms it was certainly so. It was

8

still the chink in the grimy barriers building up round me; still, in a way, my defense against Maura. The thought of selling it made me feel sick.

I slowed at the corner and tooled along to number seventy-four rather slowly, listening to a peculiar sort of rattle from the clutch every time I changed gear. This was something new. I wondered if Ratface had been tinkering with it, whether he'd been tinkering with it all along so that he'd have to repair it, but after a moment of viciousness dismissed the idea. He wasn't a bad Ratface at heart; this last was only one of a series of bills he had let me run up. By the sound of the clutch—a fiver's worth, I thought—I'd be owing him a bit more soon.

I drew in to the curb, let myself into the house, walked up the three flights. There was a note stuck under the plant on the plush tablecloth. It was in Mrs. Nolan's indelible pencil and read:

> *Mr. Whistler. Your young lady phoned. She said she phoned your office at 5:30. Will you ring her at home when you get in.* L. NOLAN.

I thought Maura could wait a bit. I hung up my mac and went out to the bathroom for a wash and came back and smoked a cigarette, sitting on the divan with my feet up on the edge of the coverlet. I wondered what I was going to tell Maura.

I had known her only for six months, but already, it seemed, for a lifetime. She was Irish, redheaded, and she had digs in a square off Gloucester Road, not far away. It was Maura who had given the Little Swine his sobriquet, and she who had maneuvered me into today's confrontation. Maura said the position was ridiculous. She said I was either a partner or I wasn't. She said anyone with thirty per cent of the firm's shares should count for something. She said the business must be making *some* profits, and where were they?

I had not even got round to that one with the Little Swine.

Even worse than her constant preoccupation with the Little Swine was her mania about my Uncle Bela. Bela was my mother's brother. He had emigrated to Canada several years before the war and now lived in Vancouver. He had never

9

married and on a trip to England to see Maminka after we had arrived from Czechoslovakia, he had told her I would be his heir.

Any family such as mine with European connections and relatives who have emigrated have figures such as Bela. I had a hazy recollection of a large, asthmatic man always supposed by my father to be excessively mean. It was a fact that he had never helped Maminka in any way, and the only present he had ever given her was a rather flashy zircon brooch which she never wore.

Bela's name was seldom absent for long from my mother's lips; she took it for granted that he would leave me at least a dollar millionaire, and her only hinted criticism was that he had not already settled the money on me.

It was probably because he had entered Maminka's mythology more than anything else that made me regard Uncle Bela as a somewhat dubious prop. She wrote to him regularly and I knew that she managed to contrive some mention of me in every letter. As he seemed to take equal pains never to refer to me in his infrequent and curiously uninformative replies, it seemed obvious he had regretted his earlier impulse. He operated a cannery and the only reference he ever made to his financial affairs was his annual comment that the fruit was very poor and very expensive.

Although Maura had never met my mother, she seemed equally credulous about Bela, and infinitely more annoying. Moreover, she knew the true state of my affairs and regarded my reluctance to solicit his help as the sheerest idiocy. In self-defense I had had to turn Uncle Bela into a joke—the ship that was going to come in, the treble chance that was going to turn up one day. I had built him up into such an unlikely shadow that, maddeningly, I was beginning to share their superstitious belief in him.

The cigarette burned down and I stubbed it out and reluctantly left the divan and went downstairs to the phone. Maura answered instantly.

"It's Nicolas," I said.

"Well?"

"Well, what?" I said irritated.

She made a little kiss down the phone and said, "What happened this afternoon? Did you see him?"

"Yes."

"You left early. I wondered if you'd had a row."

"No row." Mrs. Nolan came out of her lair behind me, and I thought I might as well put across the same news item to both parties, so I said quickly, "Look, Maura, I've had to pay a bill on the car and I haven't a sausage left this week. I can't afford to buy a bottle for tonight."

"Oh, Nicolas. You can bring a bottle of beer. They brought one to my party—"

"I can't even afford a bottle of beer," I said loudly. "I'm flat broke. I'll have to do without lunches for a couple of days. I'd better not come tonight."

Maura seemed to latch on that this was intended for another, for she said without concern, "Do you want me to leave five bob at the pub?"

"No."

"All right. I'll see you there. What did he say?"

"All right, then. Good-by." I hung up quickly. You had to be quick.

Mrs. Nolan was standing behind me, listening.

"I wonder that young lady wants to go out with you the way you treat her so sharply on the phone," she said.

I smiled at her wanly. "I'm worried about money, Mrs. Nolan."

"No rent for me this week, I suppose," she said with her own curious tone of winsome aggressiveness.

I said stoutly, "You know I wouldn't dream of letting you down with the rent, Mrs. Nolan. I'll just have to borrow it elsewhere."

"Oh, I don't mind you, ducky," she said. "It's the others. Don't you mention it or they'll all be going off to buy cars." She gave my arm a little push to show she meant no harm. "And you go off to that party tonight or someone else'll be after your young lady, and then we shall be sad. I've got a bottle of port you can take."

I followed her into the kitchen and accepted the bottle of British port she handed me from the fridge. She always kept one in this curious place.

"Don't you run off now," she said. "Dinner's in ten minutes. A nice bit of fish for Friday, same as your mother'd give you."

She said this every Friday. I had never understood what she meant by it.

I walked to the party to save petrol, still wondering what to tell Maura. I was twenty-four and she twenty-one; we had no claim on each other but increasingly in recent weeks the feeling had grown that if only I exerted myself with the Little Swine, or with Bela, or with the economic world at large—in a word, began to make something of myself—we could have some claim on each other.

This had induced a feeling of profound inadequacy. To make up for it I pressed home my somewhat decorous and well-signaled advances with greater desperation. I seemed to be making some progress here.

I heard the gramophone thumping out and turned in at the gate. The chap who was giving the party opened the door to me and cried, "It's Nicky. Come in, you terror of the City." Nobody else called me Nicky, and I disliked it and him. His name was Val and he worked in a film publicity business and lived with an aging model called Audrey. It always embarrassed me to be with them.

"What's this?" he said, breaking into laughter as he examined the bottle I had been clutching grimly. "Port-type wine, for God's sake. You City barons! Can't let it alone, can you? Bung it in the bowl, there's a good lad. It'll help out with the cup. In the kitchen," he said as the doorbell rang again.

I did as he bade and returned to the drawing room as he was introducing the two newcomers. He stopped to call attention to me. "And this type slipped in while I wasn't looking. Cheer up, Nicky. Boris Karloff will kick the bucket soon." He always called Uncle Bela by this name, and it was always good for a laugh. I had encouraged this, and did so now by crying in a cracked voice, "You'll be glad you knew me yet."

I could see Maura frowning at the other end of the room— she did not care for jokes about Uncle Bela—and I kept out of her way. By judicious shifting of position I was able to do so for most of the evening, and when we at last stood in the hall mak-

12

ing our farewells she seemed needled.

Her lips were tight as I took her arm and cut through the dark squares to her digs.

"So you didn't get the rise?" she said at last.

"I'm seeing him again next week."

"That seems satisfactory to you, does it?"

The dark seat under the tree where, all being well, I should make continued progress, was fifty yards away. I said somberly, "He wants to consider it. He agrees I'm in a special position. You've got to admit the prospects are good."

"Did you mention about the profits?"

"Yes," I said doggedly.

The pale blur of her face turned to me in the dark, but she said nothing.

We were at the seat now. "Like to take the weight off?" I said heavily.

"Do you mind if we don't, Nicolas? I'm terribly tired tonight."

"Oh."

"I've had rather a headache all day—worrying about you. You don't mind if I just go to bed?"

"No. Yes," I said dully.

Her hand touched my face for a moment. "I'll sit and smoke a cigarette with you if you like."

"No, you'd better go off to bed. I thought you were looking a bit washed out," I said.

"Well, I am," she said tartly.

"Right. I'll see you to the gate."

We walked the rest of the way in silence.

"Good night, Nicolas," she said, when we got there.

"Good night."

"On Sunday, then."

"Yes." If you're lucky, I thought bravely, walking off right away. But I knew I'd be seeing her on Sunday.

I shoved the covers over the car when I got back and let myself in and went up the three flights and undressed and crawled in, more inadequate than I'd felt for weeks. I tried to imagine myself at the wheel of the car, sun-drappled roads, sea glitter, free as a bird, but it seemed to be a different person I was watching.

13

Uncle Bela, I mouthed silently at the ceiling. *Why don't you just quietly die?* And presently he died on the ceiling in his big bed in Vancouver. The noisy asthmatic room grew silent, the smooth white sheets were still over the dome of his stomach. I bent over Uncle Bela and his pale jowl was slack in the moonlight, the mouth open like the fish on the draining board because it was Friday, and on Friday I had to see the Little Swine. The Little Swine's face was calm on the pillow in the moonlight, but always dangerous and now pallid and ratlike as he said I couldn't have it unless I paid half. So I paid him half, and there were thousands more in the wallet because I'd filled it from the dome, and I sat in the seat and backed down the alley and turned in two cool and snappy movements and then I was there, there in long-breathing rhythmical movements, there on the sun-dappled road, caressing the wheel, so warm and smooth, so warm and smooth where the stocking ended.

When I awoke in the morning the first thing I thought of was how I'd willed Uncle Bela to die and I lay there, slightly sick. Not much lower now, I thought. I'd have to do something about myself; frittering away the weeks and the months and the years. I rolled out of bed and into a dressing gown and into the bathroom.

I couldn't get it out of my head, however, about Uncle Bela, and my haunted look in the mirror frightened me. I had never been to Vancouver. I had never seen anyone die. And yet the details were horribly clear; the sudden cessation of the asthmatic breathing, the shape of the white sheets draped round his stomach; an entity of stillness and death. My eyes stared back at me superstitiously, and to banish the vision I began to scrub and towel with great vigor.

Saturday was eggs, and by saying "Eggs, *eggs!*" to myself in varying tones of wonder as I dressed I was able to cry, "Ready, Mrs. Nolan!" with a fair counterfeit of enthusiasm as I filed briskly into the dining room.

I nodded briefly to the three others already eating, sorted out my newspaper and mail from the pile on the sideboard and took my seat, which was just as well.

The moment I clapped eyes on the long white envelope, a pang went through me. The postmark was S.W.1. I turned it

14

this way and that, extraordinarily reluctant to open it. I had a desire to run with it into the kitchen and stuff it unopened in Mrs. Nolan's boiler.

All in all, such a course might have saved me a great deal of trouble. No night for me then on the Vaclavske Namesti; no dalliance by the terraces of Barrandov; no knowledge of the poor morals of Vlasta Simenova, the girl with the bomb-shaped breasts.

Some current of preknowledge must have vibrated through my frame. But I suppressed the urge to run to Mrs. Nolan's boiler. I opened the envelope and read the letter and watched my hands begin to tremble.

It was a short letter and I read it four times. It said:

Dear Sir,
   With regard to the estate of the late Mr. Bela Janda, I should be glad if you would telephone this office to arrange an early appointment.
                    Yours faithfully,
                    STEPHEN CUNLIFFE

chapter 2

"Two for you 'cos you sound hungry," Mrs. Nolan said, coming in with the eggs at this moment. She gazed at me and began shuffling about with her wig in some confusion. "Something the matter with me?"

I must have been gaping at her with rigid eyes, and now hastily averted them.

"Bad news?" Mrs. Nolan asked.

I licked my lips.

"Is it your mother?"

"No, no."

"Lost your job?"

"It's my late uncle. He's dead."

Mrs. Nolan pulled out a chair and sat down beside me. To prevent her embarrassing condolences I quickly handed her the letter, which she read at a distance.

"I'm very sorry indeed, Mr. Whistler. This'll be from the solicitor, I suppose?"

I looked at the letter again. The stationery was severely plain with the name Cunliffe & Co. in small black type in the left-hand corner. "I suppose so."

"Did you know him very well?"

"I hardly knew him at all. He lived in Canada."

"Well," said Mrs. Nolan sensibly, after a pause, "it's a bit upsetting all the same, I suppose. I'll get you a cup of strong tea."

She did so and I took the scalding draft down in one enormous mouthful that brought tears streaming down my cheeks. Mrs. Nolan blew her nose and asked the others, who had been gazing at me with religious respect, to leave the room. They trooped out with embarrassed alacrity muttering furtive condolences, and she followed them.

The moment they had gone, unable to contain myself, I sprang up and executed a brief, lunatic dance of joy around the table. Bad news? *Bad* news? Even Mrs. Nolan, that splendid creature, who could read between the lines of a lawyer's letter like anybody, had felt compelled to treat it with sad respect.

I dropped into a chair and read the letter again, very soberly. There was something so exactly right about the "late Mr. Bela Janda" that I was surprised I had not thought of him in this way before. The late Mr. Bela Janda was all right; he had spent the long years well and prudently, consolidating his assets and preparing to be late, and I told him so now, in a low mutter, nodding to his name on the letter.

Mrs. Nolan popped her head in as I sat muttering to the letter and quickly popped out again, and presently I ate my two eggs, taking only the yolks and leaving the whites with luxurious abandon.

This state of controlled hysteria lasted till I was up in my room again. There I could only bounce up and down on the divan, smoking one cigarette after another and waiting until it was time to phone this Stephen Cunliffe.

It was an address in Francis Street, Victoria, and I went bounding up the steep and narrow stairs like the long-lost heir coming to claim his inheritance, a proper way to bound in the circumstances.

I had spoken to Cunliffe's secretary on the phone and had learnt he would not be in till half past eleven. Mrs. Nolan had lent me another bottle of British port to while away the time and had seemed to find my request perfectly in order.

There had been some difficulty in starting the car, for in addition to its other ills, the battery had gone flat; but by almost kicking it to pieces in my excitement I had found a spark of life.

Cunliffe's secretary, a rather severe-sounding female with a slight foreign accent, had asked me to bring along the letter and my birth certificate, passport and any other documents to establish identity, and I had these in my hand as I knocked on the frosted glass door marked *Inquiries* and went in.

17

It was a small, very tidy room with a big ticking clock on the mantelpiece, a desk and a few files. Nobody was in the room. I closed the door behind me and shuffled my feet. An inner door opened a few inches and a woman whose middle-parting gave her face the appearance of a hot cross bun said severely, "In just one moment." She left the door open and I heard a mutter of voices for half a minute before she came out.

"My name is Nicolas Whistler. Mr. Cunliffe—"

"Yes, yes. I spoke to you on the telephone. You have the letter and other papers?"

I handed them over and she glanced at the letter before disappearing into the other room again. "Please sit down one moment, Mr. Whistler," she said over her shoulder. "Mr. Cunliffe will see you right away."

If not a damned sight quicker, I thought, somewhat irritated by this middle-parted popping in and out and suppressing a gust of gaseous British port. Bunface, it seemed to me, was treating the young master in far too officious a manner. A little servile bowing and scraping would have been perfectly in order here.

I was still brooding over this when a chair scraped in the next room and Bunface came out, her face now wearing something like a smile. "It was necessary to establish . . ." she murmured before I was in the room and facing Cunliffe.

I had to look twice to see if he was not hiding himself somewhere, for the Cunliffe I had imagined was a huge, lantern-jawed, gimlet-eyed character who might or might not have worn his hanging-judge wig during our interview. This one was practically a midget, a little dolly of a man who walked forward with quick, perfect miniature steps to take my hand in his two.

"Mr. Whistler?" he said, in a voice so deep and gravelly that I looked down at him in astonishment. "I am pleased to make your acquaintance. Take a seat."

I sat down, still unable to take my eyes off him.

"Cigarette?"

I took one from his full-sized gold case and watched with fascination as he lit one for himself and blew out a stream of smoke. There was an extra-large, emphatic quality in every gesture and for a moment I had the uncanny feeling I was watching a performance by some master ventriloquist who would shortly reveal himself.

18

"I should like to express my condolences on your bereavement," he said. "You didn't know your uncle very well, I understand?"

"No. I only met him once, actually." I was suddenly aware of his foreign accent; the shock of his appearance and voice hadn't made it register.

"I knew him very well indeed. A fine man. He had a heart attack on Wednesday afternoon and died the same evening."

"I never knew."

"No," he said dryly, and blinked. "You couldn't have." The eyes when you looked at them were exceptionally gray and large and intelligent. "You are the first member of the family I have informed. I believe he was very close to your mother? Perhaps there is some older person you would wish to break the news to her . . ."

"Yes, there's a Mr. Gabriel who lives in the same hotel in Bournemouth. He's a great friend. That's a good idea," I said, ashamed that I had not thought of this aspect.

"Yes," Cunliffe said, and fiddled with some papers on his desk, and in the pause I could hear my heart going. "You know, I suppose," he said at length, "that you figure prominently in Mr. Janda's will?"

I licked my lips. "I'd heard he was thinking of leaving me something."

"He has. The lot," said Cunliffe, the skin crinkling round his eyes.

He sat smiling at me, the little manikin, in a rather worldly-wise, sardonic manner, while the British port rose gaseously in my throat.

"Apparently he has made no alterations to the will in the possession of my Canadian associates which is the one I drew up for him in 1938. I am not able to give you a complete figure, of course, but I can give you a general idea of the size of the estate if you would like?"

Correctly interpreting my semiparalytic jerk as an affirmative, he went on, "In cash and securities—the lesser part of the estate, it is thought that he left something in the region of fifty thousand dollars—about seventeen or eighteen thousand pounds. The greater part of the estate consists of the cannery, transport and so forth, together with a fair-sized fruit farm which he bought in 1952 and which is, I understand, quite a valuable property."

"Supposing—supposing I wanted to dispose of it. Is that possible?"

"Certainly. You are the absolute legatee." He looked down at his papers again. "The last valuation was taken in 1951 before he bought the fruit farm. It is surmise only but I would say the whole estate now would realize roughly four hundred thousand dollars. Of course it is subject to death duties—"

"Four hundred thousand—"

"About a hundred and forty thousand pounds," he said. He blew his nose and began sniffing quickly.

He nipped off his chair. He seemed to be picking up a cigarette that was burning a hole in the carpet. I was staring rather closely at the back of his neck. I remember only leaning over with a sense of gratitude to kiss this little neck, and then I was in his chair sipping a glass of water and a woman was whispering, "He has had too much to drink. I smelled the brandy on his breath. Perhaps you should not have told him just now—"

"Better now?" Cunliffe asked, smiling. "The news was too much for you."

"I'm afraid it was. What was that figure again?"

"A hundred and forty thousand pounds. Thank you, Miss Vogler," he said to Bunface, who was hovering, and waited till she had gone.

In the next few minutes he gave me a brief, smiling lecture on the best way to hang on to a legacy, and himself proposed that I might like a little on account. I had been wondering how to frame this question and accepted eagerly.

"A hundred or two, perhaps?"

"Two hundred would do fine."

"I expect you would like to take cash now," he said, looking at his watch. "I had better ask Miss Vogler to slip out for you. The banks will be shut in just five minutes. Five-pound notes?"

Bunface returned at length with the money and Cunliffe produced two documents which he folded over for me to sign. "I had a suspicion you might like something on account," he said, smiling wryly. "They are already prepared. Just sign your name here and here. You see, I have filled in the exact sum—it is intuition."

I signed jerkily, moved by the impressive words "two hundred pounds" spelled on each form and slightly hypnotized by the fivers fluttering around me as he counted. The efficient Bunface whipped away the papers with two sheets of blotting paper and I watched as Cunliffe came to his final "thirty-eight, thirty-nine, forty."

"There. Are you satisfied with my count?"

"Perfectly." I could hardly keep my hands off them.

A couple of minutes later he was telling me that he would communicate with me as soon as she had more news, and was taking my hand in his two again.

"Think," he said, his large, intelligent eyes twinkling. "Mr. Janda left certain funds with me. But think before you spend. A little splash would be understandable, but don't throw it all away."

I don't remember going down the stairs. I found myself in the M.G. wondering what I should do first. For some reason, despite the British port, I felt wonderfully clearheaded for the first time that day, perhaps for the first time that week, possibly for the first time in my life.

There was a clear necessity to take myself swiftly off to some place of solitude with this miraculous two hundred quid and work out a few first principles. With this thought in mind I pressed the starter, and at once fell to swearing with great power and obscenity and leapt out like a madman with the starting handle. There was something that would have to come even before first principles and I drove round to the squalid enterprise of Ratface Rickett, pulling up in the forecourt with a scream of brakes.

Ratface was not about his usual task of gloating over his petrol pumps, and I walked round to the back to find him at work in a pit inspecting the underside of a lorry with a wandering lamp.

"Mr. Rickett."

From his crouched position he looked round quickly and turned away without speaking. This familiar and expected action filled me with such pleasurable fury that I crouched like a frog, inserted my head carefully between the two front wheels and, inflating my lungs, roared: "Rickett! Rickett! Rickett!" like some maniac baritone on a cracked record. Ratface straightened up as though shot, catching his head a stupefying blow, and began a subhuman, wordless moaning as he clutched his head. One word of apology would have had him swarming at me with a six-inch spanner and so, suppressing a desire to run and pretending not to notice what had happened, I called urgently, "Come on, Rickett, surely you can finish that later—I'm in a hurry, man!"

This attitude so surprised him that he actually crawled out after a moment or two, but his eyes were still so bloodshot and murderous that I said loudly, "Damn it, I've been yelling my head off. Didn't you hear me down there? I'm in a hell of a hurry and I want a new battery and to settle my bill."

I had meant to play with him a little over the question of payment, but since the encounter had provided such reasonable value and there was, anyway, the matter of getting off the premises without his savaging me, I reluctantly paid up and took off in triumph at the first touch on the starter.

I drove to Henley, and by a quarter past one was sitting slowly sipping a pint of beer and watching the swans.

The young master had come into his own with a vengeance. I could almost feel the gigantic sack of loot on my shoulder like some unimaginably heavy piece of nuclear material darkly awaiting conversion into other and more useful forms. Millions of miles of dappled roads, a big house for Maminka to queen it in, an island, a pub, a boat, a small group of harlots. Or one could acquire and slowly pulverize the entire affairs of the Little Swine, selling Miss Vosper into white slavery.

The swelling wonder of these reflections occupied the first pint, and it was as I was sipping the second that I approached cautiousy the problem of Maura. I had been aware all morning of a strong resistance to the idea of reasoned thinking on this subject. I hadn't wanted to tell her about the letter. I didn't want to tell her just yet about the money. There was bound to be a reason for this, I thought, nodding sagely to a swan who had come to stare at me.

It was not a difficult one to find. The presence of the money meant (a) that it was time for positive action with regard to our relationship and (b) that Maura would have ideas on what should be done with the money. Take a certain line with regard to (a) and (b) as a personal problem would cease to exist. And yet it went deeper than this. So long as I hadn't been in a position to marry the girl she had seemed, no doubt about it, a very desirable one. Desiring her had indeed been a major preoccupation for these past months. But there had been many months before Maura and there would be many months after her. Was this, in short, the girl for me?

I blew out my cheeks and considered. Marriage, it was a fact, was a serious business, and Maura had many defects. She was too damned bossy, for one thing. She looked on me as something less than heroic, for another.

All in all, it seemed to me, I needed to give this more thought; which, in its turn, meant keeping the news to myself for a while. For the time being I had two hundred pounds to spend, less Ratface's bite, and all the time in the world to decide what should be done with the remainder.

It was now getting on for two o'clock and people were strolling out to enjoy the river after their luncheon. I could not be bothered to eat and instead stayed slowly disposing of two further pints before the bar closed and I tooled gently back to town, listening with only mild interest to the noise from the gearbox. I thought I might buy Maminka a present, might run down to Bournemouth with it this evening; might even run down now.

At this point I recalled Cunliffe's advice to pass the tidings through Imre and pulled up at the first phone box to put through a call.

He came to the phone right away, and I said, "Hello, Uncle, it's Nicolas. How are you?" grinning to think of him standing there big and shapeless in his alpaca jacket, with the hairs of his nose waving in his powerful breath. He was a gentle, flabby, elephantine man.

"Nicolas," he said breathily. "It is good to hear from you, my boy. How are things with you?" His voice sounded a shade muted, as if he had just undersold another stamp. Well, there'd be enough for Imre, too, I thought with a wave of regard for the old boy, and I said cheerfully:

"Couldn't be better. I'll tell you all about it. But first how's Maminka?"

This was a mistake, but it had to be gone through. There was never anything wrong with Maminka, but the old hypochondriac could usually find something; it gave him an added reason for living with her.

"Well, my boy, I will tell you," he said confidentially, with a return to something like his usual form, "she is not so well today. There is a touch of fibrositis in the shoulder and I think she is starting a cold. I am keeping her in bed today."

"I'm sorry to hear that, Uncle. How is your own health?" I said, blowing out my cheeks and nodding to the phone.

"Me, me—you know how it is with me, Nicolas," he said, pleased, giving his little deprecatory laugh. "I need a new pair of lungs. Things are never quite right with me."

"I was thinking of running down to see you. I've got great news. Uncle Bela has died and left me all his money." This could have been expressed in other ways, and I was thinking of the words, when he said:

"What is this? What is this you say? Just a minute, Nicolas. The door is open. I cannot hear very . . ." He put the phone down and came back in a moment. "You say Bela . . ." he said breathily. "What is this, Nicolas?"

"I'm afraid Uncle Bela has died," I said. "He died on Wednesday after a heart attack. I heard from the lawyer today."

"Oh, this is bad," he said. I heard his noisy breathing for a few seconds. "It will distress her terribly."

"Yes," I said, somewhat irritably. "Not too good, is it? But I saw the lawyer today. It seems he left a considerable fortune. He left it to me."

"Well, this we knew he would do," he said. "It is no surprise. I do not know how to—I can't tell her today, Nicolas. She is not well enough for such news today."

"Well, that's rather the point. I hoped you would break the news to her before I got down."

He breathed into the phone for a while. "Nicolas," he said at last, "I think it would be better if you didn't come down this weekend. You understand, a shock like this, her only brother . . . I wouldn't like to say . . ."

"All right," I said, a little put out. "Uncle Bela left quite a lot of money."

"Of course. He was a rich man. You will tell me about it later. I must think what I should say."

"I hope Maminka's not too upset about it."

"She is bound to be upset. She will be terribly distressed. I can't prevent it."

"Well, I'll call you in a couple of days."

"In two or three days, yes. Good-by, Nicolas." He put the phone down before I did.

I got back into the car with a feeling of letdown. It seemed there was nobody I could tell about the money. The weight of the hundred and forty thousand pounds was suddenly heavy on me. The beer had left a sour taste.

I drove slowly back home, aware I shouldn't be driving at all. By a stroke of luck, Mrs. Nolan was not prowling in the hall. I went up to my room and fell onto the divan and was asleep immediately.

Only one other thing of note happened that day. I awoke at half past eight in the evening. Mrs. Nolan had gone to the pictures and one of the lodgers was knocking on the door to call me to the phone. I took myself frowstily down the three flights. It was the man Jack had mentioned who was interested in buying the car. I told him rather shortly that it was not for sale, and hung up.

I didn't take his name or number.

I called for Maura next morning, and watched her in my new role of scale-weigher. What I saw went solidly on the plus side. Nothing wrong there, I thought, as she hopped nimbly into the car. Her red hair was cut short. She was wearing a gaily colored cotton frock and a shoulder bag. Her lopsided smile could take your breath away in that sedate Sunday-morning square.

She said, "Nicolas, I was so mean the other night. I've been depressed about it."

I said, "Well," with a tremendous lift. "I've not been feeling so hot, either."

"Then let's forget it and have a wonderful day, I've got something to tell you."

"What is it?"

Her lopsided smile came on briefly. "I'll tell you later. Can we afford a run into the country?"

"I've got a secret, too," I said, and dug into my wallet for the twenty-five pounds I had brought with me. "Look. I won it."

"Nicolas, you never did!"

"At the dogs." I'd rehearsed this in the bathroom mirror, but it was coming out a bit too quickly.

"Was this last night?"

"Yes."

"You never told me you were going. You've never been before. Nicolas, you're fibbing . . ." A thought struck her and she looked at me, blinking quickly. "There wasn't anything more about the Little Swine? You weren't keeping anything back?"

"No," I said irritably. It had started to go a bit funny.

"Well, it's wonderful anyway," she said. It didn't sound so wonderful now. "Let's have a picnic, We can buy food. I was dreaming about the country. I was dreaming about Ireland."

So that seemed all right again, and I shoved in the clutch and took off like a jet through Chiswick, through Datchet, through Taplow, and we sang like little larks, not knowing what would befall.

That was a perfect July day, the best of that wild summer.

We ate in a clearing in the woods beyond Cliveden and afterwards lay back and smoked. Maura said, "Nicolas."

"What?"

"I've been thinking of going back to Ireland."

"I know. In August."

"I mean for good."

I sat up and stared at her. "Why, for God's sake?"

Her eyes, which had been closed, now opened, gray-green, and regarded me mournfully. "You know why, Nicolas."

This could only be an obscure reference to the Little Swine, it seemed to me, and I bent to kiss her to obliterate the thought. She twisted away, lifting her fingertips to my face.

"All my family are in Ireland," she said mournfully. "I've got nobody here."

"How about me?"

26

"How about you?"

"You know how I feel about you, Maura."

"I know you want to go to bed with me."

"Damn it," I said, with fright. It was the first time she had said anything like that. "There's more to it than that, Maura."

"What?"

"I love you," I said, awkwardly. The scale-weighing, it seemed to me, was not going too scientifically.

"I love you, too, Nicolas," she said. "But there doesn't seem much chance of our ever being able to do much about it, does there? Oh, I can see," she said mournfully, beginning to enjoy it, "I can see it's not going to be any use. You'll be a lifelong poor relative. The Little Swine won't do a thing unless you push him, and your uncle in Canada won't either because you don't show a spark of interest. I've tried hard to believe some miracle will happen to change you . . ."

"Well, try a bit harder," I said, echoing Ratface, and suddenly invigorated by the recollection took her head firmly in my hands. "Look, Maura, I've had more than enough of this conversation. The time has come to settle a few simple points. (a) My formative years are long past and nothing now is going to alter my character. (b) Changes of circumstance, of which there could be many, should not affect our relationship, viewed as a long-term proposition. If in your mind they do, well, you're perfectly right—it's no go. And now," I said, "let's forget it."

She wriggled her head round fast before I could get down to her. "Nicolas, what's happened to you?"

"You've happened to me," I said. She returned my kiss with enthusiasm. Her eyes were lively and alert and sparkling when we drew apart.

"If you knew how worried I've been," she said. "Is everything going to be all right now, Nicolas?"

"Yes," I said reluctantly.

"He agreed to your becoming a full partner?"

My mental defenses had shaken themselves wearily into life like a big tired bulldog. "Well, it's difficult to explain."

"All right," she said lightly. "I've got no right to know."

"Maura, you have. I'm just not able to tell you at the moment. Believe me, Maura," I said, with a desperate attempt at her

27

own line of dramatics, "I've thought about this and thought about it, and I know you've got a right to be told, but you've just got to trust me."

"No right at all," she said, but only the words were cold. Her eyes were warm and curious. "When will you be able to tell me?"

"Soon," I said, wondering how the hell I'd placed myself in this insane position. The idea had been merely to keep from her for the moment the fact that there was now no bar or impediment to marrying her. She now understood (a) that I could and (b) that her prompting to approach the Little Swine had paid off. The fact that the latter was untrue was not only irrelevant. It was damned inconvenient. My firm intention had been to see the Little Swine for just one further and rewarding session. I would now have to create a detailed day-to-day fantasy for her.

The prospect was so enervating that all thought of smooching swiftly dispersed. I lit a cigarette and lay down beside her. Our heads were together, but she did not say anything further. For a long time I could see her eyelashes from the corner of my eye, blinking rapidly and intelligently at the sky.

The next three days passed deliriously. I had a short, perfect interview with the Little Swine and with Miss Vosper, which was not so much a burning of boats as the entire disintegration of a familiar shore. I had not meant to let it go so far as this: I was drunk with good fortune.

I ordered two new suits; bought one off the peg; three silk shirts, two pairs of shoes, three motorcar tires and a gearbox, and paid off Mrs. Nolan. Her curiosity about the lawyer's letter was now warm, and, anxious that she should not let drop anything to Maura on the telephone, I told her there was a legacy but that the legal situation was complicated by other claimants and that I had pledged myself to remain silent.

This rage of spending kept me busy during the day, and I saw Maura each evening. Our relationship had now developed a curious, somewhat uncertain, but not unpleasant character. She was quieter, rather quizzical, scrupulously uninquisitive. It was as though we were meeting for the first time. Titillated but uneasy, I felt myself compelled to invent complete and detailed days in the Little Swine's service.

On the Wednesday I rang Imre again.

"Nicolas, my boy," he said breathily, "you must be patient. I have not told her yet. She has not been at all well."

"Damn it, Uncle—I must see her."

"I know, my boy, I know," he said unhappily. "She has been asking why you have not been. Perhaps if you could leave your visit till the weekend."

"Well, if you think so," I said.

"Say Saturday. It will give me more time. She is improving a little now. Saturday would be the best. We can have a little talk downstairs first."

"All right."

"Good-by," he said abruptly. Maminka must have wandered into hearing.

"Good-by," I said, after the click, and nearly smashed the phone in fury.

It seemed to me that my mother would show a rather more rugged fortitude over Bela's death than Imre gave her credit for; my interest came first with her. I felt safe, therefore, in taking her some rather grand present. With this in mind, I went up to my room and inspected the state of my finances.

I took out my wallet and emptied my pockets in a small pile on the divan and began counting. There were eight fivers, two one-pound notes and a handful of silver. I stared at it appalled. Over a hundred and forty quid gone in half a week. And I'd only paid a deposit on the two suits; that meant another eighty pounds to lay out. I wondered how I was going to explain this to little Cunliffe.

I found myself trying a few specimen interviews with him in my mind, and after a while I lit another cigarette and went downstairs to phone him. Mrs. Nolan came out of her lair as I picked up the receiver, so I dialed TIM instead, checking ostentatiously with my watch, and went out to telephone from the public box farther up the street.

Bunface put me through to Cunliffe right away.

"Yes, Mr. Whistler, what can I do for you?"

"I was just wondering if you'd heard anything further." I caught my reflection smiling in a rather sickly fashion in the small round mirror.

29

"Nothing at all. I am not expecting to for a while. Have you any particular problem?"

"Not exactly a *problem*. I was wondering if we couldn't arrange something a little more definite about money—perhaps a regular remittance."

He didn't say anything.

"There might be one or two things I want to buy," I said, sweating. "It would be useful to know the money was available."

"I don't quite understand," he said at last. "You mean you have spent the two hundred pounds?"

"Oh, no! Not at all. Rather not, Mr. Cunliffe," I said. "I merely thought—if one coud fix up something *definite*. Perhaps starting this weekend."

His gravelly laugh came over the phone. "How much of the money have you got left?"

"Well, about forty or fifty, actually," I said, relieved that the little buffer was taking it so well. "But that includes . . ."

"You don't need to explain," he said, still laughing heartily. "A certain amount of celebration is understandable, but I must say—a hundred and fifty pounds in four days is something outside my experience. We will have to have a little chat about it."

"Well, that's rather the point. I'd like to do that, Mr. Cunliffe. You see, I've sort of given up my job, and tend to be without visible means of support. There was quite a bit we didn't go into when we met . . ."

"Of course, of course," he said. "Come and see me in the morning about eleven o'clock."

"It'll be O.K., will it, to draw a bit more?"

"I am sure we can arrange something."

"Well, fine. See you tomorrow then."

"At eleven. Good-by, Mr. Whistler."

I stepped out of the box smiling vacuously with relief. The strain of keeping the news to myself and the nerve-racking mystery that had developed with Maura had conspired to start in my mind a terrifying suspicion that the whole thing was some immense practical joke. Little Cunliffe's encouraging attitude—he had not struck me as the type to laugh off the disintegration of a hundred and fifty pounds in rather less than that number of hours—filled me with such elation that I walked back feeling

30

about ten feet tall. For the first time I could really believe that Uncle Bela had left me a hundred and forty thousand pounds.

"Mr. Cunliffe is expecting you," Bunface said with a brisk bob and a smile the moment I opened the door. She hustled me in and bobbed out and little Cunliffe had slipped off his seat and was shaking me by the hand before I had properly adjusted my eyes to his level. All this was very satisfactory and I gave him a kindly good morning.

"I didn't think I would be seeing you again quite so soon," he said jovially.

"No—ah—well," I said, not knowing quite whether I was the sheepish young gentleman or the mad young rip, but prepared to oblige with either.

"Sit down, sit down. Cigarette?"

Again he produced the massive case with one of his emphatic semaphore gestures and again I watched with fascination as he lit one himself and blew out a stream of smoke. He sat himself on the desk and crossed his little legs and looked at me quizzically.

"This is a very high rate of spending, Mr. Whistler. Don't think I am criticizing—in my profession I have always found it impossible to predict or to judge other people's appetites. But how exactly have you managed to get rid of it so soon? I thought at least a week, possibly two."

He was smiling, but not actually laughing. There was still no cue for the two characters waiting at my elbow so I said neutrally, "There were a few things I had to buy." I then told him exactly what I had spent.

He made a note of it. "Yes I think I have a fair idea," he said slowly, stubbing out his cigarette. "And you say you have given up your job, too. Without ill-feeling, I hope?"

I told him about it and he laughed heartily.

"Yes, I can appreciate the situation. It is clear that you need money. I am sure we can come to some arrangement."

"I was thinking." I said tentatively, "of a regular weekly sum until I've sorted myself out for a bit."

"Yes?"

"I thought about twenty-five pounds a week would be reason-

31

able—just until the legacy comes through."

He slipped off the desk and seated himself in the swivel chair. "Possibly," he said judiciously. "I'm afraid I have a little shock for you, Mr. Whistler. There is no legacy."

For a moment I had a wild idea that the ventriloquist had gone and that the doll had seized the opportunity to say all the terrible, lunatic things it could think of.

I actually said, in a music-hall voice, "No legacy?"

"I'm afraid not."

"But Uncle Bela . . ."

"Is thriving, I dare say."

"But—but . . ." I gazed at the little madman, practically speechless. "What about the money? You gave me two hundred pounds."

"I lent it to you." He pressed a buzzer and, as Bunface popped in, said pleasantly, "Ask Mr. Pavelka to step in, please. And, Miss Vogler, you might bring in the receipts relating to Mr. Whistler."

I was still gaping at him. "What the hell . . . You *are* a solicitor?"

He inclined his head. "Once, alas. I am now a humble money-lender."

"But you know damned well I didn't borrow money . . . What exactly is this . . ."

Cunliffe got up, smiling, with his hand outstretched. An enormous gorilla of a man with the ugliest face I had ever seen had entered the room.

"This is Mr. Pavelka," Cunliffe said. "He will explain why we want you to go to Prague."

chapteR 3

Pavelka, whose face, on closer inspection, was like a St. Bernard's rather than a gorilla's, shambled forward and extended his hand.

"*Dobry den,*" he said.

"*Dobry den.*" I was still so shaken that I was unaware for the moment of the lapse into Czech.

Pavelka folded my hand in his massive paw and slowly shook it, gazing earnestly at me like some champion of his breed trying to catch the judge's eye.

"I am very glad to make your acquaintance," he said in Czech. "This is a wonderful task you have undertaken. I only hope you prove worthy of it."

"Task?" I said in Czech through dry lips—it was uncanny how natural the Czech tongue sounded; even Maminka had not spoken it to me for years. "Task?" I looked helplessly from one to the other of them, and for an instant my sole thought was escape; perhaps to throw Cunliffe at Pavelka and, clutching Bunface as a shield, bound down the stairs four at a time and rush screaming into the street.

Cunliffe smiled dryly. "Mr. Pavelka is going a little too fast. Please sit down, both of you. Ah, thank you, Miss Vogler," he said as Bunface bobbed in with the papers.

He waited until she had gone before continuing, "Very briefly, Mr. Whistler, we have been looking for some time for a young gentleman like yourself to go on a small mission for us. It is completely without danger but so unusual that we realized some inducement would be necessary. In your case we thought—I thought, as a matter of fact—that it might be best to place you in our debt in some way and then offer you the opportunity of

33

canceling the debt and, at the same time, earning yourself a handsome fee. I took the precaution of securing your signature to this standard loan certificate. Perhaps Mr. Pavelka will hold one side of it while you read it."

He handed the paper over the desk and Pavelka, with a murmured *"Prosim"* to me, took it, inclining toward me like a slightly animated Tower of Pisa.

It was a printed document. My eye went dizzily over the close columns of *pursuant to the Acts* and *hereinafters*. It was folded horizontally. Below the fold was Cunliffe's TWO HUNDRED POUNDS and below that my own jerky signature.

"You will see," Cunliffe said, at the same moment that I saw the paragraph, "that your motorcar is down as part security. At a rather low figure, I am afraid."

I think it was the sight of the car quoted at fifty pounds that, more than anything else in the last stupefying five minutes, maddened me into sudden action. With a wordless snarl, I tore the paper from Pavelka's grip, and at once found myself on the floor with my head nearly knocked off. Without moving an inch he had caught me a paralyzing clout on the ear.

"No, please!" he said in English, looking down at me with embarrassed alarm. "Why do you do this?"

I looked up at him, horribly shocked. It was the first time anybody had ever hit me. His head, the entire room, was expanding and contracting with an agonizing boiler-house roar.

"It is perfectly all right, Mr. Pavelka," I heard Cunliffe's voice grating. "I have another copy of the document, also signed. Ah, just a little torn is it? Two are better than one. I hope you are not hurt, Mr. Whistler?"

Pavelka, after handing the form back, was helping me to my feet like a troubled elderly uncle. My ear felt as if it had been hit with a hammer.

"I'm sorry I forgot to mention about Mr. Pavelka," Cunliffe said. "He used to be quite a well-known amateur wrestler. Wrestling champion of Bohemia—I think I am right, Mr. Pavelka?"

"Western Bohemia," Pavelka said.

I sat down and gazed at him through a mist of pain as he slowly took his seat. The shocked, aggrieved expression was still on his face.

"Mr. Pavelka is startled by your behavior," Cunliffe said, with an I-thought-it-would-be-so shake of his head. "The young man has been greatly upset by money troubles," he said in Czech to Pavelka. "He is not yet aware of our offer."

"And I'm not bloody well going to be," I said. "You let me out of here and I'm going straight to the police."

It was not the most inviting of offers, but I heard my voice with amazement, astonished at my own courage. Cunliffe diplomatically produced his cigarette case and passed it round.

"You are at perfect liberty to go whenever you like," he said mildly. "I don't know what exactly it is you want to tell the police. I don't think you have any letters from me?" (This had occurred to me as he was speaking; I had brought back the only letter he had sent me.) "You will find that I am a fairly well-known moneylender. To any sensible person it would be obvious that, having accepted a loan, you have rashly squandered it and are now displaying reluctance to meet your obligations. Moreover, you would force me to take the motorcar from you right away, as I am fully entitled to do."

I inhaled an enormous lungful of smoke, and it seemed to ease my ear a little. The room had ceased its painful contractions. The situation was no less mad. I leaned forward, groping for some strand of understanding.

"If all this about Bela is just—just invention, how did you get to hear about him in the first place?"

Cunliffe's eyelids drooped wryly. "You have not exactly made a secret of your expectations."

I gazed at him, appalled. Someone had been watching me, taking careful note of the absurd little jokes.

"But why me? You don't know me," I said urgently. "I'm not cut out for this sort of thing."

"You are exactly cut out for it. As I say, we have been looking for someone with just your qualifications."

"I haven't any qualifications, Mr. Cunliffe," I told him slowly and desperately. "Before you go any further, you've got to understand that. I am not qualified to do anything. I am also a coward. I don't know what it is you want me to do and I don't want to know. I'd be less than useless to you."

As I spoke I was frightening myself and the words came in a

35

gabble at the end. I didn't seem to be frightening Cunliffe, who was holding Pavelka with his eye as though to ensure that he heard every word. He gave a little nod and Pavelka, who seemed to have reassured himself about me, at once sat forward and grasped my knee.

"I like you," he said simply. "You look like your father. You have no recollection, I suppose, of Pavelka ware?"

"I know nothing at all about Czechoslovakia—"

"Nobody has today," he said bitterly. "It was excellent glass. I had the finest factory in Bohemia. Since 1934 I employed a research staff of twenty-seven—*yoh*, twenty-seven!" he repeated, wrongly interpreting as astonishment the look of despair I threw at Cunliffe. "Twenty-seven men uneconomically employed who did nothing but experiment to try and produce unbreakable glass. Not ovenproof glass, not plastic. Beautiful table glass, as delicate as the finest in my complete range. Since 1934! Now they have found it, and you are going to Prague to bring it to me."

His inhumanly large hand was gripping my knee tightly, his great creased dog's face not a foot away.

"Mr. Pavelka!" I cried. "This is incredible! The very idea—"

"*Yoh*, incredible! But it is so. Since 1934 twenty-seven men working at nothing else, and now they have it. And they will flood the world with it. You know what it means."

"I don't, Mr. Pavelka," I said. "I don't know anything about glass. I only worked in the office." His big dog eyes were looking seriously at me, but it was plain he didn't understand me, or didn't believe me, or didn't care. I glanced desperately at little Cunliffe. He gazed blandly back.

"You need have no fears, Mr. Whistler," Cunliffe said after a moment of silence. "It is the simplest job in the world. I could do it, or Mr. Pavelka here, or a reasonably intelligent Boy Scout. It is all a matter of finding someone with a legitimate reason for visiting glass factories—someone the Czechoslovak authorities would not suspect. Your father was a well-known glass importer. It is entirely natural that you should wish to start up trade again. You will go as a buyer, of course."

"They're not going to sell me this unbreakable glass!"

"No. It's not in production yet. And I gather a specimen of the glass wouldn't be very useful for our purposes. One can't hope to duplicate it after analysis because of the fusion process in glass—you'll know more about that than I would. You're bringing back the formula."

His reasonable tone had been bringing the project down to earth; the word "formula," although casually dropped in, put it back on a new mad plane. Cunliffe saw my expression and smiled. "A bit of paper with a few figures on it—you won't know anything about it. I assure you unless I told you where it was you wouldn't know you were carrying it. The whole thing has been arranged so that there is not the slightest danger to you. After all, we're going to quite a bit of trouble and expense to get that formula, and Mr. Pavelka, as you can see, has thought about scarcely anything else since 1934."

"That's just it," I said eagerly, and turned to Pavelka, who was staring moodily at a drinking glass on the desk. "There's so much trouble and money involved here that I'd be a definite weak link. I'd be frightened out of my life. They couldn't help but suspect me. You've waited years for this. For God's sake, Mr. Pavelka," I cried, "put someone you can trust on the job. I'd wreck your chances for life."

"It is very pleasing, is it not?" Cunliffe said to Pavelka, his head held a little to one side as he listened to me. "I thought I was not mistaken the first time. Modesty, circumspection, reserve, a little childish cunning. . . . I won't conceal from you, Mr. Whistler," he said to me, "that I am more and more taken with your manner. I am sure the Czechoslovak authorities will expect you to be a little—well, a little as you are. Your family was there in the old days, the former capitalist class. . . . It would be difficult to make a better choice for the job. And now to business," he said as my mouth opened.

"The moment you return with the—the bit of paper, I hand you the loan certificate. Both copies!" he said, smiling. "And on top of that we will pay you a further two hundred pounds. Moreover, if you do not feel inclined to return to your job, I dare say Mr. Pavelka will be prepared to offer you something. He has the highest hopes for the new process."

"It will be colossal," Pavelka said. "Of course you will work for me."

"There," said Cunliffe. "The prospects are unlimited and

you've got to admit the pay is princely for a few days' pleasant sightseeing with all expenses paid."

"How many days?" I asked reluctantly.

"That is not entirely clear yet. Perhaps only four or five. They will want to give you a good time. It is all a matter of how quickly you can tear yourself away."

"And when do I pick up this—this formula?"

"Probably the day after you arrive. If so, of course, you must try and cut short your stay. It is really something you must decide when you are there. They will make a program for you and one of the items will be a visit to Mr. Pavelka's factory. We have asked for that—in your name of course. Incidentally, your visa application is going through—we applied for it as soon as you brought your passport along—and we have been assured it will come through almost immediately. I expect we will have it tomorrow."

There was a long pause while I thought this over.

Pavelka said moodily, "They have changed the name, the robbers. It is the Zapotocky Works now."

"Of course."

"Somebody will give me this formula?" I asked at length.

"It will be given to you. You won't know anything about it."

"How?"

"You must leave that to us. I will explain everything before you go. It is remarkably simple and you need not have the slightest fear."

"Well," I said, and stood up. "I'll think it over."

"Of course," Cunliffe said. "You have several days. You will be leaving by plane at ten o'clock on Tuesday morning."

Pavelka unfolded himself and grasped my hand in his again. "I am relying on you," he said with his great St. Bernard face. "I only wish I could go myself."

I wished he could, too. I was too full of worried care to speak.

"You might telephone me on Sunday," Cunliffe said, slipping out of his seat to come to the door with me.

"I'll be in Bournemouth on Sunday." I had forgotten that I would be staying overnight until this moment.

"Bournemouth?" he said sharply. "Bournemouth? Ah, your

38

mother. I'm not sure," he said slowly, "if that is a very good idea."

"Well, that's too bad," I said, with a sudden idiot pleasure in crossing him. "She's expecting me and I'm going."

He looked at me consideringly. "You understand, don't you, that the only possible danger to you is if you mention any of this to anyone? *Anyone at all.* I advise you to forget everything that has been said here. Put it out of your mind."

"Right away," I said, allowing my face to lengthen in a sardonic leer. God knows what I'd got to leer about. It seemed to worry little Cunliffe. He looked at me pensively.

"Well, ring me when you get back. You can get me at this number," he said, writing it on a sheet of his diary. "You must be back on Sunday night. Ring me however late it is."

When I was back in my room and lying on the divan, the situation was so awful I couldn't think about it. I tried for a while, smoking one cigarette after another, but the entire scene, the extraordinary proposal, was so grotesque it didn't seem to concern me at all. I was conscious only of three sharp impressions. One, there was no fortune; two, I couldn't propose to Maura; three, the car didn't belong to me. The crazy flow of incident in the last few days had anesthetized me against the first two; most of the time they had seemed fantasies anyway. Number three, however, left me in such desolation that I looked distractedly round the room for something to break.

I thought of my session with Ratface, of the three new tires, the new gearbox, the new battery, of the man on the phone I had put off so brusquely. I addressed myself to each wall of the room with savagely waving arms and voiceless imprecation. This bout of silent declamatory passion slipped me into a higher gear and with a mindless sense of action I went out, got into the car and drove decisively to town.

It was after one and Jack was busy serving sandwiches and beer. I ordered a Scotch and inquired if they still had the name of the man who wanted to buy a car.

"I think we threw the bit of paper away," Jack said. "I'll find out."

39

The place was filling up. I finished the whisky slowly and the warmth of it and the buzz all round me and the masticating City jaws began to draw a veil of sanity over the bomb-lit areas of my mind left by the interview with Cunliffe. The idea of going to Prague to steal a secret formula seemed more grotesque than ever. Looking around me I decided suddenly, no nonsense and once and for all, I wouldn't do it. Enough was enough. What could Cunliffe do about it? I had the car and the logbook. If I sold it quickly and handed over the money he could have no legal claim on me.

Thinking thus, I ordered another double and with some excitement began to plot out my moves. First there was the business of getting hold of Jack's man—or, for God's sake, anyone who wanted to buy a car. There must be thousands of them. One way or another I could have a hundred and fifty quid plus within twenty-four hours. . . .

This escaped-convictlike scenting of the new landscape took me through the second whisky, and I was just beginning to perceive with a sinking heart that by working flat out I might be able to get back where I started, minus the car, minus my Little Swine prospects, probably minus Maura, when Jack came over.

"Phyllis says she threw it away. He'll probably be in again. I'll keep an eye open."

"Thanks, Jack."

"Having your ups and downs like the rest of us?"

"Like the rest of us," I said faintly. "I'll have another of these."

With the third whisky I *knew* I was back where I had started, but the prospect was not so cheerless as it might have been. Nodding dolorously to the whisky, I felt the presence of old friends here. Here was indecision and sloth and confusion. . . .

One thought seemed to be drawing clear of all the rest, it seemed to me after a while. Indecision argues an alternative. Somewhere in that blind country of the mind one of me had accepted Prague *as* an alternative.

I was waiting across the road with a splitting headache when Maura left the office at half past five. I waved limply and she came across, surprised.

40

"What are you doing here? Is anything wrong?"

I had arranged to meet her at half past seven. Since three, when I had left the Princess May, I had been dozing on a seat in Lincoln's Inn Fields wondering what the hell I ought to tell her. I seemed to spend half my life doing that. When five had struck, the prospect of waiting around for another couple of hours had become suddenly unbearable. My head was throbbing. If I went back home and crawled on the divan, the chances were I wouldn't get off it. I had taken myself queasily to wait opposite her office.

"I got away early," I said, slipping automatically into the daily fantasy of life with the Little Swine. "I thought I might as well pick you up."

She stared at me. "Have you been drinking, Nicolas?"

"I had a couple."

"Spirits?"

"Look, can we go and sit down somewhere?" People were streaming home all round us. I felt ramshackle enough to topple over and over if one of them bumped into me.

She looked at me in a decidedly odd manner, but made no comment. We walked meditatively to a Lyons teashop.

Over the tea she said quietly, "What's up, Nicolas?"

I'd been beating my tired brain to find the words for this one. I said, "It's damned awkward but something's cropped up that might interfere with my—my plans."

She didn't say anything.

"I might have to go away for a bit, Maura."

"How long for?"

"I'm not sure."

She looked at me without speaking for a long time. "I see," she said quietly. "We won't be seeing so much of each other in the future—have I got the drift right?"

"No, you haven't." I took her hand over the table. "You haven't got it right at all. I love you, Maura," I said, groaning inwardly and savagely cursing Cunliffe, Pavelka, the entire Czechoslovak Republic and my two hours of fuddled gloom. "I love you and I meant to ask you to marry me, but now a lot's happened unexpectedly. . . . I'm going to Prague," I said,

41

listening to my own voice with a certain unearthly fascination, and knowing as I said the words that I must have made the decision hours before.

"Prague?" She stared at me and her mouth dropped open. "Did you know about this at the weekend?"

"No."

"But there was something. . . . It's the glass business, isn't it?"

"Yes," I said truthfully. "But for God's sake, keep it to yourself. I shouldn't have told you at all, really. I've never done anything like this before."

"And I'm sure you'll make a success of it," she said, pressing my hand. Her eyes were shining. "Oh, Nicolas, you fool you— you don't have to pretend to me. And you don't have to prove anything to me. You're trying, and you've got him to give you this chance. That's what counts—your attitude to it. Can't you see that, Nicolas?"

I gazed at her with the shocked but dull resignation of some elderly beast after an unsuccessful attempt with the humane killer.

"It's not quite like that, Maura. Don't bank on anything concrete coming out of it."

"I'm not banking on anyone but you, Nicolas dearest. I've got complete faith in you, my darling."

There was rather more than the normal quota of endearments here and embarrassment was added to my ruined condition. I pressed her hand silently.

"Your mother will be delighted to hear the news." She knew I was going to Bournemouth over the weekend. "I'll see you on Monday, I suppose?"

This seemed doubtful. If I did go off on Tuesday, there would doubtless be many essential preliminaries to tie me up on the Monday. My head, which had eased a little when I sat down, now began to throb again. I said wearily, "I'm not dead sure when I'm going off on—on this thing. It could be Monday or Tuesday. I'll have to get in touch with you."

"Monday or Tuesday!" Her eyes opened wide. "Is it so urgent? So silly little Nicolas had to go out and get tight to tell
42

me. . . . Silly little Nicolas," she said softly, with love, brushing my mouth with her hand.

Too wrecked by the events of the day to fall in with this sort of talk easily, I could only smile like a silly little Nicolas. The attempt cannot have been successful. Maura showed immediate concern.

"Oh, Nicolas, you're looking terrible. You'd better get off to bed."

The car was where I had left it in the side street next to the Princess May. I drove Maura home and made to kiss her briefly. She grasped me in a close, love-communicating hug that jarred my head and made me grit my teeth.

I drove home slowly and left the car without covers and walked upstairs, holding my head. The divan waited solidly in the darkening room, and I embraced it with a muted groan. Almost at once, sleep, like some rhythmical, snoring vacuum cleaner, consumed the awful day.

Saturday was hot and I was up early and unrested, with that glazed efficiency of movement that often follows a drinking session. I ate breakfast, and shortly regretted it, and by nine o'clock was on the road, trembling all over with a nerveless and unidentifiable feeling of apprehension.

Somewhere around Winchester with its chain groceries and post-office vans, however, the apprehension began to diminish and I even felt a slight accession of confidence. The events of the past few days, it was a fact, were no more insane than the previous reality of life with the Little Swine. Through the New Forest the road was sun-dappled, and I sang a little, cautiously.

In my mother's presence, I thought, I would see the proposition for the grotesque and unthinkable nonsense that it was. Maminka, fairy of vision though she might be, was at least a constant in my life. The young man of affairs I knew about and could cope with. The young secret agent, never. Let him, this Cunliffe, just try and take the car, I thought. Let him just try. In the freshness of the morning, with the tree shadows falling hynotically across the bonnet, I abandoned Cunliffe; abandoned Maura too and every other complication, and felt free as

43

any bird. Who was Maura? I thought. And who the, who the, I sang as the tree shadows fell rhythmically across the bonnet, who the hell was Cunliffe?

Somewhat dazed by the rush of sun and shade and with only the mildest groundswell of despair, I drew up at the Pleasance Hotel at eleven-thirty.

Imre, who had evidently been lurking in the foyer, came out at once and stood rather helplessly like some huge, embarrassed baby in his black alpaca jacket.

"Nicolas, my boy! It is good to see you. There is so much to talk about." The hairs of his nose were waving in his powerful breath. "We will walk in the garden, it is such a pleasant day."

He was gripping my arm tightly as I walked with him. "How are you, Uncle?"

"Thank you, thank you."

"And mother?"

"She is a remarkable woman. Today she is in excellent health. Of course, she expects you. This, naturally, must be taken into account. But, Nicolas, I must tell you . . ."

He was laboring under some powerful anxiety, the hairs of his nose billowing.

"You have not told her about Bela?"

"I could not. This was an impossibility. Her health . . . I would like you to understand, Nicolas . . ."

He was in the throes of some large agitation. I said kindly, "No harm done. There are plenty of complications anyway . . ."

"Complications," he said. "*Yoh*, complications!" He stopped in the path and faced me, breathing stormily. "You will not be angry, my boy? Promise me you will not be angry."

"What is it?"

"How to explain?" he said, looking at the sky. "I decided —it seemed a sensible thing to do—that while she was not well enough to hear the sad news about Bela, she could hear the good news about you. After all, good news. . . . Your mother has wonderful recuperative powers."

"What is it you've told her?"

"It is not what I have told her," he said with some heat. "It is what she has made of it. She is a wonderfully imaginative woman. . . . I merely said," he went on hastily, noting my ex-

44

pression, "that you had had a success in business and might be traveling abroad. I wanted to work round to Canada—I suppose you will have to make a trip there—so that in a week or two perhaps we could come round to the subject of Bela. . . . And right away she took it you would be starting your father's business again in Europe. In Prague," he said nervously.

He was gazing at me apprehensively, but I said nothing.

"Your mother does not keep up with the news," he said anxiously. "She thinks Prague is as she left it. It is not possible to tell her of the changes. . . . You are very angry?" he said at length.

I was not angry. I was merely enfeebled. Short of jumping on his shoulders and tattooing with my fists on his head or driving endlessly there and back through the New Forest to resurrect my mood of nihilistic freedom, there was nothing to be done.

"I think we should go in," he said, looking round. "She will have seen your car. We must cheer up, she will expect it. You don't know what it is, my boy," he went on aggrievedly as we walked back, "when an imaginative woman gets an idea in her head."

I do, I thought with melancholy. Better than you. Better than anyone. There was a weird and lowering feeling of inevitability in my vitals as I walked up the steps to the hotel. I knew I would be going to Prague on Tuesday.

Maminka was smoking a cigarette and writing a letter at her little escritoire when we went in.

"Nicolas, *bobitchka!* But you are so thin. You are working so hard. Why have you not been to see me? Let me look at you. Come, kiss me." It was seldom necessary to speak for the first five minutes in my mother's company, and I made no attempt to do so, merely smiling at her with melancholy affection. My mother demands much affection and can always claim it. She is tall, with large, beautiful almond eyes. Her hair is gray, rinsed with blue. She has the complexion of a young girl and has enjoyed, all her life, perfect health.

She engulfed me now in kisses and caresses, speaking rapidly as Imre, only slightly subdued by our conversation, watched with somewhat proprietorial pride.

45

"Stephanie," he said at length, reproachfully, noticing her cigarette for the first time. "It is the second cigarette you have smoked this morning. You promised me. Your throat . . ."

"I have been writing letters," she said loudly. "I must smoke when I am writing letters. Of course," she said confidentially to me, "it is not my throat that worries him. It is the price of the cigarettes. Oh, you will be repaid!" she told him scornfully. "I know you keep an account of the small loans. Be so kind as to let me have a list. My son will attend to it very shortly now. Really," she said, drawing me to her again, "the creatures one has to rely on these days."

"Stephanie," said Imre, with pain, "you know this is not the case . . ."

"But you, Nicolas," said Maminka, disregarding him entirely. "I cannot tell you how delighted I am at the news. Of course, I had not the slightest doubt that you would open the offices again. Your father often spoke of it. Can you get the same building, do you think, on the Prikopy? I used to look in every day on my way to Wartski's in the Vaclavske Namesti. There was a little lift with golden gates, and such a darling old man who worked it. He had a fresh flower for me every day. Ah, those days! Will they ever return? Now sit down and tell me all."

I sat down with acute enervation. "It isn't anything important, Maminka. Just an exploratory visit. Nothing might come of it, you know. Things have changed greatly."

"Of course. Nothing stands still," said my mother, with great energy, looking swiftly at Imre. "Men of affairs have to be up and about. Are you thinking of taking Nimek with you?"

"No."

"Your father had a high opinion of his shrewdness. He is a low creature and I could never see the need for taking him into partnership, but he is undeniably shrewd. Would it not be safest to take him?" she asked wisely.

I regarded her with helpless affection. "Maminka," I said, "Nimek is running the business now. Don't you remember, I told you?"

"Certainly. Of course," she said impatiently. "It was merely a suggestion. Not that it matters. I have written you several letters of introduction to the people who count. And, of course, to Hana

46

Simkova——you remember old Baba who used to nurse you? And now," she said briskly, seating herself beside me and taking my hand, "if Mr. Gabriel could only be persuaded to respect the privacy of other people's rooms, we have much to talk about."

Poor Imre went presently. My mother's high clear voice went on and on.

Imre got me on one side before I left, on Sunday. "Those letters," he said, "I couldn't prevent her writing them. What was I to do? It made her happy."

"That's all right, Uncle."

"Even to your old nanny, Hana. Hana is dead. She died two or three years ago. Of course, I didn't tell her. Even the husband moved away somewhere. . . . She is very much behind the times, your mother," he said sadly. "You are very angry with me, Nicolas?"

"No, Uncle. I'm not angry."

"Here, give me the letters. I'll throw them away. I'll burn them."

He was so contrite and anxious to please that I did so.

I left after tea, and tooled back to Fitzwalter Square at half past eight. It was growing dark and quiet in the square. I sat in the car for a while in a mood of profound melancholy. I had no wish to see Maura. I had no wish to go up to my room. I sat and brooded, on Cunliffe, on Pavelka, on the trip to Prague. I wondered where I would be next week at this time.

Presently a few lights began to come on about the square and I got out of the car and walked to the Musketeers in the High Road. I had a drink there every Sunday. Mrs. Nolan was in the saloon bar with a friend, transfixed by the television. I ordered a pint and drank it. She did not take her eyes off the screen.

I went into the other bar from which sounds of livelier activity were emanating and saw Val and Audrey, the couple who had given the party the previous week. The aging model waved at me, and I waved back, but I didn't go across. I watched this group with some curiosity, noticing other familiar faces and wondering which, if any, of them, had been spying on me. It was a profitless speculation. I left and walked slowly back to the car and put the covers on and let myself into the house.

47

It was a quarter to ten. The hall was dark. From an upstairs room there was the soft mutter of a wireless. Somebody listening to a Sunday-night play. But nothing so strange as this play, I thought, as, with a feeling of the strangest detachment, I dropped the coppers in the box and dialed Cunliffe's number.

He answered at once, and I said, "This is Nicolas Whistler."

"Yes, Mr. Whistler."

"You asked me to ring."

"Yes. It is good of you to do so. I wished to be sure you had returned from Bournemouth. But I have already been informed of that."

My scalp began a slow and unpleasant crawl. I said, somewhat breathily, "Are you still having me watched?"

"One must exercise a little prudence. It is an important assignment you have undertaken. You are holding yourself ready to leave at ten on Tuesday?"

I did not answer, thinking of the noisy group in the Musketeers. Any one of them could have slipped out after I had left. Mrs. Nolan, even, I thought, recalling suddenly the small, transfixed figure by the television. But Mrs. Nolan had not known of the jokes about Bela. Only friends had known about Bela— friends of Maura's and mine. Could it possibly be . . . But not Maura. How Maura? Maura did not know I was back. Shamed and confused by this thought, I said loudly into the telephone, "I'm not sure yet, I haven't made up my mind."

"I understand perfectly," Cunliffe's wry voice grated in my ear. "Perhaps you could come and see me at eleven in the morning. Your visa has come through."

"I'll see."

"It's rather important," he said, and rang off at once. I replaced the phone and walked upstairs slowly in the darkness.

On the second landing I began to have an unpleasant suspicion. The muttering of the wireless had grown louder, but it had not come from the first floor, and it was not coming from the second. The only room on the third floor was mine.

I climbed the next flight softly and stood outside the room with my heart thudding. There was a crack of light under the door. The wireless was unmistakably on inside. I put my ear to the door. There was a small creaking from the divan and the rustle of paper.

I was not feeling heroic. I wondered if I should sneak just as softly right down the stairs again to get a poker or a policeman or a fire engine. I did none of these things. Reckless suddenly in the dark, I bent and took off my shoe and, holding it as a weapon, flung open the door, shouting gruffly at the same time, "Who's there?"

"I am," said Maura. She was sitting on the divan unwrapping a toffee. "I wondered how much longer you'd be."

Her lopsided smile had acquired a faint roguishness of late. She said, "Who did you expect to find in your room?"

I licked my lips. "How did you get in?"

"I rang the bell."

"Mrs. Nolan's out."

"An old man on the first floor let me in. He seemed a bit annoyed."

"How did you know I was back?"

"Your car was outside the door."

"When was that?"

"Well, really," she said, the roguishness departing swiftly. "I don't know. About half an hour ago, I suppose. Aren't you ever going to come in?" she asked impatiently. "And why have you taken your shoe off?"

The return to her old asperity was some faint comfort, but there was still rather too much to take in here. I gazed at the shoe and at her, and licked my lips again. If she had telephoned Cunliffe would she have come up and waited for me in my room? I didn't know. I didn't know about anything. It was the first time she had done this. I bent down and put on the shoe and gazed at her in some bewilderment.

She said, "Would you like to stop looking like one o'clock struck and tell me what's happening?"

"You caught me by surprise. I didn't expect to find you."

"I thought I'd look in and say hello. I might not see you before you go off. You don't mind, do you?"

"No. No. Not a bit."

She looked at me shrewdly. "The trip is still on, is it?"

49

"Yes. Absolutely."

"I expect your mother was pretty pleased."

"Yes. Delighted."

"Well, good."

"Yes."

A pistol shot suddenly went off on the wireless, and I jumped about a foot. Maura turned the wireless off and said, "Look here, Nicolas, what's up?"

"Nothing. I'm a bit tired, Maura. It was the drive back, I expect."

She looked at me consideringly for a moment, and said slowly, "Well, I'll leave you to get some sleep."

I didn't say anything.

"No idea when you'll be back?"

"In a week or two, I expect. I don't know for sure." I wondered if she did.

"Right." She stood up and stuffed her sweets into her handbag and slipped on a jacket. "Perhaps you'll look me up when you come back." Her lopsided smile came on briefly.

I wanted to take her hand then, but desisted. "I'm sorry about this, Maura. I'm terribly tired."

"That's all right. I can see myself down."

I saw her down, but I made no offer to accompany her home. In the dark hall I felt closer to her than I had been in the light, felt suddenly that I should take her in my arms and get rid of the suspicion once and for all. But I knew it wouldn't get rid of the suspicion. She said good night and went down the path without looking back.

I walked slowly back upstairs and smoked a cigarette on the divan and undressed and got into bed. Just for a moment as I swam lightheadedly into sleep, it all seemed believable.

chapter 4

As we filed into the airport bus at Cromwell Road on Tuesday morning, I could see Cunliffe watching me from his car parked across the road, so to give him a little early-morning pick-me-up, I dropped the guidebook I was carrying. It was a gesture of the merest bravado. I felt acutely frail, boneless, bodiless almost without the book.

The man behind me picked it up and gave it back to me and I thanked him, marveling that I was not sick with hysteria all over it. This book—it now seemed to me unbelievably obvious—was the nub of my mission. Beneath its flyleaf when I returned would be Pavelka's formula.

Cunliffe had explained the operation to me in endless and sickening detail. I must carry the book everywhere. I must allow it to leave my hand only once—in Pavelka's factory where I had to "forget" it on the desk in the manager's office. It would be returned to me before I left.

"That is really all you need to know," Cunliffe had said. "One may claim without immodesty that it is quite a neat little scheme. It is entirely natural for you to carry a Norstrund about—indeed, it is the only up-to-date guidebook on Czechoslovakia. You will find it invaluable. Prague is a beautiful city with many ancient monuments. Reax. Enjoy yourself. I am only sorry you have to know you will be carrying the—the bit of paper."

I was sorry, too.

I got in the bus and it shortly moved off and I turned my head to see if Cunliffe was following. His car stayed where it was. I was glad of this. I had stayed awake half the previous night toying with expedients that might prevent my departure. These included throwing an epileptic fit at the airport or locking myself

51

in the lavatory until the plane had gone.

At the airport, although I could not quite screw up the gall to throw the epileptic fit, I did lock myself in the lavatory, staying there for longer than seemed humanly or technically feasible. The party was still there when I emerged. A minute or so later the loudspeaker boomed an announcement and I found myself flowing nervelessly across the tarmac.

In four hours I was in Prague.

When you have left a town at the age of six and return eighteen years later, there is a certain quality of enchantment. The streets, the monuments, the church spires, set up a whispering in the mind. You know, with dreamlike certainty, what is coming round the next corner, and the sensation of finding you are right is inexpressibly poignant.

All this was totally unexpected, and despite the terror in which I had stepped out of the aircraft and negotiated Passport Control and Customs, I arrived at my hotel, the Slovenska, in a mood of swollen, if highly unstable, elation.

The Hotel Slovenska stands three-quarters of the way up the Vaclavske Namesti—Wenceslas Square. This thoroughfare, despite its name, is not a square but a broad avenue. At one end is a large gray Victorian museum standing in its own gardens. At the other end, crossing it like the top bar of a T, run the town's main business streets, the Narodni Trida to the left, the Prikopy to the right.

I stood outside the hotel and gazed about me, remembering it all. It was a scene of vitality in the hot sun, the pavements crowded, the little one-decker trams clanging up and down the wide cobbled street. At the far end Wenceslas, beloved figure of my childhood, glittered from his iron horse in the middle of the road. Even the hotel itself, I thought, was familiar, and after a moment realized why. Here, under another name, was the Wartski's where my mother used to take tea, the big sash windows open now to the pavement in the heat.

I was grinning at all this in a somewhat loose-jawed way, recollecting intimately the plushy darkness of the interior, the racks of newspapers, the heavy velvet curtains, the old ladies dabbing their mouths with little handkerchiefs. It was inconceivable that I should be back.

There were, however, no old ladies present when I went inside. The place was abustle with open-shirted men in sandals. At the reception desk a center-parted woman, not at all unlike Bunface, was engaged in some intense calculation over a ledger. I waited two minutes and said in English, "I have a reservation."

She looked up sharply and flicked quickly through a pile of cards.

"Pan Whistler, Nicolas?"

"That's it."

"There is a letter for you. Your room is quite ready. . . . One-forty," she said in Czech to the porter who had come to stand by my bag.

I took the letter and followed the porter into the lift. He was a bent little ancient with an immense Adam's apple and a prominent stud in his collarless shirt. He gazed at me with interest, grinning and shaking his head.

"The *pane* has been to Praha before?" he asked in Czech.

"Not for a long time."

"Many changes," he said, and hawked politely behind his hand. "Once we used to be full of businessmen. Not so many now."

"No, well. Times have changed."

He hawked again. "Still, Praha is the same city, very beautiful. I'll bet you haven't seen many cities as beautiful as Praha."

I was no longer listening to him. I had been examining the envelope and, as we came out into the corridor, had seen the small inscription: *State Glass Board*. It was evidently my program. My stomach turned rapidly to water again, and I was thus not able at first glimpse to appreciate the magnificence of room one-forty.

When the porter had deposited my bag, however, and departed, grinning, I stood in the middle of the room and gazed about me. It was, no doubt about it, a handsome apartment. It was tricked out in green and gold. A large bed, curtained all round, stood in an alcove. There was an adjoining bathroom with a shower compartment. There were easy chairs and a chaise longue and a writing desk. Double French windows stood open to a broad balcony. Cunliffe was doing me proud.

I sat down on the chaise longue and opened the envelope. There was a booklet and a two-page letter. The letter, signed *L. V. Svoboda, general manager, State Glass Board*, read:

> Dear Pan Whistler,
> It is a privilege to welcome you to Prague. I enclose you a booklet relating to our glass industry and also a program planned for your visit. The program, as you will see, is brief but quite comprehensive, and it will be a convenience if you will telephone the undersigned on your arrival to indicate if any changes should be required. Believe me, dear Pan Whistler . . .

The second page of the letter, headed *Visit of N. Whistler, representative of Bohemian Glass and Bijouterie Limited*, read:

> Wednesday 10:00. Discussions with L. V. Svoboda, State Glass Board offices, Ujezd 23. Followed by luncheon at showrooms, Vaclavske Namesti 48. Afternoon, Discussions with departmental managers, S. N. Czernin, P. Stein, B. R. Vlcek, and tour round departments.
> Thursday 10:00. Automobile to Zapotocky Glassworks (Kralovsk, 15 km.). Full day. Luncheon at works.
> Friday 10:00. Automobile to Tseblic Glassworks (Tseblic, 23 km.). Full day. Luncheon at works.
> Saturday. Free Day. Return visits or further Discussions as necessary.

As L. V. Svoboda had said, brief but quite comprehensive. The visit to Pavelka's old plant was on Thursday. That meant, all being well, that I would have the formula within forty-eight hours. It also meant I would have to carry the bloody thing around for a further forty-eight. Unless, as Cunliffe had suggested, I could cut short my stay.

I had read the program rapidly. Now, lighting a cigarette to try to control the shaking of my hands, I went through it again. No point in arousing suspicion by asking to leave immediately after visiting Pavelka's factory; especially since they had only laid on two glassworks to be visited. The Saturday free day, then.

I inhaled deeply, pondering this. A terrifying thought had struck me in the airplane that there might be some mess-up on the actual day. Cunliffe had not allowed for this. I was to "forget" the Norstrund; someone would pick it up; it would be returned to me. Fine. But what if some ill-starred maniac refused to allow me to "forget" it? What if it somehow weren't returned to me? I might be very glad of that free day with its wise provision for *Return Visits*.

As Cunliffe had said, it was natural enough for a visitor to carry a Norstrund around with him. So long as I put it promptly into service and carried on that way, all might be well. All things considered, the program was best left as it was. L. V. Svoboda should be advised of this. I should also book my return flight for Sunday.

I put down the program and realized I was still clutching the Norstrund. It had not left my hand all day and was now sticky from the perspiration that had flowed freely. I thought I might have a shower first, and also a bottle of beer. I went to the telephone and ordered the beer, and then stood under the shower for ten minutes.

I seemed to be washing off more than the grime of travel.

When I emerged, refreshed and relaxed, the room was in green semidarkness. A striped awning had been lowered on the balcony. The beer was waiting on a tray. I had heard no one come in.

I took the beer out on the balcony, and drank it, looking down on the Vaclavske Namesti. The street was acrawl with people. In the hot sun, a queue waited outside an Automat cafeteria opposite. The little trams clanged up and down. Far down the street, Wenceslas glittered in the hard light, and at the top end, by the Prikopy junction, an enormous picture of Lenin looked down, inscribed with these words: "Every hand, every brain for the building of socialism."

It seemed suddenly a very long way from London, from the Little Swine and the Princess May and Maura.

Far down the street, the trees began to move in the museum gardens and a moment later the awning above my head fluttered as a small breeze swept the street. I finished my beer and lit a cigarette and went in to phone Svoboda.

I took the Norstrund out for a walk that night. There had been a few spots of rain but the Vaclavske Namesti was warm still and noisy. The lamps were lit, the trams clanging. I crossed the cobbled street at the Prikopy junction and cut through into the old part of the town and could remember as clearly as if it had happened yesterday holding my mother's hand as I had made this same journey.

There had been no home for me since leaving here, no real security. All this was bedded firmly in my childhood, and as I walked in somewhat emotive silence, a loose smile twisted my mouth from time to time.

I walked round the dark bulk of the Karolinum and across the Staromest square to the lovely gray sleeping Klementinum. I crossed the long, stone-figured Charles bridge with the Vltava liquid and winking below, and up, by the steep Mostecka, to the palaces on the Heights: the Czernisky and the Loreta, the Schwarzenberg and the great pinnacled Hradcany.

There was a little desultory singing and the hum of talk as I passed the lighted entrances of the kavarnas in the narrow medieval streets, and the loose smile tugged at my lips. I could never have seen this in the dark before and yet I seemed to know it in my bones, and my feet found their own path.

It was cooler on the Heights. Below, through the trees, Prague glittered in the dark. I stood and looked down and remembered the shape of it and the smell of it and the places where I had played and was extraordinarily moved. Presently I walked down again and crossed the river by the three islands at the Smetanov bridge.

There was dance music coming across the water and I recognized, twinkling with lights, the old stone tower by the Manes café where often I had gone with my parents to have tea on Sunday and to bathe from the large rafts moored alongside.

I had meant to look down the Prikopy to find the office Maminka remembered with the little lift with the golden gates, but I found myself suddenly tired and lost. A policeman was walking along the embankment, alien in high boots and broad flat shoulder tabs. But his face as he passed was young and boyish with that peculiar steadfastness of the Slavs.

He put me right for the Vaclavske Namesti, and I found myself back in the broad, brightly lit street in an exceedingly curious state of mind. The crowds were still there, noisier, more vivacious than London crowds. Open necks, open faces, a new breed. They seemed to be streaming down the road together, millions of them. At the end of the street the monstrous picture of Lenin looked down, illuminated now. "Every hand, every brain for the building of socialism."

I felt oppressed and bruised by these hardy hands and brains. The town of my childhood had been taken over. It lay asleep beneath their vigorous sandals.

I badly wanted a drink, but the lounge was full of them, open necks, open faces, forward together. I went upstairs instead.

The floor waiter, a plump, immaculately tail-coated character, whom I had already encountered, was prowling about the corridors. He saw me coming and stopped to wait. He had glossy black hair, a blue chin and a gold-toothed smile.

"You have been out to take the air, *pane?*"

"Yes."

"It's cooler now. We'll have a storm, I think. I have closed the shutters but left the windows open in your room."

"Thank you."

He seemed disposed for a chat, smiling with darkling fervour and rubbing pale, plump hands. "You plan to make a long stay?"

"Just till the end of the week, I think."

"I hope you make good business. We need the businessmen back here."

"You seem pretty full already."

He shrugged and shook his head sadly. "Delegations. A different class of business. It's not like the old days."

"No, well. Times change." I felt I was repeating myself, tired as hell suddenly in the airless corridor. I put my key in the door.

"Perhaps you would like something?" he said wistfully. "A glass of beer?"

"No, thanks." I wanted only my bed now.

"Well then." His gold tooth winked. "If you should require me, I am Josef."

"Right. Good night, Josef."

"Good night, *pane.*"

By six o'clock the following evening, my apprehension was dispersing fast. Svoboda and his acolytes, Czernin, Stein and Vlcek, seemed to be businessmen like any other businessmen, if somewhat overgiven to Discussions. Svoboda himself, a kindly old character with spaniel eyes and a Mikoyan mustache, remembered my father, and this was certainly all to the good. In my service with the Little Swine I had picked up a little glass lore, but by no means enough to be a young master out buying. Any bona fides that came my way were more than welcome, and as he called huskily into the telephone for glasses of tea, I assiduously searched my memory for the names of old retainers who had worked in the warehouse. I actually recalled one or two.

There had been more tea in the glass showrooms, and an enormous meal with several toasts to trade and peace, and by midafternoon I was comatose, my face stiff with intelligence and my hand cramped from writing in a notebook. This book was now half full with largely indecipherable nonsense about delivery dates and output over which I had nodded so vigorously that as I finally emerged into the sunlight I had a splitting head-ache.

I seemed to have collected a genie, a strapping young woman who had been driving me about all day, and as I came out on the pavement I saw with some nervousness that she was waiting for me. She was, no doubt about it, a hand and brain. She was massive and tanned. She wore a white shirt and swept-back hair. She had a splendid bust and sturdy, though shapely, legs. She was studying English and had practiced on me conscientiously.

She hopped out of the car when she saw me.

"You will want the automobile again today?"

"No, thanks. I'm only going back to the hotel."

"Ah, I have wait for you."

"I'm very sorry. I didn't know."

"It is no trouble. You will require the automobile tomorrow?"

"I'm going to Kralovsk. Will you be driving me?"

"No. For longer distances is another service."

"Right. Well," I said, teetering in the hot, vigorous street. "Like a drink?" This seemed only right after the immense creature had sweltered all afternoon in the car, but I made the offer diffidently and without enthusiasm.

"Oh, thank you." Her teeth glinted. "I would like it."

"Fine. Let's go to the hotel."

She did not speak on the way, walking massive and solemn

beside me. My head thumped abominably.

We found a place in the open-necked throng and she sat down, gazing about her with interest. "I do not come here often for myself," she said. "Here is very expensive."

"Yes, well. On business one travels on expenses."

"Ah, so. You travel to many places?"

"Around and about."

"The work of a merchant must be very interesting."

"Very. What will you have?"

"Tea, please. I should like to do such work myself."

"Ah." Her bust seemed to be on a level with my eyes. I removed my gaze and said in some desperation, "You've got a very nice tan. Been on your holidays?"

"Yes. I have worked on a farm."

"Was it nice?"

"It was very interesting. It must be interesting to see many different places."

"Ah, well, Prague is very interesting."

"You like Prague?"

"It's very pleasant."

"I hate it."

I had been urging her mentally to stow it, to lap up her tea and leave the merchants in peace. But at this curious statement I stared at her with interest. She had high cheekbones, long gray eyes, a straight nose, no lipstick. Her shirt was clinging to her and her magnificent breasts stood out like bombs. It suddenly occurred to me that she could not be very much more than twenty.

I said, "What don't you like about Prague?"

"Oh, it is so dull here. The people are dull. It is very boring."

"Where would you sooner be?"

"Anywhere. London, Paris, New York. Vienna even," she said glumly. "In Vienna also is the rock and roll."

This statement from such an unlikely source struck me as so grotesque that my eyes swiveled. "Are you keen on rock and roll?"

"Not just the rock and roll. Everything."

She had dropped her voice and was beginning to look about her in some embarrassment. My headache lifted quite suddenly.

I wondered if I dare take this giant girl out. I said faintly, "Would you like to have dinner with me?"

"Oh, that would be nice." Her teeth glinted again. "I would like it. Thank you."

"About seven-thirty, here?"

"Ah, tonight is not possible. I go to evening classes for the English studies. Tomorrow I could come."

"All right."

"And it would be better if we did not meet here again. Somewhere else, perhaps."

"You say where."

"You know the Slavia kavarna? It is on the corner of the Narodni Trida, by the river."

"Slavia kavarna, seven-thirty tomorrow. Right. Well," I said. "You know my name. What's yours?"

"Vlasta. Vlasta Simenova," she said and stood up to go. I watched her leave with a somewhat mixed and fearful anticipation. She was certainly a lot of girl.

On the way up in the lift I suddenly remembered what else was going to happen tomorrow and my stomach turned over in a single paralyzing movement. I had forgotten about that. I went into the room and tossed the Norstrund on the desk and flaked out on the chaise longue.

I had put off thinking seriously about this since my arrival, but now gave myself over to it in a daydream of much detailed terror. This was no time to be thinking of taking big girls out. I wondered if, by tomorrow evening, I would be free to take myself out. I thought of all the terrifying slip-ups that could occur.

Presently I dozed off into a confused and nightmarish dream and awoke to find the room in darkness. I thought someone was there, and lay in panic for a minute, listening. But it was only the outer window rattling. It was raining outside. I got up and switched on the light and looked at my watch. It was a quarter to ten. There was a sour taste in my mouth.

I had a shower and went down for my dinner, but when it came I couldn't eat it, and went back to my room again, sick with foreboding. I slept badly.

The foreboding was still there next morning. I ate no break-fast but drank two cups of coffee and had smoked three cigarettes by the time the car turned in at the gates of the Zapotocky Glass-works.

Vlcek, a small vulpine character with receding hair and a mania for statistics, accompanied me, pouring into my ear for the entire fifteen kilometers a ceaseless stream of data. He was still at it when we got out of the car.

"Of course," he said, as we entered the office block, "I have given you the merest outline. Pan Galushka, the director, will tell us much more. Pan Galushka is a brilliant man. He is the architect of the plan for our industry. He is not perhaps," he said, and smiled uncertainly, "the easiest man to get on with."

I stared at him uneasily.

Pan Galushka awaited us in his office, and the moment we entered I thought I should be sick on the spot. The desk upon which I was discreetly to forget the Norstrund was one of the largest I had ever seen. It was also, except for an ashtray and a diary, totally bare.

Galushka walked over from his desk, hand outstretched. He was a spare man with small uneven eyes and a rather odd twisted smile. He said, "*Dobry den,* Pan Whistler."

I shook hands numbly.

"Pan Whistler has asked especially from England to see the Zapotocky works," Vlcek said in a rather ingratiating way. "I have explained a little of what you are doing, but naturally not in detail."

Galushka had still retained my hand and was looking at me rather carefully. He suddenly revealed a line of uneven and dis-colored teeth. "We are complimented," he said. "They still remember our lines in England, then, Pan Whistler?"

"Very well," I said. I licked my lips. "They were very pop-ular."

He let go my hand. "I am glad to hear it. Sit down, sit down, Vlcek. Pan Whistler, a chair for you."

There was a certain amount of kefuffle here while we were seated and while Galushka handed round cigarettes, and in the course of it, without any plan or intention to do so, I simply placed the Norstrund on the desk. I looked at it with cold fright.

61

"Well," Galushka said, "I think I can assure you—Pan Vlcek will correct me if I do not speak the truth—the glass we turn out is as good as it ever was."

"It is so," said Vlcek, speaking to me behind his hand and clowning gruesomely. "But we will not give them swollen heads. Now we have to see," he said, smiling at Galushka, "if they can fulfill the plan for the year."

"Is our increase not enough for you in Prague?"

"It is useful for a start," said Vlcek, winking at me and screwing his cigarette into a holder. "An increase of two hundred and thirty per cent in four years is certainly a useful start."

This hearty joshing about percentages and output had gone on yesterday and seemed to be the form for commencing Discussions. Vlcek, however, appeared to be working overtime to show that it was all in fun. Galushka sat relaxed, smiling with his uneven eyes and his curious mouth. He wore a lightweight gray summer suit, sandals, and a dark-blue celanese shirt, buttoned but tieless. This seemed to be the form for bosses; Svoboda, too, had worn sandals and a tieless shirt—although, it had seemed to me, somewhat apologetically. The acolytes were more formally attired.

Galushka was looking me over carefully. He said, "At any rate, you will find no change from the old Pavelka ware, except for the better. I sometimes have to remind myself that it's not called that now. I worked in this factory for many years with the old Pavelka, you know. I doubt if he would recognize the place now. We have grown. Of course it could have happened in his time if he had put the interests of the industry first."

"He was a good employer, quite a progressive manufacturer according to his lights," Vlcek said, screwing his cigarette in some embarrassment and glancing at me.

"A paternalist," said Galushka.

The conversation seemed to be taking a decidedly odd turn, and I sat frightened out of my life. I had no wish to discuss Pavelka. It was as much as I could do to keep my eyes away from the Norstrund. I had a sudden horrible suspicion that Galushka knew all about it, and was playing with me.

He was still smiling, however, as he said slowly, "I only raise the point to bring to your attention, Pan Whistler, that to make

Pavelka ware one does not need a Pavelka. Many of the men who made it are still making it—a great deal more of it and the quality has not suffered. It is important to realize this and for us to understand each other in a friendly way."

His eyes had been wandering over the Norstrund, but as he said the last words he looked up at me. There was nothing particularly friendly about his smile.

The Discussions then formally began. Cunliffe had supplied me with a list of questions and I asked them, shoving in a supplementary from time to time on information gleaned from yesterday's Discussions. Galushka, fortunately, was a man obsessed with his subject, and the moment he began to talk about glass in its technical aspects appeared to undergo a personality change distinctly for the better.

He seemed to have some minor bee in his bonnet on the subject of plate glass—not included in my queries—and made frequent and fairly flattering references to a British factory which specialized in it, apparently at St. Helens, Lancs. This seemed to please little Vlcek, who nodded encouragingly.

For myself I was obsessed only with the Norstrund lying screaming on the desk, and with Galushka's roving eye. When once, to illustrate some obscure point of pliability, he picked the book up with both hands and began vigorously to bend it this way and that, I thought my heart had stopped. But he threw the book casually down on the desk again.

After what seemed several hours, Vlcek became mildly restive, and Galushka, looking at his watch, apologized. "Pan Whistler asks questions, I must answer. But we've almost missed our lunch, my friends. Come, we can continue at table. I hope, at least, Pan Whistler, that you begin to have an idea now of how we work here."

I said I had.

He stood up. We all stood up. The Norstrund remained screaming on the desk. We left the room. I thought, *Now go to it, whoever you are. Go to it as quick as you like.*

We ate with three of the departmental managers who had been waiting for us at a round table in a secluded corner of the canteen. There were small crossed flags, British and Czech, as a decoration in the middle of the table. I found myself drinking even more than the previous day. It did nothing for my nerves but seemed, at least, to assist the food down my throat. I felt sick and lightheaded. My legs were trembling under the table. Galushka dominated the conversation, returning again and again to his preoccupation with plate glass, no doubt as some obscure compliment to me.

It emerged that the firm in St. Helens had recently installed new continuous rolling machinery which had excited lively admiration in the glass world. One of the departmental managers wanted to know if I had yet had the opportunity to inspect it.

I said, wistfully, that I hadn't.

Galushka laid his hand jovially on my shoulder. "My friend," he said, "you should come and work with us. Here few things are secret. Here an aspirant can see and learn any process he wishes to master. I think," he said, looking joshingly at me, "you are not yourself interested so much in hollow ware. I could tell it as we talked. I'm right?"

I didn't know how to answer this. Vlcek, who had been drinking cautiously, came to my assistance. "We are embarrassing Pan Whistler. Hollow ware, after all, is his subject. Can a man claim he isn't interested in his own subject?"

Galushka nodded round the table. "Isn't it a criticism of a form of society that a man is forced to specialize in a subject that doesn't interest him? I think, Pan Whistler," he said to me shrewdly, "that if you worked here with us in Kralovsk, even though you are a specialist in hollow ware, you would not miss an opportunity to inspect the continuous rolling process with plate glass. Ah!" he said, as I broke obediently into a sheepish smile and his delighted managers chortled round the table. "Ah! We'll say no more about it. We won't talk any more of plate glass, comrades. It's a forbidden subject."

I was very glad to hear it. It seemed to have put the company into the best of humors, however. When, later, the party broke up, there were hearty handshakes all round. The managers returned to their life's work. Vlcek, Galushka and I went round the factory.

Of this tour round Mr. Pavelka's old works very little remains in the mind. Glassmaking is a noisy business. A great deal of the finished product manages to get itself broken. It is also conducted in enormous sheds, very hard on the feet, and in a variety of temperatures ranging from the merely tropical to the ovenlike. It is enough to say that by half past four we had finished.

Galushka said he had some papers he wished me to take. I was very glad to hear this, having been distracted half out of my mind over the problem of maneuvering a return to his office. We went back there.

"Of course," he said, as we entered the office block, "your program is impossibly limited—you have seen only the merest outline. Have you the possibility to return before you go?"

"Saturday is a free day," Vlcek said. "Perhaps Pan Whistler will be able to use the opportunity."

I said I fervently hoped so, and followed Galushka in. I was feeling physically ill. I thought the Norstrund wouldn't be there and I would have to ask for it. I had the clearest vision of myself tottering about making conversation while it came back through the channels. Maybe it wouldn't come back at all. Maybe whoever was fiddling with it had not had enough time; had been disturbed. . . I could see a variety of cockups looming, and as I entered the office closed my eyes in a brief wordless prayer. When I opened them I looked at the desk. The Norstrund had gone.

"If you'll just wait one moment," Galushka was saying, pressing a key on his intercom, "I'll get the report on tensile strength that interested you so much. I think also you should see our papers on heat treatment and annealing. Miss Bironova," he said into the intercom, "please bring me in the reports on . . ."

"Aren't you well, Pan Whistler?" Vlcek said in alarm. "Sit down a moment. It's the heat—you're not used to it. Here, let me help you."

I sat down, sick and shaking. Galushka got me a glass of water. While they were both staring at me in some concern, his girl came in with a sheaf of papers and the Norstrund.

One of the messengers had brought it in to her, she said. Perhaps it belonged to the *anglicke pane*. I said yes, yes, it was indeed mine; I must have mislaid it . . . and sat there a few minutes longer listening to Galushka, and my own voice responding very civilly to his remarks.

Just a little while later I was on the way back to Prague.

I locked the door of the room very carefully behind me and flaked out on the chaise longue. I was not excited or even nervous. I felt merely exhausted, as if I'd been shoveling for several hours or had gone a few rounds with some nimble-footed flyweight, not a heavy puncher but fast.

I sat up presently and opened the Norstrund and examined the flyleaf. It was crinkled a little in one corner. I didn't think the mark had been there before. I couldn't see any other sign of tampering. As Cunliffe had said, unless you knew about it you couldn't tell.

It was not yet half past five. I thought I'd take a warm bath and soak, and presently got up and went into the bathroom. Despite the magnificence of the apartment, the tub was an ancient instrument standing on four clawlike legs about eighteen inches out from the wall. It lacked a soapdish. It also lacked a plug. I looked underneath and around for the plug. There was a loose bit of lead piping on the floor near the wall, and that was all. I thought it was time I made use of Josef and rang for him.

Josef brought me a plug and I drew the bath and got in, lowering myself gently horizontal. I felt extraordinarily calm. I thought of all the heart-thudding, bowel-loosening hours I had gone through. Well, it was all over now. I'd got it. All I had to do was get back with it.

I think I dozed off.

I came to at a quarter past six and got out and dried myself. I put on clean underwear and went through to the room and lay down again on the chaise longue, relaxed and pleasantly ruminative. The day wasn't over yet. I wondered what else was in store. At seven o'clock I dressed and rang for a beer and went out on the balcony.

I stayed there, sipping slowly, until the clocks began to chime the quarter past, and then went in and picked up the Norstrund and left.

Seven-thirty, she had said, at the Slavia.

chapter 5

The effect of a bath and a rest and a beer had wrought some miraculous change in me as I stepped out of the hotel and into the still-crowded Vaclavske Namesti. I felt excessively clean-limbed and English, and in the mood for Adventures.

Prague, it is a fact, is still the most Ruritanian of the capitals of Europe. Despite the hands and brains, an aura of romance lingers over the city. At sunset lamps are lit in the linden trees on the embankment. A hundred points of saffron reflect the last light of day from the pinnacled Hradcany on the Heights. As the neon slogans begin to flash in the Vaclavske Namesti, so the turreted gray buildings and the cobbled courtyards of the old town come into their own. One feels the presence of Black Michael and enigmatic young countesses; one is no more than a stone's throw from Zenda.

All this was very satisfactory and I lingered as I cut through the old town. The clocks began to boom the half past as I came out on the embankment, and I put on a spurt. Even so I was ten minutes late.

The Slavia was a big corner café with huge windows, half open to the river. It was a hive of activity in the warm evening, waiters and waitresses shuttling there and back between the crowded tables. She was sitting with a glass of tea near the window reading a newspaper in a cane rack. She was wearing an embroidered blouse and had done something to her hair. It was now coiled on top, giving her a long and rather luscious neck.

She hadn't seen me come in and I approached from behind and said, smiling, into her ear, *"Dobry vecer."*

She started and looked round. "Oh. *Dobry vecer.*"

"I'm sorry I'm late. I didn't realize how long it would take me to walk here."

"Oh, don't think . . . It isn't any matter . . ." She had flushed rather stunningly, and seemed to have run out of English in her surprise. I took the seat opposite and gazed at her with frank admiration. "You're looking very attractive. I like your hair."

"Thank you. You are gallant."

"What have you been doing today?"

She told me in a rather solemn and childlike way. I continued to gaze at her with this same frank admiration. She had a thin gold chain and a cameo suspended from her neck. The embroidered blouse did nothing to cramp her wondrous figure. There was just a touch of wildness about the high Slav cheekbones. I felt myself begin to tingle with pleasant anticipation. Whistler Nicolas, no doubt about it, could have done a great deal worse for himself.

I had taken the only available seat at the table, and the curious attentions of the other patrons seemed to be inhibiting her. When I suggested that we move elsewhere she sprang up immediately. The punched bill was on the table. I paid it and we left.

Out in the street my misgivings returned. She stood almost a head taller, and walked with a powerful loping gait. I found myself beginning to sweat with embarrassment. It didn't seem to affect the girl. She talked slowly and studiously, grappling her way through the syntax and gazing down at me with long gray candid eyes.

We ate at the Zlaty Kohoutek, the Golden Cockerel, a night-spot across the river. It looked a little gimcrack place from the outside with a flashing sign of a cockerel and musical notes in several garish colors. Inside it was rather romantic, a long room, darkish, with lamps on the tables and much gleaming napery. A five-piece band played softly and cornily during dinner.

The girl ate and drank with healthy enjoyment. I had left the choice to her. She ordered carp, roast goose, sour cream, something called Soufflé Milord, and a water ice. She also ordered powerful cocktails, a half bottle of Hungarian white and a bottle of Hungarian red wine, and Rumanian brandy with the coffee.

All this had a profound effect on me. The band at the end of the long room showed a tendency to float gently up and down. The effect on the girl seemed equally beneficial. A certain primness in her manner departed. She put her elbows on the table and smiled across at me like the Mona Lisa with her chin cupped in her hands.

She told me she was twenty, and lived with her father, a musician and a widower, at Barrandov a few miles down the river. She had been a driver for two years.

I said, "What was all this about rock and roll? Are you very keen on dancing?"

"Not the dancing. I wouldn't call it dancing. It is the gayness. Gayness?" she said, recollecting her studies.

"Gaiety."

"Yes, gaiety. It is the gaiety and youth. But I love dancing, that is true. I would have been a dancer with the ballet. My father wished it, but it was not possible. I growed too much."

"Like Topsy."

"Topsy?"

"She was a girl who growed too much. It's a joke," I said, noticing the bafflement in her eyes. "The word should be grew really."

"Ah, a joke. Thank you. I am glad when you correct me. This is the only way to learn the language, don't you think it is so?"

The band had begun its slow upward levitation. I said daringly, "They say pillow English is very effective."

"Pillow English?"

"It's just another method. Forget it," I said, alarmed suddenly at the large, brooding face.

She didn't forget it, frowning over it. "Pillow English. A pillow is for the head?"

"That's it."

Enlightenment dawned. "Ah, you mean when people are in bed together."

"I'm sorry. I shouldn't have said it."

"Oh, it's nothing. Don't be shy," she said surprisingly, smiling at me."There is such a phrase in French. I forget it. You mean people in love learn the language quicker?"

"Sort of. It was just another joke."

She was regarding me with interest, teasing a wisp of hair that had come loose. "As a merchant you travel a great deal."

"Here and there."

"You have many mistresses?"

I goggled at her. "Not really. Not many."

"How many?"

"I don't know. You know I was only really . . ."

"Have you a wife?"

"No."

There was an odd flicker in the wine-bright eyes as she smiled curiously at me. "It is so interesting to learn how other people live. I would like to learn so much more."

"Maybe I can teach you."

"Maybe you can." She laughed, rather huskily, very promisingly indeed, and leaned toward me. I took her hand.

"You'd like to dance?" she said.

I had been dreading this for some time. The band had stopped playing softly and cornily and was now playing loudly and cornily. Several people were on the floor. I wedged the Norstrund in my pocket and stood up.

It was not nearly so bad as I had expected. On the dance floor, she was limber and light on her pins, responding to the merest touch. We swung tipsily round for a couple of numbers. Nobody seemed to find anything remarkable in the performance. Several small men were dancing with large, well-found women, and wine was flowing all round the shadowy room. Her bust, all the same, was rather too near my chin for absolute comfort, and she seemed to be leaning on it fairly freely. All this opened up certain vistas, but I was glad when the music stopped.

We left at ten o'clock and went for a walk, crossing the river and strolling along the embankment in the greenish light under the linden trees. I thought I might put my arm round her waist, and did so, meeting with no objection. Indeed, she snuggled up very amiably. I was content to await events.

Presently we cut through to the Vaclavske Namesti, seething and noisy as ever and brilliantly lit. A number of stalls had opened up at the curbside, selling *parkys*—hot sausages—and pickled cucumbers.

"You'd like to eat a *parky*?" she asked.

"No, thanks."

"I think I would like to eat a *parky*."

I queued up and brought her one, marveling at her appetite. The *parky* came on a slice of black bread with a smear of mustard. She disposed of it rapidly as we strolled along.

The clocks began to boom a quarter to eleven.

"I have so enjoyed myself," she said. "Thank you very much for this evening."

"I've enjoyed it, too. Thank you for coming."

"I think I should go home now."

I said, "Right," supporting this move entirely. In the crowded street I'd had to take my arm from her waist. Barrandov, down the river, sounded pleasantly secluded. "Where do we get the tram?"

"Oh, there is no need for you to come."

"That's all right. I'd like to."

"No, please. See, we are at the tram stop. It is no trouble for me. You have work tomorrow."

"But I must take you home," I said in dismay. It seemed impossible that I had misread the signs.

"No, please. It's late. And my father waits for me. I will go alone."

She had rooted herself solidly to the pavement and seemed to have made up her mind. I was suddenly conscious again of her massive physique. She was holding out her hand to me.

I took it drearily. "Well, if you insist," I said, cursing the missed opportunities. We had passed several useful-looking courtyards off the embankment.

"We can meet again, if you wish it."

"Does your father wait for you every night?"

"Most nights," she said dryly.

There was something about her that I couldn't quite fathom, a certain off-beat humor lurking in the long eyes. I'd seen it in the restaurant. I said, "How about tomorrow?"

"Tomorrow is not possible. I have to help my father with his practice. Truly," she said, smiling apologetically. "I play the piano for him."

"Saturday, then?"

"Saturday would be very nice. Must you work in the afternoon?"

"No. I'm finished then."

71

"I also. If you wish, we could swim in the river. I go every Saturday to the bathing station at Zluta Plovarna if the weather is good. Later, we could eat at Barrandov?"

"At Barrandov?"

"The Terasy."

It seemed there was a kind of lido there, a pool scooped out of rock, flanked by terraces cut into the stone. In the evening one could dine and dance on the terraces.

I thought it would fill in the time, if not in hoped-for pursuits, and gave the program somewhat grudging approval. She gave me her telephone number, which I noted in my diary.

"Perhaps I will say one thing more," she said, stepping from one long leg to the other, and watching my face. The flicker was back in her eyes. "My father will not wait for me on Saturday."

"Oh."

"You understand me?"

"Yes. Certainly. Rather."

I wondered if I did.

"Good night, and thank you again," she said warmly.

I said good night, and walked back to the hotel, slightly punch drunk.

Vlcek picked me up again in the morning and we drove to Tseblic (23 km.). This proved to be more or less a repetition of the marathon at Kralovsk, except that the manager, a keen technical type, was clearly not in Galushka's class as a force to be reckoned with. Vlcek didn't reckon with him much. After lunch, at which he drank more freely than on the previous day, he quietly faded away—for a snooze in the car, I suspected.

It was sweltering hot, and the red dye from the Norstrund stained my hands as we trudged for endless hours round the works. Vlcek joined us again, very perky, soon after four, and by five we were driving back.

"Well, Pan Whistler, I hope the visits have left you with some favorable impressions?"

"Yes, indeed."

"I think Kralovsk interested you more. I have arranged the automobile in case you should wish to return there tomorrow."

72

"No, thanks. It won't be necessary. I've got everything I need."

"Ah, you prefer then further Discussions with Pan Svoboda?"

"No. No. I don't think I do. I shan't want anything more at all. Everything's been beautifully planned," I said, noting his disappointment. "I wouldn't have thought it possible to work in so much in the time."

Vlcek smiled with sad pleasure. "We try to do our best in Prague. It isn't always obvious to—to some people. Perhaps if you are satisfied you would not mind saying so in a letter when you return to England?"

"Of course."

"And when shall we see you back again?"

"Back again?"

"We understood this was an exploratory trip for Discussions and Visits. Pan Svoboda hoped you would return soon. With your order book," he said gaily.

"Ah, yes. Well, that's up to my directors."

"Your report will be favorable? Excuse me," he said hastily. "I do not wish to pry. In the old days I was a salesman. I booked orders from England, France, Germany, Belgium . . . One knew how to handle this one with discounts, that one with long credit . . . It's different now. Today one thinks very much more on industrial lines. Output, work flow. . . . It is very interesting," he said sadly.

"Ah, well, you'll get the foreign trade back."

"Undoubtedly. It must come," Vlcek said excitedly. "We are, after all, a trading nation. Once the industry has been firmly re-established, salesmanship will be required again. Salesmanship, salesmanship, and yet more salesmanship." His vulpine little face was alight with prophetic fervor.

He dropped me at the Slovenska. I went up in the lift. Josef was prowling in the corridor.

"Ah, Pan Whistler. You have made good business." He was rubbing his hands, smiling the darkling smile.

"Yes, thanks. A full day, anyway."

"You look hot. It is the humidity. The big storm has not come yet."

"I wish it would soon."

"Never fear. Tonight or tomorrow perhaps. I should say a

glass of Pilsener would suit you."

"I'd say the same."

"Right away," he said, with pleasure.

I went in and through to the bathroom and stripped off and stood under the shower. I hoped the big storm wasn't going to wreck tomorrow's planned events. I pondered over them for ten minutes.

The beer was waiting for me when I came out.

"In England the girls wear two pieces or one?"

"I think one-piece at the moment."

"Yes," she said sadly, "I thought it was so. I saw recently a German magazine. They are quicker in Germany with the fashion."

She was wearing two pieces herself, in black sharkskin. I could hardly keep my eyes off either of them. Below the top-piece there wasn't an ounce of surplus flesh on her magnificent body, the waist flat and golden, legs long and smooth. She was leaning over on one elbow, moodily nibbling a blade of grass, gorgeous breasts pendant.

We were lying in a river meadow, a long tram ride from town, at the bathing station of Zluta Plovarna. Willows hung limp in the heat. It was somewhat overcast. Josef's storm had not come yet. The river was narrower here and gurgled between green banks. I longed to lie about in it, but desisted. The Norstrund was wrapped in my towel; I had hired the towel and a pair of somewhat skimpy shorts at the kiosk.

The girl had seemed rather moody when we met and had been severely rationing her conversation since we came out on the grass. I wondered uneasily if some physical deficiency of mine had upset her.

I said, after a lengthy silence, "You seem sad. Is anything the matter?"

"No. No."

"Don't you like the heat?"

"I don't mind it."

"Did you wear yourself out at the piano last night?"

"No," she said, unsmiling.

I stretched out, baffled.

"You will go tomorrow!" she burst out glumly.

I looked up at her, flattered and surprised. I had taken her out only once. It was hard to know what to say. "Oh, I expect I'll come back again."

"You think so?"

"I might."

"No, you won't. Ah, I wish I could go, too," she said passionately. "How I wish I could leave this country."

"Haven't you ever been away?"

"Once. To Hungary," she said scornfully. "It was just the same."

"Well, this is a very nice country. I mean," I said lamely, "you've got beautiful scenery and everything. The weather in England is terrible."

"The people are free to travel."

"Most of them never leave the country."

"They can if they want to. Anyway, they are free there. There are so many things."

It seemed to be time to try and edge her out of it. I smiled at her. "Like knowing whether to wear a one-piece or a two-piece?"

"That's a part of it."

"And rock and roll?"

"Oh, the rock and roll! You will not forget it." She was smiling all the same and seemed to have cheered up a bit.

"Did you make good business here?"

"I did what I came to do."

"What was that?"

"Look round glassworks and have discussions." I looked up at her curiously. "You know all that."

"Nothing else?"

"What else?"

"I don't know. You're not working for the Americans—to come and see things and tell them?"

"Why should I be?" My heart had started to flutter a bit.

"One hears stories. They say all Westerners are spies for the Americans. Isn't it so?"

"Of course it isn't."

"I don't mind if you are. You know what I feel."

"Well, I'm not," I said shortly. "You mustn't believe all that

75

rubbish, Vlasta. I'm here on business."

"Would you tell me if you were working for the Americans?"
She was smiling down at me. The nasty patch seemed to be over.

"What do you think?"

"I think I could tell," she said. She tickled me with the grass
stalk. "I know your face very well now."

"You haven't seen it very often."

"I think I know it all the same." She edged nearer, tickling
my nose. "It is quite—quite a comical face. I can tell what you
are thinking, little merchant."

The twin luscious bombs in black sharkskin hung a few inches
from my face. I stared at them hypnotically.

"What am I thinking?"

"I know," she said, tickling with the grass stalk. "I know. I
know. . . ."

So that seemed all right.

The terraces of Barrandov were quite a sight. We had fallen
asleep at the bathing station and it was after dusk when we took
the tram to the Terasy. The little nightspot shimmered like an
iridescent shell in the velvety darkness. The rock pool was a
mussel-shaped depression hacked out of the rock, several yards
below ground level. Running down to it, and following the same
conformation, were the stepped terraces like the galleries of the
Roman Coliseum. Floodlights picked out bits of statuary and
shrubs in pots. A dance band was playing. Shadowy figures
were sitting and strolling around the various levels, and here
and there a few couples were dancing; it was early yet.

All this was more than satisfactory, and we swung along to
the entrance, arm in arm, full of fresh air and with healthy appetites. The girl had gone into the river for a dip when we awoke
in the half-light, and had emerged, dripping, laughing, and so
athletically radiant that I could scarcely contain myself to see
what happened on the nights her father didn't wait for her.

The band was playing from a large building adjoining the
pool. A few score people were dining and dancing inside.

"You would like to eat here or outside?"

"As you please."

"Outside is a cold buffet. It's very good," she said, smiling.

"All right, outside."

We walked through to the terraces and found a table near the pool and then walked over to the buffet. This was a large table, supervised by several efficient-looking men in short white jackets, and supporting some dozens of trays of *hors d'œuvres*. We made a selection and the plates were brought over to us.

It was very pleasant. The dancing reflections on the water gave an illusion of coolness in the warm, humid night. She was wearing a little bolero over a sun-top, and she took it off. I ordered a bottle of wine, and watched in some fascination as she cleared her plate. I was setting to myself, but had still not half finished when she wandered off to the buffet again.

"I am hungry," she said when she returned.

"So I see."

"Aren't you hungry?"

"Yes, I am."

"For the food, I mean," she said, flickering.

"That's what I mean. How's your father?" I said, responding to her smile with a leer of my own.

"He is well."

"What's he doing tonight?"

"He plays at a concert at Pilsen."

"Good show."

"What is that?"

"I hope he has a good concert. What time will he be back?"

"Very late."

"Then here's to music and Pilsen," I said, raising my glass.

She responded to the toast, eyes flickering over her glass. "I think you are a bad man, little merchant."

"Don't scream till you're hurt."

It took her a moment or two to work this out, and seemed to afford her rich amusement. She spilled her wine, fairly glowing at me over her heaped plate.

"I never scream, little merchant."

Better and better.

At eleven o'clock I said, "Like to go now?" We had drunk another bottle of wine and danced a bit.

"If you like."

She put on her bolero and we left.

The music followed us into the black void. The road was bordered by thickets; it seemed to be almost in the country.

"Do you live far away?"

"Not far."

"Anywhere to sit down round here? I thought we might smoke a cigarette."

"There is a seat by the telephone box a little farther along— on the other side of the road."

We crossed and found this seat, a sturdy rustic piece. The telephone box was unlighted, I was glad to see.

"Cigarette?"

"No, thank you."

"I don't think I will, either."

"Wasn't that what you wanted?"

"Not all I wanted."

In the dizzy, fractional pause, I kissed her.

She responded swiftly, her two arms whipping out like pythons —not, as I momentarily feared, to repel me. I found myself crushed in an embrace of powerful ardor. She wore no perfume or lipstick. She had a curious odor of her own, of tanned skin, fresh air, some kind of spice, a Slav smell, very stimulating.

"*Milacek*," she murmured a minute or two later when I found strength to draw back for air.

It was a word I had forgotten. *Milacek*. Darling. It came back powerfully over the years. . . . I returned to her in the blackness. And then all hell seemed to be let loose.

There was a single tearing razor flash of lightning, an instant eruption of thunder, and the sky fell in. A sheet of water seemed to drop solidly out of the air.

Josef's storm had begun.

It happened so quickly we were drenched even before we got off the seat. The girl cowered against me, muttering. I swore evilly.

"Quick. Nip in the telephone box," I said, and led the way. We stood pressed together inside, sodden and dripping. The night sounded suddenly like a river in full flood.

"Maybe it will soon stop," I said miserably.

She shook her head. "I think not. We have these storms sometimes. It will last one hour, perhaps two."

We stood without speaking for some time, our clothes beginning to steam in the hot, close air. One or two people raced past, splashing. The night was now brilliant with lightning, reverberating with thunder. Water streamed like a plastic film down the window.

"Now what?" I said.

"I don't know."

"Maybe it will ease off after a bit."

"Maybe. We could try to run to my home."

"Will your father be back yet?"

"Not yet. Not until twelve or one o'clock."

"All right."

We waited in the noisy, flashing darkness.

"I think it is not so bad now," she said after a few minutes. "Come, we can try. We will have to be quick. It will start again."

We pelted out of the box. It seemed suddenly cold outside, the rain still falling heavily, but not flooding down as before. The road was running, fantastically, with water, an inch or two deep already.

We splashed hand in hand for some minutes and turned right up a side road. "The white house. Look, you can see," she said, as lightning began to flash overhead again. It stood by itself, a small bungalow. A cluster of others stood near it.

The rain began to belt down fiercely again as we got to the gate. She fumbled for her key and opened the door and we stumbled in, streaming. She put the light on and looked at me and leaned against the wall, laughing. "To see yourself! You have had your swim, after all."

I sneezed, not sharing this joke.

"I am sorry. Come in. Take off the wet coat. You will catch an illness."

I thought I'd caught one already. The unusual exercise through the puddles—she had dragged me along with racing, Olympic strides—in addition to the damp and debilitating session in the box, seemed to have taken their toll.

"Give me it. I will put the electric fire on. So. It will dry a little."

My trousers were equally sodden. There didn't seem much to

be done about them. I stood there, damply uncomfortable, while she brought in towels and we dried our hair.

"Now who is sad?" she said. "Come, smile for me, little merchant." The brisk run seemed to have done her good. She was lively and cheerful, eyes sparkling. "I will make you some coffee, then I will change. Maybe I can find something of my father's for you to wear while your clothes dry."

She disappeared into the next room and I looked sourly round. There seemed to be three rooms, one of them a kitchen-dining room. A cottage piano stood in the living room. There was also a divan, made up as a bed. A large round clock was mounted on the wall. It registered a quarter to twelve. Her father would be back soon. A fine night this had turned out to be.

She came back after a minute with her hair down and in a dressing gown, inspecting a suit at arm's length. It was of brown tweed and evidently made for some circus freak. "My father is bigger than you," she said unnecessarily. "Try it anyway."

I slipped the jacket on, to her excessive merriment.

"I am sorry," she said. "Keep it on, anyway. Put on the suit."

"How about your father?"

"He cannot mind. It is only till yours is dry. Go in the next room. Oh, little merchant, you will have to grow!"

I was beginning to tire of this description, and also of the massive, humorous girl. There didn't seem much else to be done, however. I went to the next room and changed into the enormous trousers and shuffled back in them, nerving myself for the expected peals of laughter.

They didn't come. She was sitting on the floor near the electric fire, and only smiled somberly when I appeared. "So. This is the last time we meet, Nicolas."

I said, "Not necessarily," halfheartedly, and sneezed again.

"You had better have a drink. You are cold. The coffee isn't ready yet." She got up and fetched a bottle of slivovitz from a cupboard and poured a glass. It was fiery stuff with a mulelike though humanizing kick. I took a less jaundiced look round the room. It was quite large and tastefully furnished. There was a balalaika on a small table.

"Is that your father's instrument?"

"No, no. He is a cello. The balalaika is mine."

"How about a tune?"

"I don't feel for it. I will see to the coffee."

I didn't feel much like a tune myself. My suit was steaming away on a chair. It was two minutes to twelve. I wondered how the hell I was going to get back. I thought it would have to be a taxi. I had noticed a phone in the hall. I finished the slivovitz and put the glass down and sat down in an easy chair, wishing with all my heart that I was tucked up snugly in the Slovenska awaiting the morning chimes and the ten-o'clock plane.

She came in with the coffee, and we drank it rather silently.

"Another glass of slivovitz? Your suit is not yet dry."

"Thanks."

She had one herself, and raised the glass. "To the success of your business, Nicolas."

I couldn't think of much to say to this, and merely raised mine with a cheerful nod.

"Do you think you will really come back?"

"Well, it's possible. In business you never can tell."

"When could it be?"

"Hard to say. Quite soon, perhaps. I *would* like to hear you play the balalaika," I said, to change the noisome conversation.

She smiled moodily and picked up the instrument and sat down on the rug and began to play. It was a Slovak song my mother sometimes hummed, and presently she began to sing. It was something about pine trees and love and death. I listened, at first pleasantly surprised, and then astonished. She sang wonderfully, a husky, thrilling voice, mournful, perfectly attuned to the dolorous rhythm.

She ended with a final twang and let the strings die slowly in the quiet room. It was very effective. I said sincerely, "Vlasta, that was marvelous. Play another."

"You like the balalaika?"

"I like the way you do it."

"The balalaika is for firelight," she said with a mournful smile. "Switch off the light."

I did so, with an anxious look at the clock. It was a quarter past twelve. Outside the rain was still pouring steadily, thunder rumbling distantly. I took my seat again in the easy chair in the red glow of the fire. She had poured out two more drinks

81

and drained hers with a single toss before beginning to pluck the balalaika again.

I don't know how many songs she played. She poured more drinks between them. I sank back in the warm darkness, aware I should be going, unable to go, thinking just one more, and just one more. At some point she moved over to lean against me as she sang. I dropped my hands to her shoulders and played with her damp hair. Its odor came up strongly in the dimly lit room.

She swayed from side to side as she sang, and I swayed with her, head beginning to spin, fire rolling, darkness lurching. I cupped my hands under her chin, and, as the room rolled and the low voice sang, dropped them inside her dressing gown.

She didn't stop singing; bombs rolling warmly, smoothly, heavily in the dark. And then the balalaika had stopped and she had turned round and was nuzzling my face. "*Milacek.*"

"I shouldn't be here."

"Stay now."

"Your father."

"It's too late. He won't come."

"How do you know? How can you . . ."

"The concert must have ended late. He will come early in the morning. They have a motorbus. It has happened before."

My heart was thumping, mouth dry, the girl's face swaying in the dim light. I said huskily, "Vlasta, are you sure?"

She stood up and pulled the sash. Her dressing gown fell open. She had nothing on at all underneath.

"I am sure," she said.

chapter 6

I was rowing this enormous boat with a rope round my neck and the man hitting me over the head with a shovel when it gave a final lurch and I came up out of it. I opened my eyes. A large white face was circling several feet in front of me. It stopped after a while and turned into a clock, which, after much diligent frowning, I calculated to be resigstering ten minutes to seven.

There was an awful numbness at the back of my neck and my head seemed to have been crammed forward over my eyes. I lay quiet for a while puzzling why this should be and trying to think where the hell I was, and suddenly remembered and sat up in a panic. I was going home today. I was due at the airport at ten. Three hours.

I had been lying on her arm. Her large, beautiful body lay stretched out on top of the coverlet, one massive tanned leg across mine. Her bomblike breasts rose and fell profoundly. She was fast asleep and moodily magnificent.

She had loved with such ferocity last night that even in my drunken excitement I had been unnerved at the appalling strength of her. In this shattered morning state I was more than unnerved. I felt broken, ruined, and in much physical danger.

Across the chair, in some disarray, lay the inhumanly large clothes of her father. I had no wish to be around when he arrived; still less, a far graver and more urgent contingency, when his insatiable daughter should awake.

She lay sleeping like the mother of the universe. I began trying to maneuver my leg from under hers. This was no simple operation, and in the course of it her arm came round in a loose movement batting me numbingly on the ear.

83

She was turning over.

I waited in palpitating and queasy silence, but apart from a somber, muttered "*Milacek,*" she did not awake.

I drew myself slowly off the bed, watching her minutely. The Norstrund was on the floor beside the almost-empty slivovitz bottle. I picked it up and tiptoed into the bathroom.

My clothes were still damp and crumpled. I put them on swiftly. The room lurched. I rammed my tie in my pocket and left my shoe laces undone and tiptoed back to the doorway. She had turned half on her side, knees drawn up. She was sleeping soundly with the healthy and magnificent grace of some satisfied jungle beast. I said silently, Good-by, Vlasta, good-by, *milacek,* and let myself out quietly.

I walked softly up the gravel path to the side road, but once there tied up my shoe laces and began to run. It was a still morning, hot already, the sun glinting everywhere. My mouth was parched, stomach gravely uneasy.

At the main road I stopped and looked up and down. There was nothing in sight, no trucks, no farm wagons, not even a bicycle. The telegraph wires hummed softly in the silence. A tangy smell was coming up off the road in the early heat. I began to panic again. I had a terrifying feeling the girl had woken up and was storming around looking for me and would shortly come bounding up the road in amorous fury. It was a damned long way from the hotel. Too far to walk; two hours at least. And I had to pack and pay and get to the airport.

In a state of mild frenzy, I began to trot up the road, and five minutes later had to slow down, gasping. A couple of minutes after that I saw a horse and trap pulling out of a side road ahead of me and yelled like a madman for the driver to stop. He did so, staring curiously as I panted up.

"You drive to Prague?" I asked in Czech.

"*Yoh.*"

"*Dobry den,*" I said belatedly as I clambered up.

"*Dobry den.*" He was a little wizened carrot of a man, in shiny gaiters. He still looked curiously at me, but apart from a sly remark of "How goes the night work, comrade?" made no comment as we trotted down to the shining river.

We crossed the water at the Jiraskuv bridge and he dropped

me at the corner of the Mezibranska and I walked past the museum and up the Vaclavske Namesti, quiet for once in the still of this sunny Sunday morning, and got into the hotel by ten past eight. I had a shower and packed and went down for my breakfast and had paid the bill by twenty past nine. And then with nothing to do, but a compulsive need to do it, I called a taxi and left.

I was too early to go through the customs but, with a mindless sense that it might show the innocence of my luggage and of my conscience, I left my case on the inspection table and walked up and down, grateful, in a complex way, for this confusion of stomach and mind that obscured the terrors of the final handicap.

There was no need for worry. The customs officials showed no interest in my luggage. They didn't notice the Norstrund.

Five days after leaving it, only ten hours since parting from the beautiful giantess on the bed at Barrandov, I was back in Fitzwalter Square. I let myself in with my latchkey and paused for a moment in the hall, leaning against the front door, grinning with disbelief.

Mrs. Nolan came out of the kitchen with a loaded tray. "Hello, duck," she said. "Back already? You're just in time for tea," and passed into the dining room.

I had told Mrs. Nolan I was visiting my mother in Bournemouth, and having no desire to enlarge on this or indeed to do anything but flake out on the divan and gaze with hilarious relief at the plush tablecloth and the plant and the entire fusty sanity of my familiar surroundings, I remained in my room.

I couldn't believe I was back. I couldn't believe I would not shortly awake to find myself in the bed at Barrandov with the large and brooding Vlasta; or in the green and gold splendor of the Slovenska with the noisy Vaclavske Namesti outside and the Norstrund to be guarded. I couldn't believe I'd got away with it.

I picked up the Norstrund and opened the cover. It was still crinkled a little in one corner. I ran my hand all over it. It was smooth and flat and innocent, a very expert job indeed. Impossible to believe that I had here the secret of a new industry; that I had blarneyed my way past Svoboda and Czernin and

Stein and Vlcek and Galushka, had emerged from the muscular embraces of Vlasta Simenova, and had smuggled it out.

I was still somewhat dehydrated from the slivovitz, and presently went down to the bathroom and drank from the toothmug. While I was there I thought I might as well have a wash and took off my jacket and bent over the bowl. This familiar action, in shirt sleeves and braces, and the sight of my own face in the small cracked mirror, convinced me suddenly as nothing else had done that I was back. I toweled myself vigorously in the mirror and showed my teeth and smiled. I even said, "Well, Pan Whistler, you made it," and winked at my image, feeling at that moment extraordinarily debonair and alive and also, my nostrils carrying still the sharp odor of the girl at Barrandov, a bit of a young dog.

I went back to my room still smiling vacuously, but once there thought I'd better ring Cunliffe right away and picked up the Norstrund, out of habit, and went downstairs again.

Mrs. Nolan had been watching out for me.

"You're surely not going out again before you've had a cup of tea, ducky?"

I had intended phoning from the hall but now thought better of it. "I won't be a tick, Mrs. Nolan. I'm only walking up the street."

"Brought her a nice book back, have you?" She winked at me. "She's been ringing up, you know. She hasn't forgotten you."

I had not spared so much as a moment's thought for Maura, and now, reminded, felt the familiar distractions settling on me. I had no wish to see Maura yet, no wish to think about any of that at all. I said, "Did she leave any message?"

"Only for you to get in touch with her when you got back. No further news about the other thing yet, I suppose?"

It was so long ago, such a lifetime ago, that I couldn't think for the moment what the devil she was talking about.

"The other thing—your poor uncle."

"Oh, no. Nothing further. I wasn't expecting to yet."

"No, well. These things take time, don't they?" She had lowered her voice in referring to the other thing, but now raised it again. "Well, off you go then. Only don't make a meal of it. And don't you go catching her by surprise—you might get one yourself," she added with a playful little shove.

I went down the street thoughtfully, several familiar worries returning to mind. They were still in an unresolved and uncoagulated state, however, by the time I reached the telephone box and I took out the torn bit of diary sheet Cunliffe had given me and dialed his number with elation.

"Hello. This is Nicolas Whistler."

He said, "Who? Oh. You are back. Excellent. Just one moment," and went away for a while. "I am very glad to hear your voice," he grated warmly when he returned. "Did everything go as planned?"

"Yes. A few worrying moments, but no hitches. I've got the doings all right."

"That's wonderful. I don't think we should discuss it on the telephone, you know."

"No. Do you want me to come round right away?"

"I don't think," he said slowly, "I don't think that's absolutely necessary."

"Later this evening?"

There was a pause. "I don't think you should come here at all. See me in the office in the morning."

I said, "All right," with some disappointment.

"There isn't anything—nothing went wrong in any way?"

"No. It's just that I've been carrying the bloody thing around for several days. I thought it was urgent."

"It is indeed. I will see you tomorrow, Mr. Whistler. At nine o'clock. Good-by." He hung up right away.

My features in the little round mirror were sheepish and disappointed. I replaced the receiver and went outside. It was too early for a drink. I went back for tea, with the Norstrund.

In the night I woke up, parched again, but couldn't be bothered to get out of bed. For some reason I felt depressed as hell. A lot of things had come crowding back to mind and I turned over on my back and licked my lips and thought of them.

The night Maura was in this room. Just a week ago. She'd said the fellow on the first floor had let her in. I knew something was wrong with that, but couldn't place it at the time. I could now. He was deaf. Not just hard of hearing; practically stone deaf. You had to dance about like a lunatic in front of him to attract his attention, our Mr. Larkin. So he was the one who'd heard the doorbell and let her in.

I thought about Cunliffe then. He'd been surprised, no doubt about it, by my call. He hadn't known I was back. Nor had a lot of people. Nor had Maura. But she'd been ringing up to find out.

I thought, oh no, how could it be? Why should Maura have me sent out on such a dangerous mission? But it hadn't sounded very dangerous the way Cunliffe had explained it. It hadn't, in fact, been very dangerous. It might have sounded a lot better, a lot more useful and enterprising than sticking stamps for the Little Swine.

But how could Maura have met Cunliffe? He was a money-lender. She hadn't been borrowing any money. She had never mentioned any social occasion when she might conceivably have met him. She was a typist in a West End estate agency.

I turned on my side and tried to sleep, but I knew I wouldn't unless I had a drink, so I got up and had one and returned to bed and slept, heavily.

The sun was shining on Mrs. Nolan's aspidistra when I awoke and somewhere below that jolly lady sang as she bashed about with the crockery. I felt extraordinarily refreshed and full of beans. And why not? I thought, springing out of bed. I had nipped behind the Iron Curtain and found time to dally on the way. I had returned with a secret worth, say, a king's ransom. I seemed to have swapped for good one way of life and almost any change would be an improvement.

As for Maura—Maura was an imaginative girl with a talent for shoving her nose in. She'd meant for the best. And everything probably was for the best. There would be time to sort out Maura. For the present, there were things to be done this day.

The depression of the night seemed to have been a last poisonous kick out of the slivovitz, and I dressed and breakfasted and picked up the car and wove in and out of the traffic to Francis Street in a very agreeable frame of mind, arriving there sharp on nine.

Bunface had not yet arrived, but Cunliffe had left his inner office door open, and called, "Is that you, Mr. Whistler? Please come right in."

He was sitting waiting for me, still in his street coat, and I placed the Norstrund modestly on his desk and he took both my hands, smiling whimsically into my eyes without saying a word.

"You see?" he said at last, releasing my hands and picking up the Norstrund. "I told you how it would be. I never doubted for a minute that you could do it."

"No. Well," I said, dropping negligently into a chair, "there were one or two worrying moments. Is Mr. Pavelka coming along?"

"Mr. Pavelka is out looking for a factory," he said, smiling. "In Ireland at the moment, I believe. As you saw for yourself, he has the highest hopes for this—this new process."

He had opened the Norstrund and was running his fingers as I had done over the flyleaf. I thought: Ireland, looking for a factory, estate agents, Maura; and saw in that moment exactly how it must have been, Pavelka with his great creased dog's face explaining earnestly what he wanted, and Maura saying *Glass, glass—I wonder, Mr. Pavelka,* her busy little brain working on it right away.

Everything fell into place then, and I sat there grinning at Cunliffe, and he looked up from the book and caught me grinning and said, "Yes, he's a very impetuous man, Mr. Pavelka, but you should be complimented at the confidence he has in you."

And I was complimented; really quite touched. *I like you,* he had said. *You look like your father.*

I told Cunliffe everything that had happened to me in Prague then, with some personal exceptions, and he listened quietly, his large gray intelligent eyes unblinking.

"Yes," he said at the end, "it's really much as I thought. We've been getting reports out, of course. And now," he said, slipping the Norstrund in his briefcase, "I've got to go somewhere with this."

There was a pause as he fiddled with the straps of his case, and I wondered if I should ask about the money yet. It was, plainly, Pavelka's money, and he hadn't got the formula in his hand yet.

There was also the point that I was, so to speak—Pavelka had as good as told me—already in his employ.

Cunliffe looked up, smiling. "But we still have a little business to transact." He got up and opened his safe and took out a packet and tossed it lightly on the desk. Inside were four bundles of ten fivers. The full sum, I saw, with elation and astonishment, two hundred pounds.

"And these," said Cunliffe. He had taken out of the safe also the two copies of the loan agreement. "One a little bit torn, I am afraid," he said wryly. "There are no hard feelings?"

"None at all."

"You understand it was necessary to manufacture some—some inducement?"

"Absolutely. The trip sounded a lot more frightening than it was. I've no complaints at all. When will Mr. Pavelka be back?"

"Within a very few days. He's not the most predictable of men."

"I'd better keep in touch then."

"I'll get in touch with you. He'll undoubtedly want to see you as soon as he comes back."

"Well, fine," I said, my head fairly singing with relief and good fortune. The danger was all over now. Ahead lay the boundless future with Pavelka.

Cunliffe had picked up his briefcase and was waiting for me to go. I thought there was one thing I might get sorted out, and said, "There's just one point. This—this person who's been watching me. You don't feel inclined to tell me who it is now?"

"I'm afraid—not yet, Mr. Whistler," he said, smiling broadly. "There are still some little secrets until everything is fixed up."

"Not even if I named a name? I've a pretty shrewd idea who it is."

"I'm sorry."

"All right," I said, a bit put out, and went.

Outside in the car, I thought I might have made a more determined effort and decided to wait until he came out. When he didn't appear after a few minutes, however, I began to feel a bit of a fool, and since it might look as if I was waiting to see where he went, I started up and turned round in the road and buzzed back up Francis Street. Outside the Fuller's teashop on the corner, I saw Bunface standing wrapped in thought, and gave her a honk. She came out of her trance and dropped me a swift bob and walked quickly down the street.

It didn't occur to me until later that she might have been seeing me off the premises.

One day's indolence very easily breeds another. It was a beautiful time in London then, fine golden days, cooler than Prague, freer than Prague, and I awaited Pavelka's pleasure. I had a fitting for the suits I had ordered. I messed around with the car. I ran out one day to the river and tried all the pubs from Laleham to Old Windsor and slept under a tree near Runnymede.

It was a brainless time, an undemanding time, and I didn't want it to stop. But on Thursday I woke up with a mild sense of worry that something should be happening and by midday all the old apprehensions had returned.

I wanted to ring Cunliffe, but I knew he would have no news for me. I wanted to ring Imre and Maminka, but there was nothing I could tell them. I wanted to ring Maura, but the situation here was still obscure.

I wondered how she had managed to get into my room that night. Had she somehow got hold of my key and had it copied? And why hadn't she come to see me again? She would know I was back. It must have occurred to that busy brain that I might have tumbled her. You would expect her to put out a feeler or two.

Puzzling over this, I thought there was at least one thing I could clear out of the way, and I waited that afternoon for Larkin to come home. He was a queer old man, very reticent and aloof, in a world of his own with his deafness. He took his meals alone and I had not seen him since my return.

I waited in my room and heard him come in and go into the lounge with his paper as he usually did. I went downstairs and opened the lounge door and saw him buried behind his paper in an easy chair and I said, "Afternoon, Mr. Larkin."

"Afternoon," he said, without putting the paper down.

I felt a flush starting up from my neck and I closed the door slowly behind me and said, "Mr. Larkin."

He lowered the paper then and looked up irritably and I saw the wire dangling from his ear. Mr. Larkin had got himself a natty little hearing aid.

I rang Cunliffe five minutes later from the call box on the corner. He seemed glad to hear my voice but there was no news, and I said, "Mr. Cunliffe, I know how you feel about this, but it's become very important to me just now—it's this person who's watching me."

"Oh, now, Mr. Whistler. You know I can't say anything about that. It's all past and done with, just a prudent step I was bound to take before we knew each other."

"Yes, I know. I understand perfectly. I don't mind in the least. It's just—I've got to know," I grabbled rapidly, as he tried to interrupt, "if it's my girl friend, Maura Regan. I wouldn't let her know, or hold it against her or anything. It's just that I haven't the faintest bloody idea how to talk to her."

He had been going to say something else, but choked suddenly on the phone. "Your—your girl friend! Oh, dear me, no! Oh, my dear Mr. Whistler," he said, laughing heartily, "I feel perfectly safe in assuring you that it isn't. I'm dreadfully sorry. I wouldn't for anything in the world want to interfere with your love life. I had no idea . . ."

So that was that, and I put the phone down, a bit lightheaded and with my heart banging, and picked it up again and put more pennies in the box and phoned her office. It was twenty past five; just in time to catch her.

She said, "Hello," and I said, "Guess who," and there was a pause for a moment and I could imagine her lopsided smile coming on.

"Is it Nicolas?"

"Who else?" I said and grinned into the mirror, and she hung up.

I couldn't believe it. I rattled the phone. I said, "Operator." I hadn't any more pennies. I hopped out of the box, muttering like a madman, and stopped people in the street, and telephoned her again. They said she'd gone.

I got out of the box and stood in the street for a minute, muttering obscenely under my breath and wondering what in God's name this lot was about. But I knew all right; knew in an instant, the trip to Prague and the four golden days vanishing into oblivion as I found myself back in the continuing situation with Maura.

We'd parted in a queer sort of way. Quite enough for her to be miffed about in that alone. And I hadn't written, not a line, not a postcard. And she'd probably seen the car back, had almost certainly seen the car back, had probably tooled round regularly to see when it came back.

I thought, Oh, Jesus Christ, experiencing the familiar enervation at the course of wooing now called for, and started off to wait outside her digs.

I waited an hour and a half before realizing that she must have gone off somewhere right from the office. She evidently meant me to work at it a bit harder than that.

Next day, Friday, I telephoned her in the morning, and was told by a breathy, giggling girl that she wasn't there. So at lunchtime I went to wait outside the office.

She came out at one sharp, in a hell of a hurry, with another girl, and I said, "Hello, Maura," and she said, "Sorry, Nicolas, can't stop. We're off shopping," and the pair of them jumped on a 25 bus.

I stared after this bus, swearing, and said to myself wearily, Right, well, one more go and that's your lot, and was outside the office again at twenty past five.

I stood at the opposite side of the street in a deep doorway so that I would see her first, and I told myself that if she came rushing out merrily with another girl, she could continue right on.

But she was alone when she came out, at twenty to six, and she wasn't smiling and she wasn't in a hurry. She looked quickly up and down the street and didn't see me, and began walking slowly to the Tube station, looking so like a little girl, lost and miserable, that my heart began bumping and I crossed the road and fell into step beside her. She looked at me and jumped but said nothing.

I said, "Hello, Maura."

"Hello."

We continued slowly and in silence to the Tube station.

"Like to stop for a cup of tea?"

"No, thanks. I must get back."

"You've got every right to be angry with me, Maura, but you don't know what's happened."

"I don't want to know."

I stopped in the street and said, "Ah, for God's sake, Maura," with a haggard look I'd been practicing all afternoon. "I've got so much to tell you. I've been wanting to for so long and couldn't."

She wasn't really able to resist this, but followed me very coldly as I turned in to the teashop. I found an empty table and we sat down and I told her all that was good for her to know.

I told her the trip to Prague was a brilliant success. I told her I might be leaving the Little Swine and going into an enormous project with a big-time manufacturer. I told her all this was so secret that I had been sworn to silence and had not dared to get in touch with her lest I be tempted to reveal some minute part of it.

She listened in silence, looking down at her tea, completely enchanting in her small-girl pride, and when I had finished, said, "Do you mean it, Nicolas, about wanting to tell me?"

"Of course I do, Maura."

"And you still can't tell me any more about it?"

"I shouldn't be telling you this."

She stirred her tea slowly. "Everything's going to be all right, though, now, is it?"

"I hope so, Maura. I've just got to wait for a man to come back from—from somewhere."

She looked up and said, "Well!" and the lopsided smile came on across the table. "Oh, Nicolas, don't ever do that to me again. Give me some warning. I've been through torture. I couldn't stand that again."

She was pressing her leg hard against mine under the table, and I groaned inwardly, thinking of all that bottled-up melodrama, all the hours and hours of it, wondering how a girl with such attractions and so much of the right stuff could be at the same time so bloody irritating.

We ate, rather late, in Soho and had a bottle of wine; and

later waxed somewhat melodramatic on the seat under the tree. But with that out of the way our relationship blossomed wonderfully, progressing indeed so rapidly on Saturday (in Epping Forest) and on Sunday (in my room while Mrs. Nolan graced the Musketeers) and in so enjoyable a fashion that I thought, Pavelka or no Pavelka, I would soon have to do something about it.

I took her out to lunch on the Monday, and decided that I would definitely ring Cunliffe when I got back to start some action. I didn't have to start any. When I returned there was a note in Mrs. Nolan's indelible pencil on the plush tablecloth. It read: *Mr. Whistler. Please telephone Victoria 63781.* And underneath, a later addition, *Please ring your mother.*

I went down the stairs two at a time and out whistling into the street. I called Cunliffe first and Bunface answered, and I dropped her a quick bob in the mirror and asked to be put through.

"Oh, Mr. Whistler, we have tried to get you. Mr. Cunliffe is out just now. He is out with Mr. Pavelka. He asks will you come for a meeting at eleven in the morning."

I let out my breath, grinning stupidly in the mirror. "Certainly. Absolutely. Tell him yes."

"Thank you."

"Thank *you*," I said, and put the receiver down and went out into the street, still grinning. I was halfway back before I remembered about Maminka, and returned to the phone, having no wish for Mrs. Nolan to overhear this conversation either.

It was unusual for Maminka to telephone me. I wondered if Imre, with his talent for doing the wrong thing at the wrong time, had suddenly decided to tell her about Bela, and when he came to the phone, felt a wave of irritation, and said quite brusquely, "Hello, Uncle. What is it? Maminka rang me?"

"It was I, Nicolas. I called you. How are you, my boy?"

"I'm all right. Is there any trouble?"

"No trouble. Certainly not. I was worried about you. You were so downcast when you were here."

"You haven't, by any chance, told Maminka about Bela?"

"I haven't. The heat is not good for her. She walks always in the sun without a hat and is naturally fatigued. It is totally impossible to reason with her," he said, breathing noisily.

"Well, that's all right," I said. "I shouldn't bother to tell her just yet, Uncle. I'll explain later."

"You are not still angry with me?"

"Of course not. Everything's O.K. Don't worry. I'll come and see you soon."

"Oh, I am glad," he said, and sounded it. "I thought maybe you didn't wish to talk with me."

He sounded so helpless and contrite, the old booby, I wondered for one mad moment if I dare tell him, just a hint; but thought better of it instantly. There'd be time for that after I'd seen Pavelka. Only a few hours more, another night of discretion, and then I would be able to take steps in several directions.

I was not able, however, to exercise this discretion with Maura. Embracing her that night on our trysting seat something seemed, as they say, to snap inside me and I found myself asking her to marry me. I was completely unable to prevent myself; the words seemed to be washed out of me on this swelling tide of good fortune. And after a moment's silence in the dark, Maura clutched me tighter and said, "Oh, yes, Nicolas, please. I want to. I want to," and that was that settled.

She asked me no questions, the lovely creature, but when an hour later I said good night at her gate, she said, "Can I come with you to tell your mother, Nicolas? I'd like to be there then."

I said, "Of course, Maura."

"Perhaps we could pop down on Sunday and stay overnight so that I can get to know her a little. We could come back early on Monday morning."

"That's a splendid idea, Maura. I'd like that very much."

And so I left her and walked back through the dark squares rejoicing to Mrs. Nolan's, thinking how wonderful Sunday night would be, and how much I wanted to introduce Maura to Maminka; which, of course, I would have done and with much pleasure, if Sunday night had chanced to find me in Bournemouth, instead of, as it did, in Barrandov, in bed, with Vlasta.

chapter 7

"I will come right to the point, Mr. Whistler," Cunliffe said. "The formula you brought back is incomplete. We don't know how or why this should be but the fact remains—Mr. Pavelka, would you mind showing him the —the object—all that it makes is this."

Pavelka, who had been sitting massive and dejected in his chair, came slowly to life and handed over a piece of glass he had been clutching in his hand. It was part of a hollow blown sphere, cut to show the thickness. It was green and opaque. As a piece of glass, it was of quite exceptional ugliness.

I licked my lips and looked from it to Pavelka. I had known the moment I came into the room that something was wrong. Pavelka looked back at me somberly, but said nothing.

"Mr. Pavelka feels," Cunliffe said after a moment, "that the only explanation must be that the formula was written in a hurry. There were several apparent inconsistencies that puzzled our chemist, but one of them—perhaps you would elaborate, Mr. Pavelka."

"Golombek is a bloody idiot," Pavelka said heavily.

"I don't think," Cunliffe cut in smoothly, "that Mr. Whistler needs to know . . ."

"A bloody idiot!" Pavelka repeated. "In 1937 once I nearly dismissed him. I should have done it," he said bitterly. "He lets me down after all this planning! There is too much iron, *yoh*?" He was pointing one bananalike finger at the glass in my hand.

"Iron, Mr. Pavelka?"

"Iron oxide. The green is iron, *yoh*?"

"Ah. *Yoh*. Yes."

"This proportion cannot be. It is a useful glass but we are not making beer bottles. Perhaps he has transposed it with the dolomite—I wonder," he said, his great St. Bernard's face creasing suddenly. He remained in intense thought for several minutes.

Cunliffe broke the silence. "What it amounts to, Mr. Whistler, is that the formula is very nearly right, but not quite. Mr. Pavelka feels it would be possible to go ahead with research here on the basis of it, but this would almost certainly cost a great deal in money and time."

"*Yoh,* money and time!" Pavelka said darkly. "That bloody idiot! When you go back you will take him a personal letter . . ."

"If you please, Mr. Pavelka," Cunliffe said sharply. "Mr. Whistler will do nothing of the sort when he returns. We have headaches enough."

"When I what?" I said, the lunatic suggestion suddenly breaking through.

"When you return," said Cunliffe. "To Prague. To Mr. Pavelka's factory. As I was trying to point out, research here might involve a considerable investment and it would almost certainly be cheaper and quicker for you to return to Prague immediately. You could do this very simply and without bother—"

"Oh, I couldn't, Mr. Cunliffe," I said. I had come bounding out of the chair, still clutching the piece of glass and was now wringing it urgently. "I really couldn't. There's nothing simple about it at all. You don't understand." As I spoke I had the clearest possible recollection of all the heart-thudding, mouth-drying, sick-making hours I had gone through, of Vlasta, of Galushka. "There's Galushka," I said. "Galushka, for a start, would see through it. You've no idea how dangerous—"

"Galushka?" said Pavelka. "What has Galushka to do with it?"

"Oh, dear," said Cunliffe, and took out his cigarette case. "I'm afraid I took the liberty of omitting what you told me about Mr. Galushka. He annoys Mr. Pavelka intensely."

"Galushka?" said Pavelka again, breathing heavily, his massive brows beetling. "Galushka isn't anything. I sacked Galushka years ago."

"Well, he's back now, Mr. Pavelka," I said loudly. "Times have changed. He runs the factory. He's a very sharp man. We'd never get past him twice with this. You'd much better press on with your researches and later on maybe . . ."

Pavelka was staring at me thunderstruck and now began to swear horribly in Czech. "That agitator runs my factory! What can a man like that . . . You told me Golombek!" he said to Cunliffe.

"I assure you Golombek is our man," said Cunliffe patiently, offering his case. "This is really very foolish. I thought we had agreed that it was very much better that Mr. Whistler should not know any of the arrangements. I really do not share your apprehensions," he said to me. "The Czechs are interested only in trade. It is entirely natural that you should return urgently after discussion with your principals. From what you have told me, they expect it."

"But what in hell am I going to talk about? I was in deep water several times . . ."

"You will be adequately briefed, I assure you. But this is really a matter between you and Mr. Pavelka," he said, sitting back and shrugging his shoulders. "You have done the job you were asked to do—and very well, too, if I may say so. It is certainly not your fault that this has occurred."

This calming statement and the absence of the previous sort of pressure certainly put the matter in a different perspective. I sat down and looked at Pavelka. He was still smoldering over the revelation of Galushka.

"We'd use the Norstrund again?" I said.

"Why not? Nobody suspected it the first time. They will be used to seeing you with it."

"And used to my forgetting it on Galushka's desk?"

"Really, Mr. Whistler," said Cunliffe mildly. "Whoever noticed you leave it last time? But if it would make your mind easier, don't forget it. Merely ask to leave it. Say you don't want to carry it round the factory with you."

"Why should I want to see round the factory again? They've shown me it once."

"Yes," Cunliffe said, and looked at me thoughtfully. "I'll have to arrange for you to see one of the processes again." He scribbled on his pad. "He could be quite a useful young man, this one," he said to Pavelka without looking up.

"Of course," said Pavelka. "I saw right away."

There was silence for a while after that. The thing was not, after all, so fantastic. Pavelka had undoubtedly owned and run very successfully an enormous factory. I had seen it. He could do the same thing here. I said, "You consider it essential for me to go back again for this formula, Mr. Pavelka?"

"Certainly. Naturally," he said. "It would shorten our work. Come back quickly with it. We have a lot to do."

"When would I need to go?"

"Well," Cunliffe said, looking dubiously at the clock. "I've been trying to expedite matters, but I doubt if you could get away before Friday. I spent a perfectly dreadful day rushing about yesterday."

"How long would I be away?"

"If you went Friday, you could go to the factory on Saturday and be back on Sunday afternoon. Less than three days in all."

Less than three days, I thought. I should surely be able to cope with that.

Later I saw Maura and told her as much as was necessary. She said, "Oh, Nicolas! You will try and be back in time on Sunday."

"Of course I will. I'll be back at teatime. We can buzz off right away."

"I'd hate anything to interfere with that. I've been so looking forward to going there and seeing your mother and everything."

"Well, you will."

"I'd feel superstitious about us if it didn't come off now."

"That's because you're a silly little thing."

"You'll write to me while you're away?"

"I'll be gone only three days."

"Three whole days."

"And I'll see you on two of them."

"Write anyway. Write in the airplane, and write when you get there, and write on the way back. And post them. Then I'll know you were thinking of me."

"Don't you trust me?"

"No. Oh, Nicolas, I do love you. I love you so much. Do you love me?"

"No."

"Nicolas, truly."

"Well, a bit."

"How much?"

"As much as this. And this. And this."

Quite a lot of this had been going on lately.

She saw me off on the Friday morning. Cunliffe had not been too taken with this idea, but there wasn't anything I could do to stop her. He sat waiting in his car opposite while we shuffled our feet in the entrance hall. I was carrying in my case a brand-new Norstrund that he had given me that morning, and had been mildly troubled in case the flyleaf might be bulky with Pavelka's threatened letter. Cunliffe had laughed me out of that one. "Have no fears, Mr. Whistler. His bark is always much worse than his bite. You'll be carrying nothing at all on the way there—the return cargo is the point of this operation." And indeed the flyleaf was immaculate. If I hadn't known it had been specially prepared for easy opening and resealing it would have been impossible to tell.

Maura had not told them at the office that she was taking time off, and was tending to make a Departure of it. She clung silently to my arm, her face white and dramatic, eyes large and staring. This nerve-racking performance was giving me an acute and unexpected attack of the jimjams.

We moved at last, mercifully, and in the queue she gave me a quick kiss and dug in her bag. She had brought me a present, wrapped in a brown paper bag.

I said, "What is it?"

"Something to read. Maybe it will keep you out of mischief," she said with a feeble smile, and gave me a little nudge up the steps.

I spared a quick glance for Cunliffe and got in the bus, and hoped to God it would move quickly, for Maura was rooted to the spot outside like one of the women in a pit disaster.

Presently the bus did move and I turned and waved to her, and saw Cunliffe still siting in his car. And then all that was over and I sat jolting in the seat with only that curious unease of the stomach that is a part of every departure.

We were at the Chiswick roundabout before I opened the brown paper bag to see what Maura had bought me and I had drawn it halfway out of the bag before I was sure. I said quietly, "Oh, Jesus Christ, no!"

My neighbor on the seat, an immense businessman with a blue chin, horn-rimmed glasses and a valise, said, *"Pardon?"*

"I'm sorry. It was nothing."

But it was something. Maura had bought me a Norstrund. A brand-new Norstrund.

The implications of this second Norstrund were borne in on me as the bus turned up the Great West Road. A man who appeared habitually with a Norstrund might or might not arouse suspicion. A man who had another Norstrund tucked away in his case was quite a different proposition. My room at the Slovenska had possibly been searched once. It would possibly be searched again.

There was also the chance of the two copies becoming mixed up. One could always mark one of them. But better, far better, to leave Maura's behind, to deposit it somewhere, lose it.

I tried to do this. I looked out the window and let the bag bounce off my knee. My blue-chinned neighbor picked it up. I tried kicking it under the seat when we left the bus. The driver came running up with it twenty minutes later as we streamed out onto the tarmac.

It was an ill omen. The trip had started with complications. I stuffed Maura's gift in my raincoat pocket and glanced at the bulge every few minutes.

By the time we touched down at Prague all the butterflies were back in my stomach.

At the Hotel Slovenska I had been given the same room, and on all sides there were welcoming smiles. The intense receptionist nodded quite gaily, the ancient porter grinned and gawked and hawked. On the second floor, Josef awaited me with darkling fervor.

"What pleasure to see you back, Pan Whistler. We didn't hope for such a quick return."

"No, well. Business, you know."

"The *pane* thinks trade is beginning to move?"

"I hope so, Josef."

"That's good news. We miss the businessmen. I hope you are the first of many. Can I bring you something, *pane*?"

"Beer, please, Josef."

I went in and had a shower. This familiar action and my re-emergence into the green and gold splendor for my beer had a calming effect on the butterflies in my stomach. I took the beer out on the balcony and looked down on the Vaclavske Namesti. It was hot and steamy and rain had fallen, but nothing had changed. The crowds still streamed in the heat. The queue still waited outside the automat. The trams clanged up and down. Wenceslas strode his iron horse far down the street. And from his perch above the road junction, Lenin still stared down on his disciples. "Every hand, every brain for the building of socialism."

It did not seem, as it had a fortnight ago, to be a different world. London no longer seemed so remote. And the task had not the unknown dangers. Even the formidable Galushka, now that I was here, seemed not quite so frightening. There was only the complication of the Norstrunds.

I came in from the balcony, got them both out and compared them. There was no doubt about it; they were alike as two peas. Only when you looked hard could you see slight differences. Maura's was an earlier edition, 1950. Cunliffe's was 1953. I thought I had better mark it up to avoid confusion, and went to get my pen out of the jacket in the wardrobe.

The room phone rang.

I jumped about a foot. The two Norstrunds were spread out on the table. Here was where confusion could start. I swore out loud, let the phone ring, and marked a small dot in the top right hand corner of Cunliffe's copy. Then I stowed both books in my case. The damned phone hadn't stopped ringing. I picked it up with sweating hands.

"Hello."

It was Svoboda, from the Glass Board, hoping he wasn't disturbing me.

"Not at all."

"There were things in your telegram we could not grasp, Pan Whistler. Do we understand you are empowered to conclude a deal on this visit?"

"Not exactly. We wanted reassurance on some matters, and my principals desire quick action. We thought it more convenient for me to make another personal call at the Zapotocky works."

I was tending to shout with nervousness, and Svoboda drew his own conclusions. "Of course. Naturally. Do not misunderstand me. We are delighted you should return. Please tell me of any way we can help. Perhaps you wish for immediate Discussions? I can send a car right away."

I had an instant vision of the giantess of Barrandov standing in stormy silence by the car outside the hotel. "No. No, thank you. It won't be necessary."

"You wish to deal directly with Kralovsk?"

"That's it. I'd like to go tomorrow. In the morning. It shouldn't need more than an hour or two there. My principals expect me back in time for a conference on Monday morning."

"Very good," Svoboda said. "I will see everything is arranged. A car will call for you at—what? Is nine o'clock too early?"

"Nine o'clock would be fine." I had no intention of leaving the hotel tonight. A nice, quiet trip, early to bed.

"And you wish for no Discussions today?"

"No, thanks. I've got everything I need for the moment."

"Excellent," said Svoboda.

He sounded a shade muted at this dearth of Discussions.

Little Vlcek was there with the car in the morning, vulpine and informative as ever.

"I hope you have brought good weather back with you, Pan Whistler. Since you were here last we have had nine and a half centimeters of rain. Perhaps now the sun will shine."

I said, "It looks a bit overcast now." The air was steamy and stifling; I had slept badly.

"Ah, there might be a shower or two. But the meteorological service says all should be well for the parade on Sunday. That is the main thing."

"What parade is that?"

"You have not heard?" Vlcek was delighted. "It will be one of the greatest in recent years. See the stands are going up. One hundred and eight contingents are coming from outlying districts alone. The district of Brno, for instance, is sending one thousand seven hundred participants. You will see, the decorations go up today and the town will start filling tonight. There are many interesting problems in coping with such an influx . . ."

After a while I stopped listening again, and looked out the window. Vlcek went on talking ceaselessly. He had not mentioned what the parade was in aid of; I felt far too queasy in mind and stomach to ask him. We were nearing Kralovsk and my palms were sweating on the Norstrund. I was carrying Maura's copy in the pocket of my raincoat. I wondered how I was going to leave the book this time. Knowing definitely now that Galushka was not in the plot did not help. I wondered how I would stumble through the questions I had to ask him, and if he would regard them with suspicion. He had already pointed out everything that could possibly be communicated about his bloody glass. God, I thought, how I hate glass.

Vlcek, as before, was still talking as we got out of the car and went through the front hall to Galushka's office. It was some interminable nonsense about the organizational problems raised by the parade, but none of it required further response than an occasional nod. Which was just as well. I was feeling sick again.

They had buzzed through to Galushka from the front hall, and he was at his door to meet us, his small, uneven eyes roving over me in the unpleasant way I remembered.

"Well, Pan Whistler, so we are honored again." He had taken my hand in both of his and was slowly pumping it up and down. "Comrade Svoboda tells me you are troubled about some of our arrangements."

"Pan Whistler's principals, you understand," said little Vlcek, whickering slightly and showing his gold teeth with extreme uneasiness. "Before concluding a deal naturally they wish to satisfy themselves on all points. Pan Whistler, I understand, merely wished to confirm what he has already seen. I believe you were more than satisfied with Comrade Galushka's systems, Pan Whistler."

"Quite," I said. My mouth was dry and my heart pumping very unpleasantly. "We thought a further visit to the factory would be worth while in view of the impending trade agreement. We wish quick action."

"I too," Galushka said. He had released my hand and ushered us into the office. "This is the essence of our industry. Speed, efficiency and quality. You know, Vlcek," he said, "it will take much work from Prague to convince our customers—our Western customers—that our specifications are so high. Article for article our product is both better and cheaper. They are amazed. They wonder what is the drawback. Oh, there is nothing personal in this, I assure you," he said to me. "I understand very well the psychology of the Western businessman. I had excellent opportunity to observe it for thirty years. It does not surprise me and I do not resent it. We will have to educate them."

His twisted smile was quite genial. Poor Vlcek was grinning horribly from one to the other of us. "The glass is very good, undoubtedly," he said in embarrassment. "Pan Whistler, as I understand it, does not doubt it. It is merely a new market opening. One understands the problems and so forth . . ."

"Well, I am at his service entirely," Galushka said. "What exactly is it you wish to see again?"

I told him, exceedingly relieved that he should regard my return in this light. He rang round to two of his departments while Vlcek screwed a cigarette into his long holder and strove to shed amiability. Embarrassment kept him less conversational than usual, however.

"Well," Galushka said, putting down the phone. "We can go." He looked out the window and picked an umbrella from his stand. "Rain again. But leave your raincoat here if you wish, Pan Whistler. The one umbrella will do for both of us. There is not much walking between the shops."

The rain was a godsend. I had been wondering what to do with the raincoat, having no desire to leave the two Norstrunds hanging about in the room. I said, "No, I'll take it, thanks. It isn't any bother, and it will leave you the umbrella. But I'll tell you what I will do," I said, marveling at the way it came out. "I'll just leave this book here."

"Of course," Galushka said. And then, looking at it, "Ah,

you are still attached to your guidebook, I see. We must not let you forget it this time."

And that was that, the first part over.

The back of my neck was damp with sweat as we left the office. Little Vlcek came too. Nobody asked if he had a raincoat and Galushka didn't offer to share the umbrella. He got very wet.

It was just after half past nine when I had arrived at the works and it was not yet a quarter to twelve when I finished. Unless you're very keen on it, there are few things actually more boring than the mechanical production of glass. A number of dull minerals are melted in a furnace, the resulting fused "metal" being then rolled or molded, depending on what you are making with it. The questions I had asked related to the "metaling" of fine tableware and the annealing of three of the ranges on offer, processes of such total lack of interest that I remembered nothing at all from my last visit.

Gaushka proceeded on the principle that I remembered nothing at all and saw to it that I wrote everything down in my notebook. I emerged from the last of the shops with a filled notebook and my face again stiff with painful interest.

The rain had stopped and the ground was steaming in the tropical heat. The sun seemed to be trying to come out.

"You see, Pan Whistler," Vlcek said. "I said you have brought the good weather with you." He was sneezing a little but had kept very cheerful. "We were all worried in town for the parade on Sunday," he told Galushka. "But the meteorological service announced today that the sun would shine. They do not realize Pan Whistler brought it with him," he said gaily.

"Ah, the parade," said Galushka. "You are staying over to see it, Pan Whistler?"

"I'm afraid not. I must fly back tomorrow."

"You will be missing a worthwhile experience. To see the young people from every region in their national costumes, all dedicating themselves to the State—this is to understand the source of our strength."

Since I had taken down his every word he seemed kindly disposed toward me, and now showed an inclination to stand

and chat. I was in no hurry. Every minute wasted here was a minute gained for whoever was fiddling with the Norstrund. Nothing had been said about staying on to lunch. I wondered if the mysterious Golombek, that bloody fool, would have had enough time to do his work.

Presently we strolled back to the office block. The car was waiting outside.

"I hope you have now sufficient information," Vlcek said to me. "There is nothing else Comrade Galushka can tell you while you are here?"

I couldn't think of anything. It seemed impossible that there could be anything further to tell about glass. I felt the back of my neck beginning to sweat again with the strain of wondering how to draw attention to the Norstrund.

"If there is anything further," Galushka said, putting one hand on my shoulder and taking my right hand with the other, "don't hesitate to get in touch. I do not resent it," he said, his uneven eyes smiling. "I understand very well the reasons."

"Yes, well. I think I've got everything."

The sneezing but alert Vlcek came to my assistance. "Ah! Your guidebook, Pan Whistler. We have nearly forgotten it again!"

"Of course," Galushka said. "I will get it."

He seemed to be a hell of a time about it. Vlcek and I made heavy conversation among the steaming puddles. Presently Galushka reappeared. He had the Norstrund in his hand. A minute later we were cruising back to Prague.

As Cunliffe had said, once you stopped worrying there was nothing to it.

The car put me down outside the Slovenska and Vlcek took a sneezing farewell. He was a friendly little soul, and I felt sorry for him. If anyone was going to get the chopper when this lot came out, I knew who it would be.

It was half past twelve, too early for lunch. I felt wound up, too excited to go to my room. I thought I would walk up the street toward the museum, and have a drink on the way.

I was lightheaded with relief and hilarity. I knew from previous experience that the mood would not last, that very shortly

I would begin to jangle like a piano wire. But just then, at that moment, I had a heady conviction of total success. I knew I'd got it this time. There had been a certain smoothness, a certain inevitability about the whole business. All I had to do now was fill in the hours till ten in the morning.

The Vaclavske Namesti was glittering in the sun, cobbles, pavements, trees, sparkling and steaming from the rain. As Vlcek had said, the decorations were going up and there was a new air of bustle and cheerfulness about the place. Workmen were up ladders attaching banners and streamers. Outside the Zlata Husa restaurant, a group of them were swaying in a cradle fixing a giant tryptich of portraits.

Farther along by the Opletala, a banner broke across the street above the little shuttling trams: TO A LASTING PEACE. TO THE PEOPLE'S VICTORY. Young office girls out for the lunch break streamed along the pavements, gossiping and laughing, their splendid Slav bosoms straining in light summer dresses. Even the old black-clad crones, a changeless feature of the place, seemed to be sharing some common joke, toothless gums grinning as they shuffled by with shopping bags.

By the time I reached the statue of Wenceslas I'd decided to amble down to the embankment for a drink, and crossed the road, winking at him on his iron horse, and walked down the Mezibranska by the side of the museum. I walked under the linden trees to the Manes café.

It was chiming one o'clock all round when I got there and the crowds were streaming back to work. I sat at an open-air table and ordered a large beer and drank it, watching, in the hot sun, the bathers diving from the raft into the molten river.

I had no appetite for food. I stayed at the Manes café drinking the light beer till three o'clock. Then the sun went in and clouds came over again. I picked up my mac and left.

With the sun gone, the air was too thick and sticky to walk back. At the tram stop by the Smetanov bridge I caught a number seventeen for the Vaclavske Namesti, and had to stand all the way, jolted and jostled in the throbbing heat. I got off at the Prikopy junction with a violent headache.

They were trying out loudspeakers that had been installed on lampposts as I walked the few yards back to the hotel. A military march. My head throbbed, mouth sour with beer, heavy and oppressed again in the suddenly gray, hot afternoon.

Josef was lurking on the second floor.

"You have eaten well, Pan Whistler?"

"No, Josef. It was too hot to eat. I've been drinking at Manes."

"Ah, so. It's very sensible. A thunderstorm will clear the air."

"It looks as if we're going to get it."

"Yes. In an hour or two, I think. Have you further business today?"

"No. I'm going to lie out now on the bed."

"It's a good idea. You'd like another beer?"

"No, thanks. I've drunk enough."

"Try an iced Pilsener before you rest. I recommend it."

I didn't want any more beer, but he seemed installed for a chat, so I said all right to get him out of the way and went in the room. The canopy was down on the balcony, the room green and dim like the inside of an aquarium. I flaked out on the bed and edged my shoes off and kicked them on the floor.

The row of the military band came in through the open window, but presently stopped. The technicians began testing with numbers. "*Jeden . . . dva . . . tri . . . ctyri . . .*"

The throbbing in my temples had begun to ease when Josef reappeared with the Pilsener. He stood and watched me sip it, smiling in his darkling way.

"It's good?"

"Wonderful." It wasn't wonderful. It was the strong export Pilsener, too tangy for my sour mouth.

"You want to lie here all afternoon or shall I call you for tea?"

I thought I'd better write to Maura, as promised. I said, "What time does the post go?"

"From the hotel at five o'clock, from the post office until seven. Someone can always go if it is urgent—the post office is just along the street. It's a letter to England?"

"Yes."

"Better to get it in the six-o'clock post. A call at five-thirty then, *pane?*"

"Five-thirty would be fine."

110

He went and I put the beer down and lay back again. Just a short block of time to get through now. Rest until five-thirty; write, eat, drink, read until ten. Then bed. Only a few hours.

It suddenly occurred to me that I had not examined the Norstrund. I sat up and picked it up from beside me on the bed. The flyleaf was still immaculate. I hoped the man had had time to do his work. I wondered what the holdup had been in getting it back from Galushka's office. But if there'd been anything wrong I wouldn't have got it back.

My head had begun to throb again and I felt suddenly dry and sour as hell, my mouth like a birdcage. I took another sip of the Pilsener, but it was too tangy and I got up and went to the bathroom and emptied the glass and took a drink of water. It was hot in the bathroom, the single frosted-glass French window shut. I opened the window and looked out. It was still heavy and gray. A few doors along the balcony a young blonde was sitting out in a negligee, showing rather a lot of leg. She smiled at me. I went back in.

I took my jacket and shirt off and loosened my belt and flaked out again, kicking the raincoat to the foot of the bed. I shoved the Norstrund under the coverlet where I could feel it by my side, and after a minute got up again and put my passport and wallet there, too. Presently the throbbing in my head stopped again and I dozed.

A soft tapping on the door brought me out of it and I lay still with my eyes closed and let Josef come in and shake me. Josef came in, but he didn't shake me. After a bit I wondered what the hell he was doing and opened my eyes a slit. He was standing by the door, not looking at me. He was looking round the room. After a moment he picked up the glass and sniffed it.

My heart gave a lurch, a single sickening thump. I thought, *There was something in the beer*. I knew this couldn't be, that I was on edge, that there was no reason why anyone should put anything in the beer. If they suspected anything they could haul me off quickly enough. But the beer had tasted queer. It had dried my mouth. My heart began to pump very unpleasantly.

My breath must have come out sharply, and he turned and looked at me. The bed was in shadow and I closed my eyes

111

quickly. I heard him put the glass down. I felt him bending over me; warm, slightly sweaty, the faint tang of shaving lotion. Presently he moved away.

I didn't open my eyes again until I heard him over at the other side of the room. He was closing the French windows, his back broad, much broader than I'd realized in the black morning coat. He turned from the window, rubbing his hands gently, and gazed thoughtfully round the room. Then he began to search it.

chapter 8

My case was over on the slatted luggage rest and he went soundlessly across to it. The case was not locked; he went through it carefully and then moved across to the wardrobe and went through the stuff there. He ran his hands over the top and bent and peered underneath.

When he straightened up, I shut my eyes again. I thought he'd be trying the bed next, under the pillow, the mattress. I didn't know what to do if he looked under the coverlet. The Norstrund was there. I could feel it against my side. I had given no serious thought to the nightmarish contingency of being discovered. I was too appallingly frightened to do so now.

I thought, Shall I let him take the Norstrund if he finds it? God, no. But why not? He wouldn't find anything inside it, unless he was specifically looking. And if he was specifically looking, what chance would I have anyway? The only prospect then would be to try and brazen it out. I wondered where the British Embassy was, if I could somehow get down into the street, jump on a tram, hide.

My heart was going like a steam hammer. I couldn't control my breathing. I heard a rustle of cloth, and opened my eyes again. He was fumbling with something and I couldn't see what it was until he held it up. My mac, at the foot of the bed. He was feeling the pockets. He withdrew something.

Maura's Norstrund. I had forgotten it. I had totally forgotten it. But now with a single flash of inspiration, I saw a chance of salvation, a slim, slim chance. He didn't know about Maura's Norstrund. Nobody did. If he showed any kind of informed interest in it, I'd have to wake up, stall, get him out of the room

113

for a few minutes while I did something about the other one. I didn't know how I would do this. I felt sick with terror at the prospect. It seemed the only chance.

He'd turned half away from me and I couldn't see what he was doing with the damned thing. Presently he dropped the mac and took something out of his own pocket. It was a moment or two before I realized what he was about. A small delicate movement of the elbow: he was cutting. I thought, *Oh, God, he's on to it, this is it,* and, half vomiting with the beer rising in my throat, stretched and groaned and sat up.

I didn't see what he did with the Norstrund. In one movement, he bent, began tidying my shoes where they had fallen beside the bed, and picked up the mac.

"Ah, you've wakened, Pan Whistler. A good sleep?"

"Yes, thanks. God!" I said, holding my head. "How long have I slept?"

"It's early yet, not quite half past four. I came in to shut the windows. The loudspeakers were making a great noise."

"Do you have such a thing as an aspirin?"

"Right here," he said, and changed hands on the mac to fiddle in his inside tailcoat pocket, and I saw how he'd got the Norstrund, in the hand holding the mac. I thought I'd better let him leave the room with it. It would take a few minutes for him to fiddle with it and find nothing there and seal it up again.

I licked dry lips. I said, "I'd be glad of a cup of tea, Josef."

"Right away, Pan Whistler. I will just hang up your raincoat."

He turned with his darkling smile and opened the wardrobe to do this. And then the clumsy oaf dropped the book. There was no possibility of looking away. It bounced off the bottom of the wardrobe on to the floor.

His eye caught mine. He said slowly, "Ah, *pardon.* There was something in the pocket," and picked up the book. He didn't know what to do with it, and stared from it to me. I gazed at him in dull horror. He placed the book on the table and left the room.

I moved quickly off the bed, locked the door and got Cunliffe's Norstrund from under the coverlet. I didn't know what the hell to do with it. I looked round the room. No hiding place they wouldn't spot easily enough. I went through to the bath-

114

room. Nowhere here, either. The single French window was open and I looked out on the balcony. There was a flowerbox against the short stretch of wall between the bathroom and bedroom windows. It was an oblong box with a few pots of petunias standing on a gravel base.

I reached out and pulled it towards me. I took two of the pots out, scrabbled up the gravel, pushed the book into it and smoothed the gravel over again before replacing the pots. Then I pushed the box back and washed the gravel and sand off my hands.

I had worked quickly and in extreme panic and not more than half a minute had elapsed since Josef had left the room. I wondered how far he had got with Maura's Norstrund and picked it up. There was no mark on the front flyleaf. No mark on the back, either. I couldn't make out where he'd been cutting and examined the book all round. Something fell out, into my hand, a tiny strip of what looked like red leather. A bit of the binding. I saw then what he'd done. He'd sliced a shaving off the bottom of the bulging spine. I poked my little finger inside the gap. There was a loose slim shield of cambric, and something else. I edged it out. A corner of rice paper showed.

My forehead had gone cold and I felt sick as a dog. I thought, *I've hidden the wrong one. I've got them mixed up somehow.* I couldn't understand how it could have happened. I couldn't understand why the paper was hidden in the spine instead of under the flyleaf. I pulled it out. It was a single sheet, folded over, about four inches long and three wide. It was written in ink with a very fine nib, a mass of figures, letters, equations.

My body seemed to be covered with fine cold sweat all over. I was shaking like a leaf. I thought, *It can't be, it can't be.* I knew I hadn't mixed them up. This book had stayed in my raincoat pocket all the time at the glassworks. It had been the other one I'd left on the desk. There wasn't any doubt about it, no room at all for error. I'd left it on the desk, and then it had been returned to me, and I had carried it in my hand ever since, had slipped it under the coverlet when I stretched out. It was now in the flower box. Yet the formula was in this one.

I sat down on the bed, my legs shaking, staring stupidly at the book. There was no dot on it. Of course there was no dot

115

on it. I had put the dot on the other one. I had put it on in this very room. I remembered it clearly. I'd got the two books spread out in front of me. But then Svoboda had telephoned. The bloody phone had gone on ringing. Had I put the dot on the wrong one?

Now wait. Think, I told myself. *Work it out.* I had known which one was Maura's because it was an earlier edition, 1950. Cunliffe's had been 1953.

I opened the book. It said 1953.

All right, I said, streams of sweat running down my forehead, and accepting this nightmarish fact. *This one is Cunliffe's. I accidentally switched it. It was Maura's I left on the desk at the glassworks. It is Maura's that is now in the flower box. This one here in my hand is Cunliffe's. It stayed in my pocket all the time.*

Then how the hell, I thought, *does this one come to have the formula in it?* The sweat trickled over into my eyes. The answer was all too clear. There was only one way it could have the formula in it. I had brought it in with me.

There was something very peculiar going on here. I thought again, *Now wait. Think. Be absolutely certain. Check the other book again.*

I got up, went through to the bathroom at a shambling trot, pulled the flower box to me again and got out the Norstrund. I brushed it off in the washbasin, checked the publication date. 1950. It was undoubtedly Maura's. I got out my penknife, ripped open the flyleaf, front and back. I ripped off the bottom of the spine. Nothing. Nothing at all. Yet this was the one I had left at the works. There could now be no doubt at all.

I buried the book in the flower box again and went through to the bedroom. The formula was lying on the table next to Cunliffe's Norstrund. It floated onto the floor in the draft of my hand as I reached for it. I bent and picked it up. I had examined it briefly before. Now as I held it close in the dim green light, I saw that the top line was in clearer notations and stood slightly away from the rest. I screwed up my eyes and read it. The top line said: *Amend Aldermaston 8, 3rd stage, Banshee.*

I crumpled the paper up in my hands at once. I said aloud,

"Oh, Jesus Christ, no." My knees began literally to knock. I looked wildly round the room, licking my lips. There was only one place for this. I went through to the bathroom again, somewhat unsteadily, dropped the screw of paper in the w.c. and flushed it down. My face in the mirror was ghastly and shiny with sweat.

I thought I heard the rattle of tea things along the corridor and belted back to the bedroom in a panic. I unlocked the door, closed the Norstrund on the table and lay back on the bed again. Aldermaston had rung a bell in my mind. Something secret. Something atomic. I had just realized what it was. Aldermaston was the place where they developed nuclear weapons. The Banshee was the latest. I turned away from the door, more terrified, and with better cause, than ever before in my life.

Josef came into the room. "Pan Whistler," he said. "Wake up, Pan Whistler. Your tea, Pan Whistler."

In the moment before I sat up I decided what I had to do. I had to get out of the room in some smooth and plausible fashion. I had to go downstairs, out of the hotel, find the British Embassy. I had noticed a row of telephone directories on the shelf beside the zealous receptionist. There would doubtless be another row in the post office—a few yards up the street, Josef had said.

I turned over, sat up, groaned.

Josef was standing there, relaxed and smiling. He had put the tray down on the table where the Norstrund had been. It wasn't there now.

"You have slept again, Pan Whistler," he said jovially. "You have drunk too much beer."

"I must have."

"Well now, refresh yourself." He was pouring out the tea. "Maybe you'd like to write your letter now. You can catch the earlier post."

My heart was thumping wildly. "I think I'll make it a postcard. Are there any picture postcards downstairs?" I knew there were. I had seen a display of them.

"Certainly. I'll send up a selection."

"Don't bother. I need to wake up. I'll go down myself."

"As you prefer," he said. I thought he seemed rather pleased at this. It would probably give him an opportunity to nip back in the room again with the Norstrund.

I waited till he had gone, then slipped off the bed, poured the tea out in the washbasin and rinsed my face. I felt cold and sick. I picked up my jacket and went out of the room. There was no one in the corridor. I walked down the stairs, across the hall. It was crowded, open shirts, sandals, perfectly normal. I didn't think anyone noticed me; not even the receptionist looked up. I strolled slowly and thoughtfully to the entrance. Then I was out, in the street.

It was still gray and hot outside. I was shivering, my teeth chattering, limbs rubbery. As I'd told Cunliffe, I was no hero. I was not cut out for this deperate nonsense. If some hand should fall on my shoulder now, I knew quite certainly I would be sick on the spot.

No hand fell on my shoulder. Nipping in and out of the endlessly streaming crowds, I was at the post office in three minutes. It was a big place, crowded, the huge hall full of that curious shifting dreariness that seemed to go with long lines of open collars.

I found the telephone booths, looked up the British Embassy. B. *Britske Velvyslanectvi. Thunovska 14, Malostranske Namesti.* 66144.

I didn't know where the Malostranske was, couldn't place it. I'd never been in such a jittery, knee-knocking, teeth-chattering panic in my life before. I had a sudden overpowering urge to hear a British voice. I went into a booth, rang 66144.

The number went on ringing.

"There is no reply," said the Czech operator.

The box was terribly airless. My heart was beating dully. I said faintly, "There must be a reply. Try it again, please."

The ringing began again, went on. Suddenly the receiver was taken off. A testy Cockney voice said: "Hello, hello. British Embassy."

I said, "Thank Christ for that. Whereabouts are you?"

"Who is that speaking, sir?"

"My name's Whistler. I'm a British citizen. I've got to come round there. Whereabouts are you?"

118

"Thunovska, just off the Malostranske. Know it?"

"No. How do I get there?"

"Got a car, have you, sir?"

"No. No, I haven't. I'm in the Vaclavske Namesti."

"Right. Take a number five or nine tram over the river. Then change at the first stop over the other side, that's the Ujezd. You then want a number twelve coming up to Malostranske. It's three stops. All right?"

"Right," I said, scribbling frantically on a cigarette packet. "I'll be along right away."

"Oh, I shouldn't do that, sir. Nobody here now—they've all gone for the night."

I had felt a warm wave of relief sweeping over me at this splendid, solid, understandable sort of fellow at the other end. My toes now began to curl inside my shoes. I felt my voice dry up in my throat. I actually said in a kind of falsetto, "All gone for the night?"

"That's right, sir. Open again at ten in the morning."

"But I've got to get there tonight," I said. I suddenly found my voice. "I'm in serious trouble. I'm in deadly danger. I'm a British subject. I've got to have protection."

"Run into a spot of bother, have you?"

"Bother!" I said. "Look, the secret police will be after me any minute now. They're probably looking for me right this very moment. You've got to—"

"Well, it's no use telling me about it on this phone, sir," he broke in tartly. "It's an open line—follow what I mean?"

I followed what he meant. I found myself idiotically dropping my voice. I whispered into the phone, "Look, I've simply got to get to the Embassy. I can't explain now . . ."

"All right, sir," he said. "I live here. Keep a cool head. Things aren't always as serious as they seem in this country, you know. We'd be called in if you was in any real difficulty. I should sleep on it if I was you, sir. And don't forget to bring your passport. Can't let you in without that." He hung up right away.

A few minutes later I found myself walking up the Vaclavske Namesti, dazed and shaking. *I live here,* he had said. *Don't forget to bring your passport. Can't let you in without it.* What did he mean? What else but come round right away, I'll let you

119

in and you can stay here. If the line was tapped he couldn't say more. And the business about sleeping on it? Obviously to put off anyone else who might be listening. *Keep a cool head,* he had said. My head was cool enough. It was dripping with icy sweat.

There was a number nine at the tram stop and I got on it, and went swaying and lurching down the Narodni Trida to the river, crammed between two strapping girls and kept upright by their simply enormous busts. This served to distract me for a minute or two from my problems, and presently I began to feel some faint return of confidence. Nobody seemed to be following me. It had all happened very quickly. In twenty minutes or so I could be safe inside the Embassy telling this reassuring Cockney all about it.

By the time the tram ground to a halt at the National Theater on the river embankment, the reaction from danger had set in, and I was beginning to feel a certain lunatic hilarity. I wondered what the Cockney would make of the crazy rigmarole I had to tell him. He must be an old embassy retainer of some kind, an old soldier, a sergeant probably. Keep a cool head, sir. Don't let the bleeders rattle you. Got your credentials, sir? Don't forget your passport. Can't let you in without it.

The conductress planted herself against me with her ticket machine. I couldn't get to the money in my trouser pocket. I felt in my breast pocket for my wallet. There was a sudden ghastly hollow in the pit of my stomach. I felt the other side, in both jacket pockets to make sure. But I was never surer of anything in my life. My wallet was back at the Slovenska. It was under the coverlet in room one-forty. So was my passport.

A few spots of rain were falling and the clocks were chiming six all round as I walked back to the Vaclavske Namesti. I had had two stiff vodkas in the Slavia while pondering my best course of action. I had got off the tram in a panic, but once off had had second thoughts and had wandered about for a few minutes distracted with indecision.

I thought, He'd have let me into the Embassy. How could he throw me out after hearing my story? But it wasn't the likeliest of stories. And I'd have to admit that I'd been engaged

120

in smuggling. I would not be too popular at the Embassy *with* a passport. Without one they would probably prefer to wash their hands of me.

I saw all this as I teetered, sweating, under the linden trees. I certainly didn't fancy going to the Embassy without a passport. I didn't fancy going back to the hotel to get it, either. And time was ticking by.

The vodka had a calming effect. For the first time I thought about the whole mission. It was plain I had been tricked all along. Smooth little Cunliffe who'd fooled me once about the legacy had fooled me again about the formula. It was beyond belief that I could ever have accepted the story. And yet there had been a crazy logic about it at the time. It was easy now to be wise after the event.

They had wanted someone who would have a plausible reason for visiting an Iron Curtain country. Czechoslovakia was the easiest; it traded with the West; had a large glass industry. Find someone with connections with the industy. Rig up a story to convince him he is bringing something out, some character like myself who wouldn't dare to examine the thing he was supposed to be bringing out.

I could imagine the consternation in the glassworks when they had found nothing in the Norstrund. No wonder there had been some delay in getting it back. They must have stripped the thing. There must have been a quick message to the hotel to search my room; to drug and search me, too, when I got back.

But why drug me? Why not arrest me? Why such finesse?

Because, it seemed to me, after much intensive thought, perhaps they weren't absolutely sure I'd brought anything with me. They might suspect some slip-up, some last-minute change of plan in London. . . . Every mission, after all, would not go as smoothly as the first.

I began to see that I might have acted rashly in dashing from the hotel. They would have let me return home. The courier had proved useful once. Why destroy his usefulness for the future?

Once I'd got as far as this, I thought of plenty of small details to support this view. Little Vlcek had dropped me willingly enough at the hotel and had not waited to see me go in. I had

121

not been followed to the Manes café, and there had been no anxious inquiries on my return. Josef had not sought to detain me after the bit of business with the beer. There had been no restraint on my movements since. As far as I could tell, no one was following me now.

I thought it was time to go back.

Although it was only just after six, the lowering clouds had brought premature darkness. The trams were lit up and, as I rounded the corner of the Vaclavske Namesti, the floodlighting suddenly went on all down the street. One by one the banners and portraits sprang to life. There were "oohs" and "ahs" from the crowds, people came clustering out of offices and shops to look, and as I arrived at the hotel the entrance filled up with an assortment of hands and brains hurrying out from inside.

It seemed a propitious moment to pop in unnoticed.

I hadn't made up my mind quite what to do. If no further alarms were offered, it seemed to me that my best bet was to remain in the hotel and demonstrate visible unconcern. If anything suspicious should occur, I should keep ready to slide swiftly out again. I didn't know what might rank as a reasonable suspicion. I didn't know if I'd be allowed to slide out again. All in all, it seemed safest to use the stairs instead of the lift.

I had taken my room key out with me and had it in my hand as I reached the second floor. Josef was not lurking as usual, but I saw, further along the corridor, his tailcoated behind as he leaned out a window overlooking the floodlit street.

He heard me coming and drew in his head.

My heart began to thud again.

"Ah, Pan Whistler. You're feeling better now?"

"Much better, thanks."

"You've been out?" His smile was perfectly genial.

"Yes. I took a breath of fresh air. The floodlighting is quite a spectacle."

"They say it's even better on the Heights. You should take a look later." He was rubbing his hands gently, prepared for a chat. He had searched my room and found nothing. All part of the day's work.

I suddenly realized what a muggins I had been to panic and make a dash for it, but in the same moment knew that I had

122

nothing to worry about. I was the simpleton who thought he was smuggling something out of the country. Any signs of nervousness or eccentricity were perfectly understandable.

I gave Josef a cheerful good evening and opened the room door, my mind at rest and operating a good deal more clearly than at any time since I had left London.

This was just as well. Two things stopped me short like some stricken beast in the doorway. One was the sight of both Norstrunds lying neatly side by side on the table with my passport and wallet. The other was two men out on the balcony. As I stood there stock-still, they turned and came into the room. Behind me Josef firmly closed the door.

They were wearing long pale raincoats, unbuttoned, and both of them had their hats on. They had been chatting on the balcony and were still smiling as they came into the room. One, somewhat shorter than the other, said conversationally, "Whistler, Nicolas?"

I said, "Yes," and licked my lips.

"We must ask you some questions. Please take a seat."

I said, "Who are you?"

"S.N.B."

The taller man withdrew a wallet from his breast pocket and opened it in front of me. The wallet had a glazed window. Inside was a card with his portrait and the words STATNI NARODNI BEZPECNOST. State Security Police.

I seemed to have stopped breathing some time ago. My chest was tight and suffocating. My hands, feet, scalp, lips had begun to throb. I didn't think I could get to the chair he indicated. I sat down heavily on the arm of the easy chair.

"We've been waiting quite a long time for you, Pan Whistler. We wondered where you'd gone."

"I went out for a walk. I had a drink." My voice seemed several tones higher than usual.

"Where?"

"Somewhere." I couldn't think. It had gone out of my mind. I thought, *Two Norstrunds. They'd found it then in the flower box. They knew I'd hidden it. They had an idea now what had happened.* "I don't know the name of the place," I said.

"Have you been there before?"

"I think so."

"Was it the Manes café?"

"No, no."

"You've been to Manes before, haven't you, Pan Whistler? You were there earlier today."

"It wasn't there. I can't think where it was. Somewhere by the National Theater. Why do you want to know?"

"Was it the Slavia?"

"The Slavia, that's it."

"How long were you there?"

"I don't know. I had a couple of drinks."

"Did you speak to anybody while you were there?"

"No."

"Not even the waiter?"

"Well, the waiter, of course the waiter."

"What did he look like?"

"I can't remember. It was a woman," I gabbled suddenly, as though this feat of memory could help me in any way. "I can't remember what she looked like. Why should I remember what she looked like?" My breathing was not getting any easier. "What do you want to know all this for?"

"Did you meet anybody during your walk?"

"No."

"You walked there and back?"

"Yes. No," I said, confused. "I took the tram there."

"Why did you do that, Pan Whistler?"

"I don't know. I felt like it."

"But you say you went for a walk."

"I did. It was too hot to walk when I got outside. I just took the tram."

"You knew where you wanted to go?"

"I wasn't going anywhere. I thought I'd just get off somewhere on the way."

"And you got off at the Slavia?"

"Yes."

"And spoke to nobody there?"

"I've already told you."

The smaller man looked at his companion, who had replaced

his wallet and was now jotting down notes on a pad. The taller man put down his pad and regarded me speculatively.

"You're not frightened of us, Pan Whistler?"

I licked my lips. "Why should I be?"

"I don't know," he said.

Suddenly he hit me full in the face.

The force of the blow took me clean off the chair. I tumbled over clumsily backward and hit my head on the wardrobe. I stared up at them in shock and pain. My nose felt as if it had been squashed over my face. The excruciating pain had filled my eyes with tears. I was too shocked to utter a sound.

"Get up," the tall man said.

I got up slowly, holding my nose.

He hit me again, very hard, on the side of the face, his knuckles jarring my head and sending me stumbling back against the wardrobe. I bent double, trying desperately to shield my head and face, thinking, *Oh God, oh God, this is going to go on now. This is what happens. It will go on and on.*

But no further blows landed. The other man said conversationally, as though nothing had happened, "You were telling us where you had been, Pan Whistler. You said you took a tram to the Slavia. What happened there exactly?"

I straightened up slowly, head and face singing with pain. The taller man was still regarding me speculatively, gently rubbing his knuckles. My jaw was trembling.

"Is our friend here inhibiting you?"

I nodded.

"He's only trying to help. If you tell the truth, there will be no more work for him. Who was it you saw at the Slavia?"

"Nobody. I'm telling the truth," I gabbled quickly. "You can check up. Someone must have seen me there. I'll tell you whatever you want. I'll tell you anything I can. I don't know what it is you want of me." I thought the bastard would suddenly hit me again. You couldn't tell. I hadn't been able to tell before. He had just hit me very quickly.

"Yes, you do know, Pan Whistler." The smaller man picked up the two Norstrunds and dropped them. There was a bit of sand on one and he brushed it off slowly. "You know very well. You're trying to think of some lie that might satisfy us. You'll have to learn that only the truth will do. We know why you came here. We know why you suddenly left the hotel. We know that you were away for an hour and a half. We are sure you met someone and gave them something. We don't know—I am honest about it, you see—just who this person was. But we can find out. We intend to find out. The only question for you is whether you tell us somewhat unwillingly now or very willingly indeed later on. There isn't any doubt that you *will* tell us. Do you understand?"

A trickle of blood was edging down my lip. My whole face seemed to be swelling outward like a pig's head. Outside, the loudspeakers suddenly started up again with a jaunty march. The French windows were still open.

I said, "I swear to you that I gave nothing to anyone."

"Why did you leave the hotel in such a hurry?"

"I was frightened."

"What of?"

"I saw the waiter searching the room. I thought he would find the—the thing I was trying to hide."

"But you found it instead, didn't you?"

"No."

There was nothing quick about it this time. The tall man put out one hand to steady me and hit me, as hard as he could, with the other. It was in the stomach. I doubled over, gasping and retching, and he stepped back and let me fall on the floor.

I was sick.

Presently the smaller man said, "Get up now, Pan Whistler."

I tried and couldn't. He helped me to my feet. "Sit down if you want."

I sat on the arm of the chair.

"If only you told the truth right away none of this would be necessary. It is stupid to lie. We will find out the truth, you know. We know you found the paper. Admit it."

I nodded.

"And you wished to get rid of it quickly in case it was found on you. That is so, isn't it?"

I nodded again, still too sick to speak. And yet curiously, in this moment of physical horror, I found my brain suddenly beginning to function again. They couldn't really know I had found the paper. They had to assume it from my dash from the hotel. But why should they also assume I had given it to someone? I had thought myself a courier of glass secrets from the country, not nuclear secrets into it. If I had seen the paper, it was obvious what I would have done with it—destroy it at once in a panic. Then why assume I had passed it on to someone else?

I suddenly saw why, in a flash of inspiration. They didn't known if I'd understood what it was. There was still a possibility that I hadn't rumbled what was going on. That was the point of all these questions. They didn't think I'd given it to anyone. They were giving me the opportunity of saying, *Why the hell should I have given it to anyone? I destroyed it. I flushed it down the lavatory pan.* Then they would know that I knew. Then I'd be cooked.

I said, "Can I have a drink of water?"

The small man went and got me one in the bathroom. The other man sat down on the bed, still rubbing his knuckles gently, looking at me without hostility, looking me all over as though selecting the next place. The small man came back with the water and gave me it and sat down himself on the bed, side by side with his thoughtful colleague.

He said, after a while, "So, Pan Whistler, let's try again. I'll give you one last chance. I don't need to tell you what a serious matter this is. We know well what it was that you were carrying. There is still the possibility that it can be stopped from leaving the country. If that should prove to be the case, it might not go so badly with you. If not, I can promise you the highest penalty. It is in your own interest to tell us what you did with it."

I said slowly, "Can I believe that—that it will be better for me if you get it back?"

"Certainly."

"Well, I just hope you can," I said. "I posted it." The idea had come to me as he spoke. It sprang to life fully documented, without fumbling or hesitation. It wasn't going to save me. It might give me a few hours' respite.

They were taken utterly by surprise. They looked at each other.

"When did you post it?"

"The minute I left the hotel. I went right out to the post office.

It should have caught the five-o'clock post."

"To whom did you send it?"

"To a man called Cunliffe, the man who sent me, in London."

"You thought it would go through the post without examination?"

"I didn't know what to think. I was in a panic."

Nobody said anything for a minute. The loudspeakers boomed outside. It had begun to rain heavily. I could hear it splashing down off the awning on the balcony. I began to tingle all over, pain forgotten for the moment. There was just a chance, I thought.

The small man said slowly, "It didn't occur to you to destroy the paper? That would have been the quickest and safest way."

Think now. Think. I said, "I wish to hell I had done. But I'd come all the way to get it. I thought there was just a chance it would go through. There was nothing to connect me with it. I just put it in an envelope and addressed it."

Silence again for a minute. "Very well," he said at last, heavily. "We will see, Pan Whistler. I hope, for your sake, that you are telling the truth this time. Get your coat."

I turned to get it from the wardrobe, heart pounding. I knew there was nothing to lose. I thought, *Oh God, I'll never do it.*

I took the raincoat off the hanger and turned round with it. They were both looking at me thoughtfully, side by side on the bed. The raincoat was creased from the morning's rain. I shook it out. I seemed to be shaking it out for about two hours, everything suddenly in slow motion in the last paralyzing moment before action. Then I thought, *Here it is. Now. Now,* and did it.

I threw the raincoat over them. I punched both heads together with a crack. I switched off the light, opened the room door, yelled at the top of my voice. Then I hared back across the room, out onto the balcony. The bloody flower box was in the way and I tripped over it. I scrambled up, kicked the flower box slanting in the opposite direction and went in quietly through the bathroom window, pulling it to behind me.

I don't know how many seconds it took. I was shaking all over. I got down behind the bath in the gap between it and the

128

wall. I crouched there, holding my bruised stomach and trying not to be sick again.

There was a confused row from the next room, people stumbling about. The room light went on again. Josef's voice. "He didn't come this way. I was in the corridor." Then they were on the balcony. "This way. See. He tripped over the flower box."

Footsteps running in the opposite direction. I couldn't hear if they got as far as the fire escape at the opposite end. The loudspeakers drowned everything. But they'd certainly be coming back. I had perhaps half a minute to get out through the bedroom. I couldn't tell if Josef had gone with them.

My stomach was painful as hell. I levered myself up from the floor in the narrow space, found something there at the side of the bath. The bit of piping I'd seen there, weeks, years ago. I picked it up, edged out of the gap, careful to make no sound. I tiptoed over to the half-open door to the bedroom. No one was there and I went in.

Josef stepped in from the balcony.

He stood stock-still for a moment, jaw dropping with surprise. I ran across the room with the piping. He said, "No, no," caught me by the shoulder and half turned me round. But I managed to lift the thing and hit him once, as hard as I could. It landed above the ear. His eyes turned up, he gave a single, heavily exhaled breath and fell against me. I stepped back and he folded up on the floor. I didn't know if I'd killed him. It was the first time I'd ever hit anyone.

I said aloud, "Oh, Christ," panting, half sobbing. I looked quickly round the room, saw my passport and wallet and stuffed them in my pocket. I didn't know how I was going to get out of the hotel. I was sure they'd have people watching, a full description of me.

The moment I thought of this, and with a mindless sense of inevitability, I began tugging Josef's tailcoat off him. He was like a sack of lead, head banging on the floor. I yanked him round, split the seams at the shoulder as I pulled it off. He had no shirt underneath, just a wide dicky, taped back and front, and a clip-on bow. I got the whole lot off, then his trousers, tugging and jerking in a panic. I thought they'd be running

129

back along the balcony at any moment. I wondered if I should drag Josef into some other room, but dare not risk the corridor.

He was shorter and broader than me. I was in his trousers in less than half a minute; had trouble with the dicky and let it hang loose at the back. There was no time to examine the bow tie in the mirror. I bundled him under the bed, kicked the pile of clothes after him, transferred the money and passport, and went into the corridor.

Rain was bouncing in at the open window there. I thought I'd better get a raincoat; it would look suspicious going out without one. I couldn't take my own. The raincoats were different here, long, thin, pale-colored. I knocked on the first door along the corridor. The room was empty, unused. I tried the next without knocking. The blonde I had noticed earlier on the balcony was sitting naked before the dressing table mirror, carefully examining one breast. I said, *"Prosim,"* shut the door quickly and tried the next one.

There were clothes scattered on the bed, a case open on the luggage rack, splashing coming from the bathroom. I opened the wardrobe door, saw a man's raincoat inside, and took it.

I had noticed some back stairs at the other end of the corridor and wondered if these were the service stairs. I walked quickly back again, my feet soundless on the carpet, terrified the men would come suddenly bursting out of the room. I didn't see a soul. The steps were narrow and badly lit. There was a dark little cubbyhole on the first landing and an old chambermaid sat on a three-legged stool eating a piece of bread. She looked at me curiously as I passed, but said politely, *"Dobry vecer."* I wished her the same and went on quickly down the stairs.

They let out into a dim, tiled hall with a concrete floor. There was a green baize notice board and a clock on the wall. Two boys in tailcoats, evidently young trainees, were pushing and shoving each other around, laughing. They froze when they saw me, muttering subdued *Dobry vecers*. There was a swing door at the end, and a double door beyond that. I went out through it. Outside a man in a hat and raincoat stood in the shelter of the doorway out of the rain. He raised his arm to hold me back. "I'm sorry, no one is to leave."

I said, "I know, comrade, I know. They've got him. He's upstairs now. I'm the floor waiter."

He watched me getting into my raincoat, somewhat sourly. "Where do you think you're going?"

"To the chemist's," I said, my stomach turning over and over. "They need something quickly. Ring up and find out if you want, only for God's sake don't hold me up. He's a delicate little soul liable to pass out any minute. You won't be very popular if he does."

He said, "Wait here," and went in through the double doors.

I heard the swing door going, and ran up the alley. It was unlit, black, black as hell, a canyon between two tall buildings. I wondered if there was any way out into a side street that would bring me into the Prikopy, but it was a cul-de-sac, and I turned and belted back, panting in the dark. Presently the alley curved and I saw the lights at the end.

Nobody stopped me this time. I walked out into the Vaclavske Namesti.

chapter 9

There is something about coshing a man for the first time that inspires a certain wild but unstable confidence. One moment you are faced with a powerful and unnerving obstacle; the next, without thought or subtlety, you have overcome it. By disengaging from the habits of a lifetime you have slipped into a new effortless gear in which all things seem possible. Minutes afterward the adrenalin aftertaste still tickles the roots of the tongue, nauseous, exultant, the unique flavor of rewarded violence.

I had buttoned the raincoat up to my chin, and was clutching the piece of lead piping in my pocket. Despite the rain the street was still thronged with hardy hands and brains. The crowds seemed denser farther down the street where the floodlighting was brightest, and I instinctively moved toward them, shuffling briskly and head down past the hotel entrance.

I knew that my only hope was to get to the Malostranske as quickly as possible, and to effect, as they say, an entrance to the British Embassy. The grotesque picture of myself as a fugitive from the secret police in this crowded and hostile city did not, in those first moments, seem at all incredible. I felt extraordinarily alive and effective, not at all the familiar coward.

The Malostranske lay at the other side of the river, perhaps a mile and a half away. I had suddenly a clear picture of the thoroughfare that I had forgotten so completely in my panic earlier on. It lay at the end of the Mostecka. I must have passed it on my walk to the Heights on my first visit. It would take me half an hour to walk there in the crowded streets. I thought I'd better get the tram.

I walked over to the island in the middle of the road. The little trams were dingdonging by, packed to the steps, but three number nines came in quick succession, and I managed to get on the last. No fares were being taken. It was impossible for the conductress to move. I stood on the step, battered, bruised, my stomach still stiff and aching from the last blow, but wonderfully alive as we swayed and lurched down the brilliant, seething street.

I thought, I've got away with it. Not half an hour ago I was being beaten up by the secret police. I fooled them. I knocked out a man who tried to stop me. Incredible but true. It was wonderful what you could do when you tried.

In my desire to get away from the hotel and make for the thickest crowds, I had walked down the street. The tram now took me back up it, past the hotel, to the huge picture of Lenin at the junction. My cockiness lasted until approximately this point, where the tram ground to a halt. It seemed to be stationary longer than usual. I leaned out to see what was happening. The whole line of trams had stopped at the junction. I felt a premonitory sickness in my stomach again.

The conductress presently struggled off, muttering, and after a minute or two came back. "Anyone in a hurry had better get off," she said. "You'd do better to walk. They're looking for something in front."

A noisy, larky bunch of teen-agers tumbled off the tram. I tumbled off with them, crossed to the pavement, and made my way up to the junction. There was really no need for me to look. The sickness in my stomach had provided accurate forewarning. The passengers were coming off the leading trams singly, each opening his coat as he got off, each showing his papers. Two men in hats and raincoats stood by each of the three leading trams. It was all very businesslike. They'd not wasted a lot of time.

I continued numbly to the corner, saw the same performance taking place on the pavement with pedestrians wishing to debouch into the Narodni Trida and into the Prikopy, and turned and made my way back down the street.

There are nine main roads running off the Vaclavske Namesti, five of them in the direction of the river, four of them away

133

from it. It took me forty minutes in the crowded street to investigate them all. I could have given up after the first. The five streets running to the river were covered; the four running away from it were covered. As I'd seen from the start, it was a businesslike operation. I wasn't going to the British Embassy tonight. I wasn't going to leave the Vaclavske Namesti. I was cobbled.

By half past ten the street showed no sign of clearing, but the rain, although it had slowed to a drizzle, had mercifully not stopped. I kept the raincoat buttoned up to my chin and trudged wearily up the street again. I was sick of the sight of it, having gone there and back six times. The loudspeakers, after repeating a medley of marches, were now rendering selections from *The Bartered Bride*. I was dropping with exhaustion.

The future, it seemed to me, was short and brutally unpromising. There were perhaps twenty thousand people in the stretch between Lenin and the museum. They would all have to go to bed at some time—say in an hour, two at the most. There was nothing for the police to do but wait.

In my perambulations up and down the street I had gone endlessly into the problem of how to get rid of the tailcoat. There was no public lavatory in the Vaclavske Namesti—and I wouldn't have dared to enter it if there were—or any enclosed building where men might be waiting. I couldn't get out of the tailcoat in the street. Even if I did manage this contortionist feat, there would still be the question of papers. There was no way out. I was trapped.

I was obsessed with a horrifying vision of the old movie, the one where the character is walking up the empty street and they start coming for him out of doorways and he runs off down a sewer. I didn't know where to look for a sewer in this noisy fairground of a street. I knew it wouldn't end like that for me. I would merely get more and more tired, it would get later and later, and all the people would drift off. Then the police would begin to round up stragglers. "Open your coat. Where are your papers?" There was nowhere for me to run. There would be no point in struggling. Just a brief ride in a closed van, and then they would start hitting me again.

134

I thought, *Oh Christ,* and turned round and started back again, seventh circuit. I thought, If I could just sit down for a minute. If I could just take the weight off, have a drink, think calmly. There was no chance of that. I had to keep moving, one of the crowd. I trudged on, shoes letting in water, stomach sickly empty, mouth parched.

I had counted six *parky* stalls up and down the street, their naphtha flares pale in the floodlighting. My stomach revolted at the thought of the hot, greasy sausages and the coarse black bread. It would make me thirstier than ever. But I knew suddenly that I had to sit down. I didn't think I could keep going five minutes longer without a rest. There was a wooden box outside the next stall, and a woman sitting on it, eating.

I teetered around the stall until she had finished, and then I quickly claimed the box. Four or five people waiting to be served looked at me. The stallkeeper said morosely, "In the queue, comrade. There are others before you."

"I'll wait. I'm in no hurry."

"Maybe someone else wants the seat."

They said they didn't want the seat. He grunted, turned back to his pan again and served the others. There was a naphtha flare at each end of the stall. Fumes from the pan hung in the harsh yellow glare. I thought I was going to be sick and turned my head.

The man said, "How many?"

It seemed to be my turn. "One, please."

"Mustard? Mustard?" he said and leaned over to look at me. "Is something wrong, comrade?"

It had risen in my throat. I couldn't speak. I said faintly after a moment, "I feel sick."

"You want some mineral water?"

"Yes, please."

I hadn't seen any bottles. He moved away inside somewhere and came out of a side door with a glass. "I'm sorry, comrade. I didn't see you were ill. People are shoving and pushing their way to the front everywhere tonight. Here, drink."

A few other people had come up and he went back inside and served them. I sat on the box and drank the mineral water and presently felt well enough to eat the *parky* and black bread

135

he had left on the counter for me. I wondered where he had got the bottle from. I wondered what else he had in there. The stall about six feet long, four wide, a wooden shack on iron barrow wheels. The counter flap was not more than a yard long. There must be some sort of compartment between it and the side door. I felt the stirrings of something.

"All right now, comrade?"

"Yes, thank you."

"Maybe you walked too much in the crowds. There are too many of them shoving and pushing tonight."

"Maybe that was it."

"Leave the glass there. Don't bother to get up. Rest for a while."

"That's all right," I said and went round to the side door and handed the glass in to him. You could step right inside and not be seen from the street. Two or three people could step inside. There were a few shelves with bottles, raw sausages, loaves of bread, a dark area about a yard square.

I thanked him and continued slowly along the street, hope beginning to expand again like bubbles in some steamy swamp. I wondered if all the other stalls were the same. I thought they would be. I thought there should be something one could do about this.

I suddenly realized exactly what I could do about it and stood stock-still on the pavement, the back of my neck beginning to sweat. It would have to be a very small stallkeeper, I thought. I couldn't cope with anything bigger than a dwarf in my ruined condition. And it would be better if it were on the other side of the road where the streets ran off to the river.

I had a dim recollection of a gnomelike figure superintending a stall at the corner of the Stepanska, and crossed the road and made my way to it. The naphtha flare was not more than ten yards from the corner. There were four or five people waiting at the counter. The side door was ajar. I went past the front of the stall and came back again. I hadn't been wrong. He was a little skinny fellow with a marked resemblance to Ratface Rickett only about two hundred years older. He wore a peaked cap and a shiny plastic jacket. It was several sizes too large for him, I was glad to see.

136

I got in the queue and had another *parky* and looked carefully inside. It seemed identical with the other stall. It waited till there was a lull in trade and went round to the side door, trembling. I pushed the door open and went in.

He saw me right away and said irritably, "Round at the front, round at the front."

I said, "I've got something for you."

"What is it? What do you want?"

He came over with a string of sausages and a knife in his hand and he was so damned old and bent I could hardly bring myself to do it. I hit him quite gently on the head with the piping. His cap fell off and he clutched his head, staring at me in horrified silence. I thought, *Oh Christ, Oh Christ,* and hit him again in a panic, and he fell down. I said silently, *I'm sorry. I'm sorry, old man,* getting quickly out of my coat and the damned tailcoat. I ripped off the bow and the dicky, and bundled the lot on a shelf, and pulled his jacket off and got into it myself.

I hadn't realized there was no floor to the stall. The road was directly underneath, and his cap had rolled in the gutter. I picked it up quickly and put it on, and in the same moment someone began rapping on the counter and calling, *"Prosim, prosim. Parky, prosim,"* and a man leaned over and saw me as I was straightening up.

I said, "Coming, coming."

"I should hope so, comrade," he said jovially. "The customers are waiting."

I went over to the counter, sweating. There were half a dozen of them there. They'd materialized suddenly. I didn't think I could have been more than a minute or two.

"Three," the man said. "With mustard."

A pan of *parkys* was stinking away on the stove. I fiddled about with them, my heart beating dully, and wondered how I was going to cope with this. I didn't think the old man could possibly be seen, but shoved him over with my foot nearer the backboard, just in case. The bread was sliced and I forked three *parkys* out of the pan and handed them over.

I had never seen more than half a dozen people at a stall all night, but now for some ill-starred and damnable reason this one became suddenly popular. In no time there was a queue of a dozen or so, and I shambled there and back, emptying and replenishing the *parky* pan in the yellow malodorous glare until I was faint with nausea and fatigue.

I heard eleven o'clock strike and then a quarter past, and shortly after that the loudspeakers stopped and the stream of customers dried up. I thought it was time I got the hell out of it. I bent and looked at the old man. He had not stirred, but he was breathing. I couldn't see any blood. I thought he'd gone off to sleep. I went back to the counter again and looked out into the street. The crowds had definitely thinned. On the corner of the Stepanska, a few yards away, a couple of raincoated S.N.B. men were on duty, big solid fellows. They were stopping everyone who entered the street. Open your coat. Show your papers. Well, I thought; I could show mine. I looked swiftly in the pocket of the plastic jacket and found the old man's wallet. His papers said he was Vaclav Borsky, seventy-four, one hundred and sixty-one centimeters, born Kutna Hora. I was not too bothered about this discrepancy in age. They weren't really looking at the papers, just seeing that everyone had them. They knew Whistler Nicolas, the well-known spy, hadn't.

I left the counter and walked out of the side door and went haring back in again faster than I'd ever moved in my life. One of the S.N.B. men was walking over.

He said gruffly, "You're packing up early."

I said, "No. No."

"Do us a couple quick, comrade, and the same for my friend. We're dropping there."

I said, "Certainly. Of course."

He watched while I fiddled with the *parkys*. I kept my head down, terrified he would have some minute description of my face. He was looking hungrily at the *parkys,* however, and stuffed his in his mouth as soon as I handed it over. I felt some comment might be called for, and said in a kind of soprano, "What's all the excitement been, comrade?"

"Ah, don't bother your head. It's an enemy of the people at large."

"What's he done?"

"Nothing to what we'll do when we get him. He's a famous
138

American criminal, an expert in disguise. He escaped dressed as a waiter."

"I hope you catch him."

"We will," he said, walking off with his colleague's *parkys*. He had not paid.

I remained inside the stall, quivering like a leaf. I sat down on a box. I poured myself a glass of mineral water. The stall was in plain view of the men on the corner. Now that the streets had thinned they could see me perfectly. There seemed no prospect of walking away. In a matter of minutes the street had gone quiet, and I was suddenly aware the trams had stopped. An ominous silence set in. There was presently a subdued rumbling, and after a few moments the two men on the corner turned to stare at me. One of them walked over.

I almost fell off the box in my haste to be up.

"Are you staying here all night, comrade?"

I said, "What? No. I must have dropped off. Time to be off, eh?"

"Your friends are all going. Better get that rattle trap off the street now. There might be some shooting soon."

I came out of the side door. The floodlighting went off suddenly. Up and down the street the naphtha flares were moving, iron barrow wheels rumbling over the cobbles.

"Look sharp now. The inspector will be round any minute. He wants to find the street empty."

I said, "Right away," and went numbly back inside, wondering where the hell to start. I picked up the frying pan and then thought of something else and nearly collapsed in panic. The inspector wouldn't be finding the street empty. Vaclav Borsky was lying about in it, at present under the stall and snoring rhythmically.

The other policeman stepped over to join his mate, saying irritably, "Come on, come on now. What's the trouble? Smirtov will be here any moment. Here, give him a hand."

I came out of the side door at a rush, crying, "No. Wait. Don't trouble yourself, comrades. I've just got to go somewhere a minute. Watch the stall for me, please. I'm bursting," and hurried off, making motions indicative of a violent need to urinate.

139

I don't know if they believed me. I was beyond caring if they believed me. I thought it would take a minute or two for them to suspect, a little longer for them to know definitely. I had about three minutes.

I went round the corner of the Stepanska like a whippet. The street looked long and hideously straight. A few yards round the corner the huge bulk of a hotel glimmered dimly, but after that it was black as hell. My footsteps rang back from the high walls at both sides. I stopped and wrenched my shoes off, panting and sobbing, and hared on again in my socks.

I thought there must be an alley or an entry. I couldn't see anything. Tall buildings; blank walls. I'd picked the wrong street. After a minute or two I was winded, stomach hurting like hell, and had to slow down to a trot, breathing heavily. Suddenly I heard a single enraged shout at the other end of the street and took off again like a rocket. Almost immediately, I fell over. The pavement had ended. I went sprawling on cobbles.

I got up, lost one of the damned shoes, scrambled frantically for it on the wet cobbles, found it. There was a light somewhere, a tiny glimmer. I couldn't make it out, took a second or two to contact. I'd found my alley.

I went up the alley slowly, puzzled by the light. A hospital, police station, cul-de-sac of some sort? I suddenly heard my breathing echoing back, realized I was in a roofed place, and stopped and held my breath, trying to work it out. It seemed to be an archway. In the silence the gutters gurgled steadily outside. The rain had stopped. A still, close night. My elbow was throbbing. I must have fallen on it. Suddenly a car revved up and came whooshing down the street. Men shouting. Another car starting up. I couldn't stay here, would either have to take my chance on it being a cul-de-sac or get out in the street again and find another alley.

I went on through the archway.

After a few paces I saw what the light was. A statue. A madonna, with a little oil lamp over her head. A few flowers showed whitely in an urn at the base. A cobbled, medieval courtyard; not, evidently, a churchyard; no obvious church; big blank buildings all round. There might be an alley running off at the
140

other side. I ran across the cobbles in my socks and suddenly stopped, quite still.

There was someone there.

I stepped back to the wall, unable to place the direction. A girl laughed, over to the right, and I saw them, a single shape that became two, then one again. A man and a girl scuffling and laughing softly in the angle of two walls. A bicycle showed dully nearby.

The muttering went on; giggling again. The man's voice, gruff and wheedling, "Ah, why not? You said you would."

I thought I could safely leave them to it, and edged round, keeping close to the wall. The courtyard was a rectangle. Railings; basements; everything in darkness. The backs of business premises, I thought. From somewhere close by a clock chimed half past eleven, and all round other clocks began to strike.

There was an opening at the next corner, a cobbled path not a yard wide. I couldn't see where it went, everything pitch black. Another car went by in the street, and men running. I was in no position to choose. I went swiftly into the opening, feeling my way with my right hand outstretched. The wall curved right, left, right again. No chance to escape if anyone came in after me in either direction.

My outstretched hand suddenly fetched up against a blank wall. Dead end. Panic. *Wait. Wait,* I thought. How dead end? Why dead end? The path must go somewhere. There had been no doors or gates opening off it. I felt all round, found that it turned sharply at ninety degrees to the left, hurried on, sobbing with relief. From all round now there seemed to be a fair amount of activity. Car doors banging, men shouting. I'd lost all sense of direction. I knew I mustn't be caught up this alley. I began to run.

Immediately I tripped, stumbled, went floundering down a flight of steps, and landed heavily on my backside. There was something underneath me, something alive and shrieking. A cat. A bloody cat. It tore out from under me, clawing and spitting, and a dustbin lid clanged a yard away. I scrabbled to my feet, terrified of the row, and at the same moment a light came on from an upstairs room in front of me. I was outside a gate, the end of the path, railings at both sides. Really dead end now.

A woman's voice called, "Franti?"

I couldn't somehow move, stiff from my fall and hypnotized by the light. There was a group of buildings beyond the gate. The woman came out onto a balcony and stood silhouetted against the light.

She said, "Frantisek? See you put the bicycle away tonight. It will rain again."

I tried to edge into the shadow. She was leaning over a small coping, peering at me. A flight of steps ran up to the balcony. "What, lost your tongue? Ah, there's no need to sneak in, you fornicating beast. I've been waiting for you. Who was it tonight?"

I couldn't understand the layout of the buildings. Not houses. Not warehouses. A large formal structure, many windowed, a Gothic arch.

"All right. Stay dumb. You can stay out, too. Maybe she'll give you a bed. Or see if you can find a girl again in the gymnasium. You filthy beast!" she said bitterly, and went in and slammed and bolted the door.

I thought, gymnasium. A school, perhaps. The caretaker's lodge. I tried the gate. There was a simple iron latch. It opened easily, but I didn't go in. There would be a front entrance on a street, a naked public street. My instinct was to remain in the dark alleys. I couldn't somehow think. I was aching all over, desperately tired. I suddenly realized I'd been on my feet for the best part of seven hours. I felt behind me for the steps and sat down, holding my head and trying to work it out. In the silence I could hear the cars still, a confused distant row. I couldn't tell how far I'd gone. But I knew I couldn't stay here. The fornicating Frantisek would be along any minute with his bike. No point in going back down the alley for the same reason. Nothing else but the gate.

I got up and pushed it and went in.

A wide quadrangle, dark, no visible features except the bulk of the buildings. I skirted them on the left, found a high wall and followed it round. I followed it for several hundred yards and came up against a building. Dead end. I cut back across

142

the quadrangle to try the other way, and suddenly a finger of light swung across and I froze. A bicycle lamp. I heard the faint clang of the gate latch and then the light went off. I remained quite still in the ocean of darkness, listening for him. The faint hiss of tires on the wet surface. I couldn't place the direction, wondered if he wasn't coming toward me to put the bicycle away in some shed, and backed quickly to the wall.

I lost him completely then. Total silence. Suddenly a light came on under the balcony where the woman had appeared. The pool of light spread all the way to the gate. I saw him leaning the bike against the wall. He seemed in no hurry. He wiped his face and collar carefully with a handerchief, fumbled around in his pocket, and I saw the weak spurt of a match. The flame leapt. He was lighting a pipe.

I told him silently, *Go, damn you, go.* He didn't go. He began to walk up and down smoking the pipe, breathing deeply. I leaned against the wall, sick and aching. My feet were cold and wet in the socks. I wondered if I might sit on the ground, and lowered myself painfully but surely right into a bloody puddle. I was so dead beat I couldn't bear to move and sat there, watching him.

A quarter to twelve struck.

He knocked out the pipe and walked back to the bike and the light suddenly went off. I levered myself to my feet again. I heard the faint sound of him going up the stairs, and started moving. He'd be down again pretty soon, I thought. I knew one fornicator who wouldn't be entering the conjugal home tonight.

I actually managed to trot on my maltreated feet past the gate and away over to the other side of the quadrangle, but after a few seconds slowed to a painful walk again. The sky seemed to be lightening a bit. The clouds were breaking up, a dim radiance appearing. I saw the outline of the wall now, and then the main gates.

Beyond the gates, the street seemed deserted. I peered through them in both directions. I had no idea at all where I was. I felt it couldn't be far from the river. I didn't know what I was going to do when I got there. They would have the approaches to the Embassy well covered by now. It seemed pointless to try to get there. But what was the point of trying to get any-

143

where? I couldn't hide indefinitely in Prague. I couldn't spend the rest of my life running up and down alleys. They were going to catch me sometime. My only hope lay in trying to get to the Embassy. If I failed, then it meant failing earlier instead of later. This meant I had to cross the river. I would have to boat or swim across, both prospects so grimly unattractive that I groaned faintly in the dark.

I wondered at which point of the river embankment the street led out. There was only one way to find out, and I turned the handle of the gate and pulled gently. Nothing happened. I tried the other way, pushed, pulled, wrenched, swore obscenely. The gate was locked. It seemed about a mile high; straight vertical bars, too difficult to climb, too risky to climb, exposing me against the skyline to anyone who might be patrolling in the street.

The sky was brightening rapidly, tattered, luminous-edged clouds scudding across now. A breeze fluttered over the quadrangle, cold against my wet trousers. I looked round the school walls, saw a cluster of buildings beyond the wall on my left, and, farther along, an unexpected godsend, a builder's ladder. I made for the ladder, planted it firmly against the wall and climbed up. At the other side of the wall there was a collection of lorries and handcarts; a big building with hanger doors; a warehouse of some kind. Away to the right the street wall continued. I could see over it now. It was dark and quiet out there. There was a faint yellow light perhaps fifty yards along; evidently the corner, the river embankment.

The lorries were parked in line at the side of the warehouse. I thought there must be a gate or door at the far end that would open directly onto the embankment. Perhaps there would be a gap or a keyhole through which I could check my position.

There was a handcart directly below at the other side of the wall. I pulled myself on the wall, dropped the shoes on the handcart and went cautiously after them. A cobbled yard, faint stink of diesel oil, and something else—polish, wood, shavings? I went carefully down the line of lorries, found blank double doors, padlocked, no gap, no keyhole.

I went back again, round the warehouse, to the hanger doors, and suddenly stopped. A glimpse of light, a crack in the door.

I seesawed my head from side to side to catch it again, couldn't, and stepped back a pace. It wasn't a crack in the door. The door was open, not quite pulled to, a gap of an inch or so.

I pushed gently, waiting for the creak, but there was no creak. It opened ponderously, but quite smoothly.

The light was coming from big plate-glass windows at the other end, faint yellow lighting from street lamps on the main road. I went slowly in, and stood for a moment just inside, sizing it up.

Furniture. Chairs, dressing tables, beds, standard lamps. Toward the window the stuff was laid out in suites. A clock suddenly struck and I dropped one of the shoes in panic, and picked it up, sweating, swearing, nervy as hell. The other clocks chimed in then. Twelve o'clock. Three-quarters of an hour since I'd left the *parky* stall. Only five hours since I'd coshed Josef and run for it. It seemed a lifetime. But I was free still. I'd got away with it so far. I'd got to the river.

With a faint resurgence of hope I moved in to the wall in the shadow of a line of wardrobes and went slowly up to the windows. As I got there the moon came out. A silvery luminescence swam over the street like a filmy curtain going up at a theater. There was someone out there. It needed only one look to see who.

Silent and alone in the moonlit street he bestrode his great horse, sword raised, iron eyes staring sightlessly along his broad imperial way. Like some homing pigeon I had come back to him again. Like some demented rat I had run back into my trap. Like a bloody fool I sat down and wept.

I must have been about twelve when I had wept last. I didn't know why I was weeping now. I hadn't wept when the policeman had knocked me about in the bedroom. I sat on a little coffee table and felt the tears streaming uncontrollably down my face, and thought what a right Charley I had been. It had been such a hellishly long day, such a nerve-shatteringly long night, I thought I'd got away with it. I thought I was miles away.

I snapped out of it presently and, edging back into the shadow, sat down on something more comfortable to take stock of the

145

situation. The river was obviously in the opposite direction. I'd come round in a half circle. There was nothing to be gained by going back up the alley. It led only to the Stepanska.

The alternative seemed to be to get into the side street. I went drearily over the operations necessary to achieve this. Then what? It would be best to keep off the street. Nip in and out of alleys, work my way round to a point below the bridges, and cross the water as best I could. That would take—how long? An hour? Two? I thought it wouldn't hurt to have a rest first.

I sat down on a settee, the seat and back wrapped with brown paper, and then slowly and luxuriously lifted up my legs and stretched out. It was warm in the room and stuffy with the smell of furniture. I could feel the seat of my pants wet from the puddle, my feet damp and throbbing in the soggy socks.

The street was bathed now in brilliant moonlight, the cold ghostly figure of Wenceslas leaping as clouds went swiftly over. It was utterly still out there, no cars racing now, no men running. I wondered where they were searching for me. Obviously along the river; they would know where I had to get. They would be at it for hours yet; plenty of river front to search.

It suddenly occurred to me in the warm musty darkness that one of the few places where they wouldn't think of looking was on a settee in a showroom on the Vaclavske Namesti.

I lay there, blinking rapidly at Wenceslas, working out the implications of this one.

It was stupid. I couldn't stay here all night. How would I get out in the morning? Where could I hide in daylight?

But why should I have to hide in daylight? Why should I have to creep down alleys when the streets were crowded with people? I could get out early when the first trams started, join the streaming workers in the streets. They would be unlikely to carry out further checks in the Vaclavske Namesti. But how to cross the river in daylight? There might still be checks on the bridges. . . .

The blissful, spreading comfort of the settee was overpowering. If tonight had taught me anything, it was not to think too much, not to plan too far ahead. I shifted the piece of piping out of my pocket and moved over into a new marvelous position. A crumpled dustsheet was lying at the end of the settee, and

146

I pulled it over me. I didn't think I was visible from the street. The settee was in shadow. But the moon would slip round.

I thought I'd better will myself to get up every time the hour struck so that I wouldn't drift off into a deep sleep. I thought the first trams would be along about six o'clock. Six hours.

I got up when one struck, and again at two, and walked about stretching myself in the shadow at the back of the showroom. I was stiff as hell. After that I stayed where I was. I knew I wasn't going to sleep. I thought I might be too exhausted for sleep, too nervous, brain going busily back and forth over it all.

I must have watched Wenceslas for longer than anyone in the world. I can still see him when I close my eyes, leaping on his iron horse in the ragged moonlight. Soon after the chorus of clocks struck five, my eyes closed and I dozed off for a bit.

It didn't seem more than five minutes, but next time I opened them it was broad daylight, a tram was dingdonging by, and a man was looking down at me. He had the piece of piping in his hand and he said, "Don't move. Stay where you are, or I'll brain you."

chapter 10

The piece of piping was a couple of feet from my head. He must have picked it up from the side of the settee. He was an elderly man, broad, grizzled, wearing an alpaca jacket and carpet slippers. His eyes were intensely blue and Slav, and, at that moment, very hostile.

He said, "How did you get in here?"

I licked my lips, shaken as hell. I said, "The door was open."

"It was locked. I locked it myself last thing at night. You must have forced it."

The alpaca jacket and carpet slippers registered then. He was the caretaker. Not a very careful caretaker. I sat up, felt the seat of my pants still warmly damp, each individual bone aching and unrested. I said, "It was open, comrade. Just a crack. Maybe you locked it later." I knew he couldn't have done, unless he made a practice of locking up sometime after five o'clock in the morning. It seemed a useful loophole to offer him. "I must have been drunk. I had nowhere to sleep. I hope it won't get you into trouble, comrade."

He had taken this latter point, of course, long before it had occurred to me. He still held the piece of piping at a workmanlike angle, however. "How did you get into the yard?"

"I came over the wall. I was out drinking with a fellow—Frantisek something. He said he would put me up, but his slut of a wife kicked us both out. He told me you had a kind heart. He said you would fix me up. He brought me a ladder to climb the wall."

This inspired lie, delivered in whining and wheedling tones, sprang to life ready-made like some work of art. I listened to

148

it with astonishment. It seemed to be registering with the caretaker. The hand holding the pipe dropped. "I should hand you over to the police," he said without much conviction. "You ought to have come and seen me first."

"I tried to, comrade. I looked all round for you, but it was dark. I thought I would just rest for a minute until you came on your rounds. Frantisek said you never missed your rounds. He told me what a kind heart you had."

He grunted and looked me over, not unfriendly. "That Frantisek—he takes too many liberties. You're just up for the parade, I suppose?"

"The parade, that's it entirely, the parade," I said eagerly.

"And what about this? What did you mean to do with this?" he said, raising the lead piping.

"That. Well, that, now," I said, thinking rapidly. "I took it off a fellow. There was this big brute came at Frantisek when he'd had a few too many. That's how we came together. Ah, you don't get that where I come from," I said, my wheedling tone leading me effortlessly into the accusing burr of some Czech village idiot. "Where I come from they don't go around coshing people when they've had a few too many. They see a chap home to his bed. They're glad to give him a bed—and his breakfast in the morning," I added, shaking my head reproachfully as I recalled suddenly that the automats might not be open on Sunday morning.

The grizzled caretaker seemed somewhat taken aback by this rustic rebuke. He made no attempt to prevent me getting off the settee. He said, rather uncertainly, "Well, no harm done, I suppose. Whereabouts are you from, comrade?"

"Round Brno way. You wouldn't know it. Just a little village. Ah, you can keep your big towns," I said, carried away by my performance, and improving every minute. "Folks aren't friendly here. Just tell me where a fellow can get his breakfast and a wash-up in a town like this, comrade, and I won't trouble you any longer."

The caretaker scratched his head. He watched me stretching myself. He said, "Where's your national costume, then? Don't you country fellows dress up in national costume when you come to town?"

I said, "National costume," and licked my lips. "Don't talk to me about national costume. You can have one, Jiri, they said to me, if you join the Party. Otherwise you can go up to Prague looking the tramp you are. We're a bit short of national costumes, Jiri, they said. Party members only, see? So I told them what they could do with their national costume, I did. A fellow's got to do too many things already these days. He's got to know all the reasons why he was ever born these days. No, comrade," I said, shaking my head with wooden defiance at the little caretaker, "you won't get me to do that, so it's no use your trying. I've got no time for it, and I won't waste any more of yours if you'll just put me on my way."

The caretaker had brightened considerably during this rebellious speech, and now took my arm warmly. "Not so fast, countryman, not so fast," he said, dropping the "comrade" and smiling indulgently. "Get your boots on first. I dare say I can fix you up with a bit of breakfast and a wash. It's just that a fellow's got to be so careful these days. I'm here on my own, see? It's hard to know who's an enemy of the people and who isn't. This way now. No harm done. Just follow me."

He gave me an excellent breakfast in his small and shipshape flat above the warehouse, which I repaid with a detailed fantasy of life in the small village near Brno. Despite the horrors of the previous night, I felt full of a wild and febrile confidence. I could hear my own voice and was in that lightheaded state when nothing about my own body or immediate surroundings seemed at all real.

The caretaker's steadfast Slav eyes hung on my words. He said at length regretfully, "Well, countryman, time for you to be off, I suppose. It's getting on for nine. The rest of your party will be up at the camp, eh?"

"The camp?"

"Isn't that where they bed them out? The camp at the other side of the Charles bridge, just before the Mostecka."

The Mostecka, I thought. Surely that was near the Malostranske, the British Embassy. . . . I felt the beginning of something and said slowly, "The Mostecka, is it? Yes, yes. That's it, of course. The Mostecka. Now what's the name of the square near the Mostecka? They said we had to rally there."

"A square near the Mostecka? Let me see, that must be the Malostranske."

"Malostranske!" I said. "That's the one. How's a fellow to find that now?"

"Why," said the caretaker, jumping up promptly, "I'll take you there myself, countryman. In just one moment."

He hurried out, and I executed a brief bob to his departing back, and considered how well things went when you left them alone. What I needed was a spot of cover while reconnoitering the Malostranske, and here was this grizzled ancient, heaven-sent and tailor-made to provide it.

I walked over to the window and looked out. As little Vlcek and his meteorological friends had promised, it was a magnificent day, with that shining, pristine quality that mornings sometimes have in very old cities. Already the street crawled; splashes of color from wandering groups in national costume; queues inevitably forming at stands and tram stops. The caretaker had told me the parade would begin at eleven and that trams would stop at ten. There would be a good deal of shifting movement all over the town, particularly over the bridges. There couldn't be much attempt at searching in these conditions.

The old man reappeared, very spruce in a blue serge suit and brown shoes, and we went out, down the side street and past the school gates toward the embankment. As we walked I began to realize how damned lucky I'd been. The warehouse was miles from the river. The street led into a broad thoroughfare, the Zitna, which ran through botanical gardens to another street, the Myslikova, before reaching the embankment. The Stepanska, down which I had originally fled, also ran into this complex: I could imagine the activity there while I had lain quietly in the stuffy darkness watching Wenceslas.

We walked under the linden trees past the bathing platform and the three islands to the Charles bridge. There seemed to be no check of any kind, but my rising spirits were damped somewhat by the old man's growing suspicion that we were going the wrong way. There were now increasing numbers of national costumes, all moving in the opposite direction.

"They're coming away from the Malostranske, countryman. Are you sure you got the instructions right?"

"Yes, yes. I'm sure. A square near the Mostecka is what they told me."

"Couldn't it have been the Mezibranska? That would be back by the museum, you see. That would be at the beginning of the parade, countryman. It sounds more likely."

"No, no," I said doggedly. "Malostranske is what they said."

"What about all these people then? Don't you recognize any of them? Over there, look—isn't that a Moravian costume? That'll be from somewhere near Brno. Shouldn't I stop and ask them, countryman?"

"You must do what you want," I said, suppressing a powerful urge to stuff his cap in his mouth and bundle him briskly along in my arms. "I know what my instructions are. Just put me on my road, countryman, and I'll be obliged to you."

This sort of thing went on until we reached the Malostranske, where the caretaker held my arm, gasping and wheezing—I had walked at a swift pace up the steep Mostecka. "There, countryman, there! Not a sign of a rally, look. You must have mistaken it. Let's get back quickly now."

"I can't understand it," I said, shaking my head stubbornly and gazing rapidly about the square. "What about the other side of the square?"

"Nothing, countryman, nothing at all there. Come quickly now. We'll never get back in time."

"And that little street?" I said, my heart suddenly leaping. I had glimpsed the Union Jack fluttering limply in the morning breeze. "Doesn't that lead anywhere?"

"Ah, that's only the Thunovska. It's a cul-de-sac. There's just one of the foreign embassies there. Come, countryman, everybody's leaving."

But everybody wasn't leaving. I had looked for them, and now I saw them. Four men, two on each corner, stood by the entrance to the Thunovska. Even at this distance one could discern the characteristic look of the S.N.B. They turned to stare at us as we stood wrangling in the square. I was suddenly sharply aware that I was wearing the cap and jacket of Vaclav Borsky. I said, "Perhaps you're right, countryman, let's go," and we turned and went back down the Mostecka.

Even though I had expected the Embassy to be covered, my spirits had swiftly sunk. With four men commanding the entrance to the narrow cul-de-sac it had been obvious at a glance that I wasn't going to get in by merely walking in. But at least I had spied out the lay of the land. At some point I would have to return. The journey had not been wasted.

The problem of my return to the Malostranske, nerve-racking as it was, was not, however, so immediately urgent as two others that now sprang to mind. There was the question of Vaclav Borsky's clothes. Excellent cover on a weekday, they constituted on this day of high festival an all-too-obvious solecism. Like the caretaker, everyone in the street was got up in his best. Once the parade started I would be jammed stationary in the crowd, an easy mark in my cap and plastic jacket for roving eyes.

The second problem was the caretaker, now deeply intent on handing me over as soon as possible to my compatriots from Brno. It seemed only a matter of time before he encountered the right group. I would have to give him the slip.

The opportunity came at the next crossroads, a busy intersection jammed with people. I clapped the caretaker on the back, and, with a rustic cackle of "I see them, countryman, I see them—wait here for me," at once crossed the road, waving my hand and walking very fast for a hundred yards. I cut across the intersection, recrossed the road and looked back. The caretaker was patiently watching, staring in the wrong direction. I continued down the street, found that it ran into the Narodni Trida, and here took stock of the situation.

It was now a quarter past ten and the parade was due to start at eleven. It was plain that I must stay with the crowds, just as plain that I should not be trapped immovably in the Vaclavske Namesti. A single stand farther down the street indicated that the parade would come down here, the fact that it was only a single stand that less dense crowds were expected. The Narodni Trida seemed to be the place for me.

There were two or three automats down the street, only one, the largest, open. I hovered near it. There was bound to be a rush for food after the parade. I thought I'd better be among the first.

It was already growing warm and my feet had begun to ache again. I padded there and back in front of the automat. The street was filling up, the fatigue of jostling crowds coming on me again like toothache. I was sick to death with them. I wished they would get the damned thing over. I wondered when I was going to be able to sit down again and how I would fill up the rest of the day. It stretched before me, hours and hours of it, hot and complicated and dangerous.

It was forty-five minutes before the first contingents came marching round from the Vaclavske Namesti. The loudspeakers had been announcing their progress for the last fifteen of them, and excitement had been building up steadily in the cavernous Narodni Trida. Between the steep and somber buildings the red banners hung. Garlands and slogans crisscrossed the road; the pavements seethed. As the first line of bob-bobbing flags turned the corner, the whole street seemed to ignite and roar like a forest fire.

There were a hundred thousand marchers, peasants in costume, hearty girls in gym slips, factory workers in overalls, sokols in white vests swinging their gymnastic clubs. They chanted as they marched, a dozen different jingles roaring in the seething street.

> *Ceskoslovensko is our land,*
> *We want no other,*
> *Socialism is our creed,*
> *Every man our brother.*
> NAZDAR!

Nazdar! cried the hysterical announcer over the loudspeakers every half minute. *Nazdar!* cried the marchers. *Nazdar!* echoed the crowds.

> *Fight for peace and down with war,*
> *Good will to all nations,*
> *Marx and Lenin show the way,*
> *Comrades, Action Stations!*
> NAZDAR!

There was an appalling row going on, the street roaring and baying rhythmically as the river of marchers flowed on; garlands flying through the air, flags waving, an occasional hand and

154

brain rushing out into the street to embrace the marchers. The girl assistants from the automat had come rushing out to watch. I kept on the move, never straying far from them.

A large float came trundling down presently, decked with flowers and paper doves. A battalion of laughing amazons on board were tossing the cargo to the crowds, who enthusiastically flung it back. The parade seemed to be nearing its end. The assistants went back into the automat. I took my station outside, stepping from one aching foot to the other and watching for the first sign of a movement of customers. When it came, I was in like a trivet.

I took my seat with a gasp of relief. It was painfully obvious I wouldn't be able to stay on my feet all day. I was weary all over, every bone aching, my stomach still stiff from the beating-up in the hotel. I would have to find somewhere to lie out, the botanical gardens or a park, perhaps. The sun was beating down fiercely outside. It might be possible to divest myself of Vaclav Borsky's cap and jacket and acquire others.

I had a cup of coffee and a sandwich, and over it was smitten by inspiration. My eyes had been attracted to a poster on the wall. Below a picture of a serious-looking man in a bathing cap was the legend *Swimming Is Healthy*, and under that *Visit Zluta Plovarna*. Zluta Plovarna! I was amazed I hadn't thought of it before. With one stretched-out body looking like another, it was the ideal place to stay anonymous. There would also be a large variety of unattached clothing.

I tried to remember how they ordered the disposal of clothing at Zluta Plovarna. There was a bit of business with an armband. . . .

I finished my coffee and left.

It was twenty past one, the white and glaring deadspot of the afternoon. The street was like an oven even in the shade of the shops. The sun blinds flapped and rattled dryly in the hot breeze from the river. There were few people about. It might not have been such a good idea to leave so early. I wondered if the watchers were out in the street.

I walked slowly down to the embankment, stiffer than ever but keeping a wary eye open. I didn't think I would be able to run very far or very fast if they came for me now. Some

155

vital damage seemed to have been done to my stomach. It caught me every time I breathed. Not, I thought, that this would be anything to what would happen if they laid hands on me again.

The thought was so peculiarly horrible in the hot afternoon that I actually managed to hobble a bit faster, and got down to the tram stop just as half past one was striking.

Despite the emptiness of the streets, there was the usual queue for the tram. I elbowed my way onto a number twenty-one and stood all the way, emerging so dazed and weak at the other end that I had stumbled almost to the entrance of the bathing station before I pulled myself together a bit and looked the place over.

It looked safe enough. It was hard to tell. I remembered it clearly from my last visit. Two old women, heads protected by newspaper cones, sat at turnstiles in a wicket fence. Farther back, grass sloped down to the river. It was early yet, too soon after the parade for large crowds to be here. A bit of picnicking was going on. A few young men and girls were splashing about at the river's edge. A few children were in the water. There seemed to be nobody standing around watching.

The gritty street was swooning in the heat. I took my place in the queue of people from the tram, went through the clicking turnstile and over to the changing huts. There was a sweaty shed with piles of wire baskets. I hired a pair of drawers and a towel, was given a basket by the old crone in charge, and went off to one of the huts to change.

In the hut, I locked the door and painfully undressed, saying good-by, one by one, to Vaclav Borsky's cap and jacket and Josef's trousers. I took everything out of the pockets and wrapped them in the towel. I got into the shorts and examined my stomach. There was nothing to see, no discoloration even. A little cracked mirror was hanging on the door and I inspected my face in it. The nose was slightly reddened, as if by the sun. Not a lot to show for a beating-up by the S.N.B. I wondered if anyone would believe me. I wondered if I'd ever have the opportunity to try to make anyone believe me, and sighing to my reflection, loaded the wire basket and went out to the sweaty shed.

The old crone took the basket and handed me a red rubber tag with a number on it. I slipped it on my wrist and went out onto the grass. It was long and green and luxuriant from the rain and I found a spot under half shade and sank down in it.

In the heat of the early afternoon there was a slow-motion, dreamlike quality about the bathing station. Willows waved gently against the sky. The river glooped and gurgled between its banks. Voices droned like bees on the air, and over the grass the sound of gramophone music wafted thinly.

All this was so exactly what was called for that I lay back with a faint moan and closed my eyes and floated away in the bland honey light, stomach easing, limbs twitching remotely, nothing at all in the world but the cool lushness of grass and the drifting sibilance of water.

There was something else in the world, of course; but no hurry yet, I thought, coming back after a little while. Rest. Recuperate. Restore the tissues for the lunatic business at the Malostranske tonight. . . .

When I woke up, the sweat was pouring off me and I was in full sun. The place had filled up. I sat up, licking my lips, and gazed about me. I was hemmed in on all sides. Thousands of them, chattering, knitting, eating, drying off children, thumping about with balls. I looked at my watch. Five o'clock. I had slept nearly three hours. I was dry as hell. There were tables outside the café now, and people sitting with drinks. I picked up the towel and went over there.

I bought myself an ice-cold Pilsener and drank it right off in the café and then bought another and took the long misted glass out to one of the tables and sat down. I ran a hand over my stomach. A slight soreness; nothing to bother about. The sleep in the open air had done me good. I felt fine, relaxed, a new man.

I lit a cigarette and smoked it, gazing around at the animated scene. One of these characters must be around my size. Before I had dozed off I'd had the germ of an idea how to switch arm-bands. It came back to me now, ready-made.

Dusk would be coming on at around seven o'clock. I thought I'd better be at the Malostranske then to watch anyone who might be popping in or out of the Embassy for dinner. I didn't know who actually lived at the Embassy or if this kind of activity took place on Sunday night. There was a lot to be found out.

I finished off the cigarette, marveling how even a type so essentially unheroic as myself could attune himself so swiftly to danger. I had no idea where I would sleep tonight. The chances were rather better than average that I would be picked up, beaten up, maimed, killed even; certainly not allowed to leave the country. I seemed to have ingested all these murderous data like some electronic brain and to have made the necessary compensations to restore equilibrium. I thought I must have become warier, better organized mentally. Certainly my planning, such as it was, was now all foreshortened: I had to prepare only for the hour or two ahead.

I thought I'd better get on with it.

I stubbed out my cigarette and went and bought an essential bottle of sun lotion at the shop. I then strolled back over the grass, weaving in and out between the groups, stepping over recumbent figures, and suddenly almost dropped with shock and turned and made swiftly in the opposite direction.

I had seen Vlasta.

There was no possible doubt about it. She was lying on the grass, leaning on one elbow facing me. She was in her black sharkskin two-piece, talking moodily to a man whose back was to me. Her magnificent breast alone would have been unmistakable in any crowd.

I loped quickly away, nerves jangling. The one person in the whole of Prague who could identify me as easily undressed as dressed! I tripped over an old man smoking a calabash pipe and went full length on the grass and picked myself up, swearing with nervousness, and scrambled on again to the other side of the bathing station.

The people were as thick on the ground here as at the opposite end, and I stepped slowly among them, nerves still jumpy, looking for the right type. This was not an operation that could be hurried. Feet and neck size were at least as important as any other dimension. In addition I wanted someone who was on his own, and not too quick on the uptake.

It took me a few minutes to find him, a young stringy character with a forehead so narrow it was hardly there. He was

158

lying flat on his back and sleeping soundly with his mouth wide open. I stretched out beside him. There was not a fraction of an inch difference in height. His legs were apart, toes pointing upwards, and I carefully measured my foot against his. We might have been twins.

There was a thin film of sweat all over his face and body and he was sleeping so soundly he might have been dead. The open mouth and rudimentary forehead suggested promising qualities. His armband was a few inches up his wrist. I thought I'd better get it over with quickly.

I took off my own armband, lit a cigarette and pressed it unhurriedly against his wrist. He came right up off the grass like a leaping salmon, and with a single profound oath began hopping about staring at his wrist in consternation.

I said, "What is it? What's the trouble, comrade?"

"I been shot," he said. "I been blank blank well shot."

"Let me see. Give it here, comrade."

He was hissing slightly, hugging the wrist to his chest like an only child. I prised it away. A fleck of white ash showed immediately below the armband. I said, "Ah, it's just a burn. I must have done it with my cigarette. Here, we'll soon fix it up. I've got some lotion. We'll just get this off," I said, quickly stripping off his armband and dropping it on the grass. I poured some of the lotion onto my handkerchief, dabbed his wrist and gave him the wrong armband back, all with some speed and talking incessantly before he had gathered his scattered wits.

"There. That'll be all right now, comrade. It's only a little burn. You won't feel it in a minute."

"I can bloody well feel it now," he said truculently.

"I'm sorry, comrade. I didn't even notice."

"I thought I been shot. I was fast asleep! You want to watch what you're doing," he said. There was a lowering look about him. It seemed tactless to offer him a cigarette. There didn't seem to be anything else I could offer him. I apologized again, picked up my things and walked off with his armband.

I worked cautiously round to the shed, watching out for Vlasta. She was lying in the same position on one elbow. I wondered if the man was her father. He looked big enough.

There was a queue in the shed, and the old crone was shuffling

159

about in a temper. She snatched the armband from me. I waited with some interest to inspect my new wardrobe. She was unaccountably smiling when she returned.

"Had a good day?"

"Very nice, thanks."

She dumped the wire basket on the counter. "We ordered the right weather for you, anyway."

"Yes. Yes, you did," I said, wondering what all this was about; and suddenly caught sight of what was in the basket and felt my toes curling up.

"What's up? It's the right one, isn't it? Nine-three-eight," she said, shuffling about with the basket, and examined the armband again. "There's no mistake, is there?"

"No. No mistake," I said and picked up the basket and moved off in a trance.

"Wait. There's your hat. I hung it up," she said, bringing the thing over. "We don't want to spoil the lovely feather, do we?"

It was a little cockeyed green thing like a demented midget bowler. There was an enormous peacock feather hanging from the side. She put it on my head, and I said, "Thank you," bloodlessly, and walked off to the changing huts.

I thought the caretaker, at least, would be satisfied. I'd won myself a national costume.

I stepped off the tram like a cripple in the gigantic jackboots. Each seemed to weigh about a ton. I was wearing baggy trousers, an embroidered blouse, a little red bolero with brass buttons and a large rosette. I had scrambled into this lunatic assortment as quickly as possible, terrified its owner would soon be claiming it. I didn't know if I'd got any of it on properly, but it seemed to be effective. In the tram there had been kindly smiles. A woman had even got up to give me her seat.

I clumped along the embankment numb with horror, wondering what I should do if I met a party in the same getup. Luckily, dusk was falling.

I was bang on schedule, anyway.

It was a quarter to seven. Across the river the floodlit palaces on the Heights winked in the uncertain light. Below the linden trees the crowds shuffled, murmuring. The lights in the branches cast a greenish aura. As I crossed the bridge the loudspeakers came on suddenly, Smetana's *My Homeland*, liquid and mournful across the darkling, flowing Vltava.

There was a shifting mass of people in the Malostranske. I dawdled nearer the entrance. A church—St. Mikulase, I remembered suddenly from childhood—had its cupola levitating in floodlighting, as though trying to cast off from its centuries-old but now ungrateful anchorage. I dawdled near the entrance to the Thunovska and saw them still there, two on each corner, not talking, just looking. I slowly gravitated nearer. No one seemed to be coming in or out of the Thunovska. A single light shone in the cul-de-sac. The buildings were in darkness.

After half an hour an open-necked man wheeling a bicycle came out of the Thunovska. He was stopped for his papers. Ten minutes later, he went back again. He was again stopped for his papers. My heart sank. It seemed almost utterly hopeless.

I stepped from one foot to another, wondering what the hell I should do. My mind was made up for me almost immediately. One of the S.N.B. men walked over.

"Waiting for someone?"

My lips seemed to be stuck together. I mumbled, "Yes. Yes. My comrades."

"Where are you from?"

"Banska Bystrica." That's what it said in the papers in the pocket of the bolero.

"Your papers."

I handed them over.

The S.N.B. man glanced at them and handed them back. His nod was not unfriendly, but he had a good look at me. He sauntered away.

I stood there for a further few minutes, trembling all over, but afraid to attract attention by moving too soon. I waited till the clock struck eight, then ambled across the square and got to hell out of it as quickly as possible.

I had no idea what to do. I knew I had to keep away now from other national costumes and the police. The peasant and his friends would be looking out for me. I walked aimlessly on and presently found myself in the Ujezd. Svoboda had his

161

offices here. I thought I remembered a kavarna somewhere nearby, and when I saw its lights dimly shining, turned in there, too distracted to think on my feet any longer.

The place was empty. An old woman served me with a large slivovitz, and I tossed it down and ordered another and took it to a small table. As I sat down the landlord appeared.

"Well, countryman," he said convivially, "a find day, eh?"

"Yes. Yes."

"You won't forget it in a hurry."

"I won't," I said sincerely.

"Slipped away from your comrades for a quick drink?"

"That's it."

He wiped the table and sat down. "What time do you go?"

"Go?" I said; but understood him entirely in that debilitating moment. Countrymen came. Countrymen would have to go. Trainloads of them. There wouldn't be a national costume in the whole of Prague tomorrow. Except one.

"You all go back tonight, don't you?"

"Yes. Yes. Not for a bit yet."

"You'll have tramped a few miles today, eh? You look bushed."

"I think I'd like another slivovitz," I said bleakly.

He went to get it and I sat, lumpen in my boots and my bolero, seeing the end of the line close in sight. I couldn't risk another night of dodging up and down alleys. There could be no question of showing myself out of doors tomorrow. I had to go to earth now. I needed a place to rest and eat. I needed a friend now.

I suppose the idea had been there ever since I'd seen her, a last desperate expedient. I felt in my pocket for my wallet. My diary was there, her number still scribbled in it. The landlord came back with the slivovitz and I drank it quickly and left.

There was a telephone box farther along and I went in and rang the number. I wondered if her father was with her. I thought if a man answered I would hang up right away, and waited, heart thudding.

A man didn't answer. Nobody answered. The phone went on ringing for three minutes. I hung up and went out into the street and stood there in the dark with a feeling of sick desolation, trying to think just what there was for me to do. I couldn't hang about here. I couldn't stay in Prague. I would soon be the only peasant left in the place. I thought I'd better get over there to Barrandov, while I was able to, and wait for her.

I set off, walking, keeping to the darker side of the street, the feathered hat in my hand.

It was getting on for half past nine when I approached the terraces, glittering in the dark. There was a dance on, figures twirling on the several levels, dance music beating out. Across the road, a hundred yards or so beyond, was the rustic seat where I had sat with her and just beside it—I had forgotten it—the telephone box. I went in the box and rang her again. There was still no reply.

I left the box and went on to the house, hugging the shrubbery. The side road was in pitch darkness. There was no light in the house. I waited on the corner for a few minutes, but there was no cover here. I wondered if Vlasta herself was being watched, if they had discovered that I had taken her out and spent the night with her, my only contact. It seemed best to get back to the shrubbery again.

There was a thicket near the telephone box. I crawled into it, and sat down on the ground to wait. A few couples came and went from the dance. A bit of hanky-panky went on on the seat. I nosed out from time to time when the coast was clear.

I called her twice more from the box. The last time, at a quarter to twelve, she answered.

I said in English, "Vlasta, it's Nicolas. Nicolas Whistler."

"Nicolas! What are you doing here?"

"Is anybody with you, Vlasta? Is your father there?"

"No. No. I am all alone. Nicolas, this is wonderful. I don't understand . . ."

"I'll explain everything when I see you. Can I come along now?"

"But, *milacek,* of course. I was just going to bed. Ah, this is wonderful."

"Well, carry on to bed. Don't wait up for me. Put the lights out."

"But of course I will wait up for you! How long will you . . ."

163

"Vlasta, please do as I say. I don't want to attract attention. I don't know how long I'll be."

"Ah, so. Well, then, I will leave the door open. Just push it. I will be waiting for you, *milacek*."

I put the phone down, grinning with relief, and went out into the street.

As luck would have it, a couple were lying on the grass at the entrance to the side road. I went back to the shrubbery and waited for them to go.

Thirty minutes later they were still at it.

It was getting on for half past twelve and the moon was well up when I at last went down the side road. I stopped before the gate, watching and listening. The place was in darkness, silent as the grave.

The gate creaked a little as I opened it. I crunched softly up the gravel path.

As she'd said, the door was open. I pushed it and went in.

chapteR 11

        She had not gone to bed. She was waiting for me in a dressing gown in the living room. There was a little table lamp on, the curtains securely drawn, and she was lying smoking a cigarette on the divan.

She had her eye on the door, and sat up sharply when I came in.

"Who is it?"

"It's me, Vlasta. Nicolas."

She sprang up. "Nicolas. What are you—what clothes have you got on?"

She stretched out her hands to hold me at arm's length, goggling.

"It's a hell of a long story. Vlasta, do you have such a thing as a drink?"

Now I was inside, in safety, in the warm, dimly lit room, the reaction had come on, I felt myself beginning to tremble.

She threw her arms round me, the long, somber face twisting loosely with a smile at the curious sight I must have presented. "*Milacek*, of course. You look so funny. You're tired. Come, sit down."

I was sitting even before she'd told me, sinking heavily back on the divan. She looked curiously at me, but asked no further questions and went to get a bottle and two glasses.

She poured me an enormous glass of slivovitz, which I drank immediately.

"Another?"

"Please."

I took a little of it and sat back again, sighing and uncoiling

165

as the neat spirit exploded wonderfully inside me. She lit a cigarette and placed it in my mouth and I inhaled deeply and closed my eyes, wondering how the hell to begin.

"Vlasta, has anyone been asking you about me?"

"No. No. Why should they?"

"When is your father returning?"

"Wednesday, perhaps. He is giving a concert in Bratislava."

"You're not expecting anyone to visit you here?"

"No. Nicolas, what is it?"

I said, "Vlasta, I'm in serious trouble. I need your help."

She drew the dressing gown more tightly round her. She looked not exactly frightened but a shade reserved. "What is it you want me to do?"

"I've got to hide, Vlasta. I want you to let me stay here."

"What is it you've done?"

"It might be better if you knew nothing about it."

"Is it—something against the State?"

"In a way."

She said quietly, "You're not a spy, Nicolas?"

"No, Vlasta. Not really. It's very complicated to explain. I need to get in touch with the British Embassy. I've tried already but the place is covered by S.N.B. men."

"S.N.B." She stubbed out her cigarette, gazing at me. "How serious would it be for us—for my father and me—if they found you had stayed here?"

"It could be very serious indeed. But I've got nowhere else to go, Vlasta. I've just got to have a night's rest. I've been on the run for two days. They'll kill me if they catch me. I'll go tomorrow if you want me to."

The Slav temperament is built to respond to melodrama. She was deeply touched. She leaned over me with her heavy breasts and took my head. "*Milacek*, of course you will stay. Tonight, anyway. You're exhausted. Maybe it isn't so bad. We'll think of something. You will tell me about it."

I had no intention of telling her about it. It seemed to me the fewer people who knew the better. The whole episode was so grotesque the effort of explaining it once only would be quite enough.

"Have you eaten?"

166

"I don't want anything."

She refilled my glass, and took one herself and we sat there on the divan in silence. With the third glass of slivovitz the dim room was showing its remembered tendency to roll. I thought of the S.N.B. men in the hotel bedroom, of the hours spent trudging in the swarming Vaclavske Namesti, of Vaclav Borsky, and the endless alleys. I remembered how I had spent last night, the damp fug, Wenceslas leaping in the moonlight. It was all, I thought, each and every bit of it, totally unbelievable. A series of horrifying hallucinations in the dim, rolling room.

"Milacek, come to bed."

She was leaning over me, somberly, nuzzling my face.

"In a minute."

"It's better in bed. Lie out."

"Yes."

"It's no use worrying."

"No."

"Maybe I can go to the Embassy for you."

"Yes." I was not listening to her, rolling warmly in the rolling room; the statuesque creature no more real than Vaclav Borsky or the S.N.B. As I heard this, however, I swiveled round to gaze at her. "The Embassy? How do you mean the Embassy? Have you been to the Embassy?"

"But of course. Two or three times a month. Even more often lately. There are many messages because of the forthcoming trade agreement."

"Well, for God's sake!" I said, seeing in the one moment a whole range of new vistas. A letter from me; a car drawing up one night; myself in the back under a rug. Safe. "Vlasta, do you think you could do it?"

"I don't know. Why not? It's dangerous?"

Suddenly the telephone rang. I was off the divan and practically in her lap with fright. She stared at me, jaw dropping.

"Who could it be? Your father?"

"I don't know." She went to answer it. I sat palpitating. It was nearly one o'clock. A damned funny time to ring up. Unless he had just arrived back in town. I strained to listen.

"No, no. No trouble. I wasn't in bed yet. Very well indeed, gracious pane," she said in Czech. *"He is in Bratislava. On Wed-*

nesday I expect him. Certainly I will tell him. Please do not concern yourself. It is nothing at all. Thank you. You are very gracious."

She slammed down the receiver and came back, face stormy. "One of his musical friends. They ring at all hours." She paced around the room angrily, and stopped by me, softening.

"Milacek, stop worrying. You're too tired. Come, we'll go to bed now."

So we did.

She pulled off my boots, whickering slightly at the bizarre collection of clothing decorating my sparse frame. She had nothing on herself underneath the dressing gown, but with some obscure feeling that seriousness was called for, put on a loose nightie before getting into bed.

As she'd said, it was better in bed. The sheer voluptuousness of it, the massive, well-remembered embrace, took me in a breath far from the horror.

"You've stopped thinking about it?" she said in my ear after a moment.

"Trying to."

"Too tired to think about anything else?"

"Pretty tired."

She gave me a mournful hug.

I sank into a dreamless doze, and drifted awake, and dozed, and woke again, ear warmly damp with her breath. "Still too tired?" the husky voice said softly, at some time. The slivovitz, the soft warmth, the rolling curtain of sleep, had destroyed all strain, all knowledge, all identity in the darkness.

I don't know what I said, but in a trice she had whipped off the nightie. Just for a moment, as she came swarming down again, I remembered where I was supposed to be tonight. Bournemouth, my mother, Maura. All a long way away. A world away. Far, far away from the breathy blackness of Barrandov.

I don't know how much later it was when I woke up again. She was sleeping softly with her head in the crook of my neck. The slivovitz had left me gravely parched, and I licked my lips, seeing the situation with sudden clarity in that moment.

Her father was coming back Wednesday. I had two days here.

Two days in which the police would have no sign or news of me, no abandoned clothing, no Borskys left lying about.

They would have to face three possibilities: (a) that despite the national costume I was somehow managing to sleep out and to steal food; (b) that I had slipped out of Prague; (c) that someone was sheltering me. Of them all, only the last was a probability. The question would then be who was likely to do so. Cunliffe would have passed on the information that I had no contacts left in Prague—I recalled that he had asked me specifically about this. That meant I had either made some or had somehow managed to get in touch with the Embassy.

The fact that no question had been asked of Vlasta indicated that this contact at least was unknown. After all, she'd been circumspect about it. She'd declined to have dinner with me at the hotel that first visit. I was pretty sure I'd not been followed when I went out with her. It was a fact that the S.N.B. men had been genuinely unaware of my movements when I dashed from the hotel. That seemed to indicate that I'd never been followed. They had been pretty sure of me.

All in all, it seemed to me, they would be driven to the conclusion that I was being sheltered by one of the Embassy staff. So they would watch the Embassy staff. They would watch their homes and their cars. All this was going to be a headache at some stage. The snags would have to be indicated in my letter. They would also—it was only fair—have to be indicated to Vlasta.

I had begun to stir about a bit in the bed with this appraisal of the situation. The gorgeous giantess moved murmurously at my side.

"Vlasta."

"*Milacek.*"

"I've been thinking of what you said, Vlasta, about going to the Embassy."

"Yes, *milacek*. Later. We'll talk of it later."

"I think we should talk of it now. You'll have to get up in a few hours."

She flung one arm around me in a hug that drove the breath from my body, and sleepily sat up and put the bedside light on. She regarded me somberly. "You want to get to the Embassy

169

as soon as possible, little merchant."

"That's the idea."

"Then this is the last time we'll be together." Her wondrous torso stood out in the lamplight. She leaned massively and mournfully against me. "You'll never come back again. Never. Never."

"No, well," I said plaintively. "Vlasta, there are things I've got to tell you."

She planted a kiss on each side of my nose. "Well then, Nicolas," she said with a sigh, "tell me."

This I proceeded to do in a revised, edited and severely expurgated version. I told her I had come to Prague for Pavelka to learn confidentially of the glass process he had initiated; that I'd had to come back again to learn of a new development, and that this second time the police had learned what I was doing, necessitating flight and several disguises.

She was frowning when I finished. "It sounds serious, certainly," she said. "But they wouldn't kill you for that. You are too nervous, my Nicolas."

I ground my teeth a little. "There were a couple of things I didn't mention. There was a *formula*," I said earnestly. "You don't need to know about that. The point is they're looking for me, and my only hope is to get to the Embassy."

"So. And you wish me to go for you. Yes, *milacek*."

I didn't think she was quite on wavelength. She was looking in a certain way at my nose as though about to return to her main preoccupation. I said, "I want you to take a letter there, Vlasta. I want them to try to smuggle me in, in a car. I don't want the car to come here, do you understand? I'll have to get out of here."

"Yes, yes. We can arrange everything. There's plenty of time yet. It's not so serious."

I ground my teeth again. The girl was proving quite exceptionally tiresome. I seriously considered rolling about with her for a bit to wake her up; but persevered once more. "It is damnably serious, Vlasta. I'm trying very hard to save my life. I've got to put all this in a rather complicated letter, which I should be writing now. But I had to tell you the main details. Do you think you understand?"

"Yes, I understand. You do not wish to bring danger to this house."

"You're sure you can get to the Embassy tomorrow—today?"

"Monday is not a busy day. I should be able to manage."

"You go right inside, do you?"

"To the reception desk."

"Is it an Englishman at the desk?"

"No. A Czech."

"Does he open whatever it is you normally take there?"

"I don't think so. I don't know."

"Could you get hold of a Glass Board envelope and write 'Urgent, Personal, For the Ambassador's Attention Only' on it?"

"I think so. Yes, yes, I think so." She had woken up a bit now, and seemed abreast of the situation. Her mournful eyes were blinking slowly and thoughtfully. She absently scratched one bomblike breast. She got up presently and put on her dressing gown and loped about gathering writing materials and a suit of her father's. After this she went into the kitchen and made coffee.

I sat up in bed, smoking, and enumerating all the things that could go wrong. I was aware of a feeling of deep but shamefaced gratitude to the immense creature. Apart from her initial reservations at the dangers to her father and herself, she had not stinted her help or her generous affections. She could very easily end up in a concentration camp. I found myself liking her very much indeed. I got out of bed and slipped on the peasant trousers and walked through to the kitchen. She was standing by the gas stove waiting for the coffee to heat, and I took her somewhat awkwardly by the shoulders and kissed her on the neck.

She leaned back against me but did not turn or speak. I kissed her again, gently, and felt her shoulders begin to shake. I realized with alarm that she was crying.

"Vlasta."

She shook her head.

"What is it, Vlasta?"

"It's nothing. It's the last I'll see of you," she said.

"Oh, now, Vlasta," I said awkwardly. "Maybe we'll meet again. You'll always be in my thoughts." If only I get to hell out of here, I thought; if only I'm left with any thoughts to think; but touched all the same.

She took a handkerchief out of her dressing-gown pocket and blew her nose sadly. "Write your letter, Nicolas."

I went into the drawing room and began writing on the divan, and presently she came in with the coffee and sat over me.

"You're copying out your passport number?"

I was, together with every other bit of personal information that would make the crazy rigmarole even faintly believable.

She watched me for a bit. "And the formula? You're putting that in?"

"No," I said briefly, not even allowing myself to think of the impossibility of explaining this to her.

"I don't mind taking it, Nicolas. There is no danger to me. Don't think about me."

"I'm not, Vlasta. There isn't a formula. It doesn't exist."

"I don't want you to tell me anything you don't want to."

"Right," I said; and was presently aware that the divan was shaking slightly. She was crying again. "Ah, Vlasta, what is it?"

She put her head on my shoulders, sobbing quietly but powerfully. I put my arm awkwardly round her.

"You're thinking only of me. You say they'll kill you if they find this thing."

"No, no, Vlasta. It isn't like that. I haven't got the damned thing."

"I love you, *milacek*. I hate myself for not being able to help you more."

"You can't help me any more than you are doing."

"I can't bear to think of you in danger in this terrible country, little merchant. Let me share it with you. Let me take this thing for you."

I rolled my eyes horribly. There was a degree of obtuseness about this otherwise splendid girl that made all normal communications impossible. I said wearily, "Dearest Vlasta, I haven't got the formula. It isn't of any importance. I'm telling you the truth."

She looked at me through tear-stained eyes. "You only say this to comfort me, *milacek*. Who else would you have given it to? There was only the old person your nanny, and she is dead. The husband? Would you trust him more than me because he is a man?"

"No, of course I wouldn't. I can't even remember him.

172

Vlasta . . ." It was useless, of course, but I made the effort. "That formula, Vlasta. It wasn't the right one. It was something else. I got rid of it. I've forgotten it. All I want to do now is get to the Embassy. You're the only one who can help me do that. You can't do more, Vlasta. Please believe me, *milacek*."

I had talked myself into a state of some emotion, and now fell to covering her ample, tear-stained face with kisses. I was not sure if she believed me, her mournful eyes indicating only recognition of large areas of nobility in my protestations.

It was now four o'clock and she had to be up at seven. I could finish the letter in the morning. I got back into bed with her.

Between the sheets she was still tearful and massively emotive. I felt suddenly shaken and unsure of myself. There was a lowering, keening quality about her murmurous embrace that was unnerving. But it wasn't that, I thought. Something else; some factor that I hadn't bargained for. It hung about, cloudlike, on the fringe of consciousness. I tried to identify it; couldn't. Presently I went off to sleep in her arms, still troubled.

The tall S.N.B. man had got me up against the wardrobe and I couldn't move. I knew he was going to hit me again. He'd got hold of my chin with one hand, and he was going to smash it with the other. He was looking at me thoughtfully, without malice, and I could hear myself grunting with the effort to shift my head. The sweat was pouring down my face. I was bleeding and sick, and it was going on and on, with the other one, the little one, waiting quietly to go on with his interrogation. But I couldn't stand any more. I couldn't stand being hit again. My neck felt stiff and half broken against the wardrobe, but I thought I'll break it, I don't care, he mustn't hit me again, and I wrenched my neck sideways and broke it and got away, swum away, threshed away out of the room and into the blackness at Barrandov.

Her elbow was under my chin. I had somehow kicked away from her in my nightmare. She was sleeping heavily in the perspiring bed, and I lay there for a moment thinking, *Oh God, still nighttime. Which night?* the interrogation still going on and on in my mind. *Who did you give it to? You'll have to tell us.*

Now or later, as you please. We know you gave it to someone. Who is it you trust more than us? Did you give it to the husband of the old person, your nanny?

But no, I thought, heart sickly beating, that was Vlasta, not the interrogators; the obtuse girl going on and on about it. Everybody going on and on about the bloody formula. And I didn't care about the formula. It should be obvious I didn't care about the formula. Why should I care about it with my life at stake? There was some great mass delusion in this insane country. They all thought alike. Maybe this was how their own nationals would behave. Hanging on at all costs to the formula, the slogan, the message, the chant.

The big uncomplicated creature slept heavily beside me, unknowable, Slav, wanting to get away from the country but part of it, her reactions the same. Wanting to suffer, to have her steadfastness tested; with some new element added, some hand-and-brain element that thirsted to be trusted as a comrade. Would I not trust her as much as the husband of the old person my nanny, because he was a man?

But wait, wait, I thought, heart still sickly beating. Who said anything about this old person my nanny? Who the hell so much as mentioned this old person?

I thought back frenziedly over each and every conversation with the girl. No nannies. No occasion when nannies might have arisen. With sudden sinking recognition, I realized what had troubled me before I went off to sleep.

This girl knew something about me that I had never told her.

I thought, *Oh, God, no.* Something gravely wrong here; and in the same moment saw a whole series of other wrong things. This spacious bungalow just for her father and herself in a town where space was at a premium. The telephone call at one o'clock in the morning. Her insistence on the bloody formula.

I sat wildly up in the bed. In an instant she was wide awake beside me. She had not moved. The quality of her breathing had merely changed. I saw now that it must have been like this the other time. I felt my teeth begin to chatter. I put one foot out of bed.

"What is it, *milacek*?"

"Toilet."

174

"You know where the light is."

I knew where the light was. I went in, trembling, but didn't switch it on, imagining the police camped out there. A hell of a lot of things had come flashing to mind. Her tears; the old Slav keening quality that had come into her voice. She had become fond of me in her way, I thought, but it wouldn't stop her doing whatever she had to do. I had walked right into it.

I sat nervelessly on the lavatory seat, shivering in the draft from the open window, and wondered what the hell to do now. It was growing light outside. I had taken off my watch and left it on the bedside table. Five, six o'clock? She'd be getting up soon. No prospect of escape this time. The instant she was out they'd be in to nab me. That mysterious telephone call . . . checking up that all was well. And all had been well; *Milacek* installed and ready to perform and spill the beans. But what beans? What had I been expected to spill to the girl that they couldn't knock out of me in half an hour?

I held my head in my hands and racked my weary brain.

"Are you all right, *milacek*?"

I came off the lavatory seat as if it had caught fire.

"Quite all right."

I washed my hands and went back into the room. She had the bedside light on and was sitting up moodily rubbing her breasts in the draft from the open door.

"You're so restless, *milacek*. You're worrying still."

"Just a bit."

"Was it anything else you wanted to tell me?"

"No," I said, getting into bed; but in the same moment saw that indeed there was.

The formula! The unspeakable, unmentionable, thrice-cursed formula! That was it. They genuinely didn't know what had happened to it. There had been a fatal gap in the reconnaissance system when I had dashed from the hotel. There was just a possibility—it could be no more than a possibility—that I had hidden it somewhere, passed it on to someone. They could knock me about and find out. But I had proved slippery enough already. Here was an easier way. One night with the insatiable giantess, with the illusion of safety, and I would tell her everything.

The tireless creature had thrown her arms round me again

and was nibbling my cheek. "*Milacek,* why are you so worried? You don't trust me enough."

"I do, Vlasta, I do," I said, and sighed. "It's just that—I'm beginning to doubt if the Embassy will believe that letter. They'll think it a trick."

"What else is there?"

"Just one thing . . . I daren't ask you to do it."

"Nicolas, Nicolas, I've told you a thousand times, I'll do anything."

I paused, heart beating in a sick sort of way. I thought she must feel it thumping there under her supercharged superstructure. "It's that formula, Vlasta. I didn't destroy it. It's a lot more important than I am. And it could just save me. That's something they would have to believe. If only you could take it with the letter."

"*Milacek,* I've been pleading with you to let me take it."

"You don't understand, Vasta. I haven't got it. I told you the truth about that at least. It's hidden."

She was silent. I wondered if I'd ladled it on a bit too thick. She said after a moment, "You want me to go and get it?"

"No, Vlasta. There are other people involved. You wouldn't get it. I would have to get it myself and meet you in town. And that's why I daren't ask you to do it. If I'm spotted, it would be the end for you, too."

Again she was silent. She released me, blinking thoughtfully. She said slowly, "Is this the truth, Nicolas? Is this all that's worrying you?"

"It's enough."

"It's nothing at all. Oh, I know the police. And the S.N.B.," she said scornfully. "I live here, little merchant. Do you think we don't all of us know what they look like!"

"Vlasta, it's dreadful asking you to do this. It's so terribly dangerous."

"*Milacek,* stop worrying now."

"But of course," I said, just in time as she fell on me again, "if I'm followed anywhere, I'll cancel the plan. I daren't compromise you or my—my colleagues. I'll die before I give anything away."

This improbable statement gave her fractional pause. She

176

shivered suddenly. "Forget it now," she said in my ear. "Don't worry about anything more, *milacek*," and returned to her more fundamental preoccupation.

The milkman shattered the last of the night at ten minutes to seven. I had been lying in a sleepless daze for the past half hour listening to him exclaiming to his horse and turning over in my mind a succession of increasingly lunatic plans.

I felt time-worn rather than tired. An enormous number of things seemed to have happened to me; a roar of events like water over some crumbling fall. Now, I thought, as the milkman holloahed and yoicked, the water had exposed bedrock, gleaming calcified strata to be identified as the essential particulars of Whistler Nicolas. Here were the layers of fraud and deception; here the unsuspected catlike qualities of survival. Here too, I thought, as the vast slumbrous thing beside me yawned to life, stamina of an even more unsuspected and, in happier times, more useful order.

I shut my eyes as she woke up.

"Nicolas. Time to get up, Nicolas."

She was clear-eyed, relaxed, a little gay even. It hadn't been a bad night for her, I supposed. She gave me an affectionate buss on the chin and sprang out of bed. I turned out more slowly.

"It's late. I forgot I have an early job this morning. I'll have to make a telephone call," she said, when she had washed and dressed.

I had been wondering how she would cope with the change of arrangements, and listened with interest as she went to the phone. "*Agnes, I'm afraid I will be late this morning. The early job will have to be put off. No, no, nothing wrong. I'll alter the schedule myself when I come in. There is no need for you to do anything, Agnes dear, nothing at all.*"

I finished the letter in the kitchen while she ate her breakfast, and watched with some fascination her magnificent jungle appetite.

"You know what you've got to do, Vlasta."

"I am to put this in a Glass Board envelope and mark it 'Urgent, Personal, For the Attention of the Ambassador Only.'"

"In English, remember. You want me to write it out for you?"

"No, no. I can remember it."

"And you meet me where?"

"At the Slavia at twelve. If you're not there by ten minutes past, I go away."

"And then?"

"I am to telephone you here from a call box at two o'clock. If there is no reply I go back to the Slavia again at five. If you are not there, I take the letter as it is to the Embassy without the formula."

"That's it," I said. A bit of elaboration had seemed worthwhile. I took both of her hands and looked sincerely into her eyes. She looked sincerely back, champing her jaws. "I won't try to thank you, Vlasta. You know how I feel. But for both our sakes, keep exactly to the instructions. If I don't keep any of the arrangements, it means the police are on to me. Don't take any chances. Don't hang about. Go right to the Embassy. It means the formula won't exist any longer."

"You won't let them take it?"

I shook my head slowly. "They'll never do that, Vlasta. It's on rice paper. I'll eat it."

Her jaws paused fractionally.

She went ten minutes later. I sat on, smoking a cigarette and staring at her empty plate. She had eaten three slices of cold veal, half a loaf of bread, a dish of sour cream and a large bowl of coffee. Even after everything that had happened this feat still had the power to surprise me. Even after everything that was still to happen, it is the thing I remember best about her. That and a certain smell and a bomblike shadow on a wall in lamplight.

I left the house at half past ten, and realized as I came out into the side street that I had forgotten my watch on the bed-side table. I didn't go back for it. It was hot already with the tangy smell coming up off the road. Men were hosing down the *terasy*, and the sun glinted back hard and white off the wet rock. I felt lightheaded and momentous, a convict on parole, far from home and blindingly exposed.

I thought I had four or five hours of relative freedom of movement. Over three cups of coffee and four cigarettes I had considered how to use them. I thought I had better find out first how relative the freedom was.

I caught a juddering Skoda bus into town, and changed there to a tram which took me north of the river to the Stromovka district. There was a park here that I had seen advertised, the Julius Fucik Park of Culture and Rest. I went through the park gates and along the main path to the opposite entrance. There were a few gardeners hoeing and hosing; no one else. I paused outside the gates, lit a cigarette, went trudging back. The gardeners did not look up. Nobody had followed me. I left the park and returned to town.

All this took time and was hard on the feet. I had bulked out her father's enormous shoes with two pairs of thick socks. They still slopped up and down, rubbing at my heels. The heat enabled me to carry the jacket over my arm, which was just as well; it fitted me like an overcoat. The trousers had needed turning up four inches and I had secured them with a pair of bicycle clips I had found in a drawer. There had also been a hammer in the drawer. It now weighed down my right-hand jacket pocket. I thought I might need it.

I got off the tram before it reached the river and changed to another that would bring me out on the Embassy side. I had given much thought to my movements, and alighted when the conductress shouted, "For the Hradcany."

I was on the Heights. The molten river glinted through the trees, and over the old town the air shimmered in the heat. I could see the little trams shuttling like toys along the embankment and hear the distant sound of them, coming up in waves. A number of workmen, stripped to the waist, were laying cables on the hill. A warm breeze swayed the foliage.

I stood for a while getting my bearings. It was nearly twelve o'clock. The cluster of glistening palaces swam in the air currents. Below, a few hundred yards beyond the wavering pinnacles of the Hradcany, I could see a familiar cupola and steeple. I thought this would be the church of St. Mikulase in the Malostranske. This was where I wanted to be.

It was hot as hell, a dry incinerator heat disturbed only slightly by the breeze rattling the foliage. I held my jacket by its hanger over my shoulder and mopped my forehead. Suddenly a factory

179

hooter went and from the old town below the clocks began to dong and boom. Twelve o'clock. Vlasta would be at the Slavia. The workmen had stopped on the instant, and were now squatting on the hillside drinking from bottles. I thought I needed a drink myself.

A steep path ran down through the greenery. I followed it, coming out to a street which skirted the Hradcany, and crossed over to the Schwarzenberg Palace square. I had walked here on the first night of my first visit. It was still familiar, hauntingly familiar as childhood. There were a number of kavarnas. I stopped in one and had a glass of ice-cold Pilsener, and continued on down. Not a lot of time for what I had to do.

I entered the Malostranske from the far side, where I had not been formerly, and found the square as I expected, crowded in the white lunchtime heat. The shops and offices were still letting out, girls arm in arm, chattering, gesticulating, bicycles weaving in and out, bells jangling.

I passed the Thunovska, saw the men still there, two on each corner, and went down the next street, running parallel with it. It was a narrow street of tall buildings, reeling in the heat. There were a number of small kavarnas and bars, all crowded; each, I hoped, with its quota of caretakers wetting their whistles. I didn't want to meet any caretakers.

I went into the first big building, saw a lift shaft, stairs going up and down. I went down. There were broad stone steps, a green-tiled wall, a half landing. I continued on down. At the bottom of the stairs was a little glass-enclosed cubbyhole of the kind one finds in public lavatories. The electric light was on. I waited for a moment, listening. No one was there. Beyond the cubbyhole was a door, half opened and leading to a boiler room and a small urinal. A naked light bulb shone in the boiler room. A strong smell of fuel oil. I looked all round. No windows. No back way out. A little ventilation grating high up in the urinal; not, evidently, very effective.

I inspected all these features at speed, and went back up the stairs and out into the street again. A man was sitting on a camp stool eating bread and sausage in the next building. After that a kavarna; four small shops; another office building— deserted. I went inside, found the same arrangement as in the first building, and went down the stairs again. Landing. Cubbyhole. Door to boiler room.

It was in rather better shape than the first, a strong smell of carbolic predominating. The boiler was a large cylindrical affair with, beside it, a large heap of coke. I had seen no coke in the other building, and now looked around for a chute. There was no chute. There was a round iron ceiling hatch with a hinged iron ladder, folded back and clipped to a hook on the wall.

I unclipped the ladder, drew it into position and climbed up. I waited for a moment under the hatch, listening for sounds of movement on top. None were discernible. I raised my arms and pushed.

The hatch was jammed.

I pushed, shoved, thumped, swore, sweated. The hatch remained jammed. I went up a rung, bent my head, got the back of my neck and shoulders to it, strained, heaved on the ladder. There was a slight sucking, glooping noise. The hatch gave. I went down a rung, paused, sweat running in my eyes, and tried again with my hands. It was heavy as hell, a slab of apparently solid iron, but it went up quite easily. I shifted it to one side, climbed up into the open air and found myself in an enclosed yard. There were a number of dustbins, a builder's cart, a pile of assorted lumber. There was also a pair of double doors, bolted and padlocked. The lock looked rusty, but the key turned without trouble. I took off the lock, undid the bolts and stepped out into an alley. I drew the doors carefully behind me and went quickly up the alley. It ran back into the side street.

With something of the elation of Columbus catching his first sight of that good old stuff, dry land, I nipped back down the alley, locked and bolted the doors, hurried down the coal tip, pulled the hatch back in position and replaced the ladder. All that was called for now was some hours of the deepest and most impregnable seclusion. I was through with running away now. I meant to walk directly into the Embassy. Give it eighteen hours, I thought, and I'd either be in there astounding all with my ingenuity or I'd be in quite a different establishment, hoping, rather urgently, for death in some quick and hygienic form.

chapter 12

Boiler rooms in Czech commercial premises tend to be spacious and rambling apartments. For six months of the year the country is frozen; a powerful heating unit and a comprehensive system of plumbing are the minimal requirements for all centers of human congress.

The building I had chosen did not fall below the norm in this respect. The boiler room measured some forty feet square. There were enough cocks, taps, levers, dials and asbestos-covered piping for the control room of a submarine. There were also two small cupboardlike rooms letting off it. One contained a broken chair, a camp bed, a bag of soot and numerous stoking implements; the other, logs—no doubt an emergency fuel supply. There were no locks or bolts to either door. I took to the timber.

After a couple of hours I was beginning to regret it. I had scooped a hole for myself in the logs in one of the corners farthest from the door and lay there painfully uncomfortable and half stupefied in the musty heat.

I had learned to identify the sounds of the building: the sucking whine of the lift shaft, chairs scraping, the distant patter of typewriters. From time to time the caretaker came into the boiler room. I heard him lighting his pipe once. He hawked and spat. But he didn't come to the log cupboard. I lay in blackness, watching the crack of light under the door. Once when I moved there was a petrifying rumble of falling logs. After that I remained where I was, sweat trickling incessantly and itchingly all over my body.

I dozed and woke and dozed and woke, three or four times, I think. The last time when I blearily came to, the crack of light had vanished. I lay silent for a while, listening. The whine of the lift shaft had stopped. There was no movement of feet above; merely the shift and creak of an old building.

I clambered drunkenly out of the log pile, felt for the door and went into the boiler room. It was dark, but with a welcome sense of space. I waited in the center of the room for a minute, listening. There was just the creak and rustle; distant sounds of traffic. I lit a match and went to the door. It was locked.

I'd forgotten to check where the light switch was, and spent several minutes fumbling around with matches before it occurred to me that it was probably on the other side of the door. I swore a bit at that. I had four matches left—and four cigarettes that I had brought with me from Barrandov. It would be a long night.

I thought I might as well make myself as comfortable as possible and got the camp bed out of the other cupboard. It was a telescopic affair of metal tubes and somewhat smelly canvas, and collapsed twice before I got the hang of it. I found myself operating with preternaturally delicate movements, afraid of the sound in the dark. I took my shoes off and lay out flat in the cavernous blackness and let my bruised and aching limbs throb back to life. The air was still warm and stuffy. I lay listening to my breathing and the dull churning of my heart.

I think I went off to sleep like that. I was tired as hell, sluggish and dazed with the crazy sequence of events. I came to after a bit with one leg lying numb on a metal support and my neck stiff. I wondered what time it was, and regretted the watch left on the bedside table at Barrandov. I sat up and lit a cigarette and went round the room with the match looking for a clock among the dials. There was no clock. It was very silent. My body seemed heavy but rested. I thought I must have lain there for an hour or two. That would be, what—seven, eight o'clock? It might be dark outside. I thought I might risk opening the hatch.

I finished the cigarette and put my shoes back on and released the ladder. I went up slowly and listened at the top, and pushed the hatch up and listened again before sliding it to one side. Sky dark blue; welcome cool wetness. It was raining out there. I went up a couple of rungs and poked my head out. Gurgle

183

of drains; wonderfully pleasant splashing—rainwater running out of loose guttering. Distantly clocks began chiming. Half past. Half past what?

I left the hatch off and went back down again and sat on the camp bed, listening. There were quite a lot of sounds. Trams, cars, bicycle bells; even a train hooting somewhere. The moon was not up yet; even so the night sky was surprisingly light; a circle of indigo in the black ceiling.

Another quarter struck. I thought I'd better leave the hatch off all night. There was little chance of anyone poking around in the yard. I thought over the plan I had conceived while lying in bed at Barrandov. Crazy. Wild. As crazy and wild as all the other things that had happened to me. But they had happened.

I lay back on the bed, but found it so uncomfortable now that I got up and fetched a log and draped my jacket round it as a neck rest. I smoked another cigarette like that. Two left.

The clocks began to chime. I counted. Seven, eight, nine, ten. Ten o'clock. About another eight hours to go, I thought. I ought to try and get some more sleep.

I was suddenly aware that I was hungry and felt in the jacket pocket for the packet of bread and sausage I had brought with me from Barrandov, and ate a hunk, lying back and watching the hatch and the rain glancing in.

They would be looking all over the town for me again in the rain, I thought. The Thunovska covered; all the approaches covered; standing there dripping in the rain. I wondered what Vlasta was doing. I wondered if they had taken in Baba's husband for questioning, if they were knocking the poor devil about. I couldn't remember him; could hardly remember Baba; a vague impression of a stout woman, a broad, warm lap, a wart near her eyebrow. She couldn't have been very old; the Little Swine was her elder brother. He was—what? Fifty-five? Maminka was fifty-three. She would be about Maminka's age. I wondered what she had died of.

I slept presently.

The boiler room was chill and gray when I awoke, and I sat up in a panic, thinking I'd overslept. But I hadn't overslept.

The clocks were chiming the preliminaries, and I heard the first hour-stroke sound. It was five o'clock. I counted, shivering with cold and fear. I'd remembered what I had to do the instant I sat up and my stomach had turned over.

My teeth were chattering. I got off the camp bed and put on the jacket and moved around stretching my body. I could see no possibility of going through with the plan. I felt acutely ill, stiff and clumsy, physically incapable of the effort required. I thought the minute I got out into the street the S.N.B. men would be on me like a shot, and would march me away numb and speechless.

I wondered if I should make provision to kill myself in the event of failure: to get in first and make it quicker. I had the hammer. But how the hell did you kill yourself with a hammer?

The door of the wood cupboard was open. There was a strong temptation to go back in there again, to bury myself and warm up, to live through another drugged and drowsy day.

I didn't go back to the wood cupboard. I walked about the boiler room, circling the ladder. I lit another cigarette—one left—and smoked it in quick, nervous drags. The quarter past sounded. The half past. I was empty and hungry. But when, presently, I opened the packet of bread and sausage and tried to eat, I was sick. This physical misery, distracting me from the immediate problem, left me feeling a good deal calmer, and after it I sat quiet on the camp bed beneath the hatch, waiting.

Small, distant sounds of activity were coming from the waking world above. A train hooted, a car changed gear. There was no sound yet of the trams, or of that other special noise that I awaited.

Just before six o'clock I lit my last cigarette and smoked it lingeringly down to a small stub, and stamped it out.

It was time to be off.

I went up the ladder.

It was a still, gray morning, misty. I crossed the yard and unlocked the padlock and went out into the alley. The street was gray and damp from last night's rain. It was quite deserted, the buildings sober and silent.

I made my way up to the top where it ran out to the Malostranske, and withdrew into a deep doorway. A few hundred

185

yards away in the parallel Thunovska the watchers would be waiting, too. We seemed to have the damp, silent world to ourselves.

It seemed a hell of a long time between the quarter and the half past. But at last the first stroke sounded. Immediately after—so close to the stroke that I wondered if I'd been mistaken—there was the sound I was expecting. I came out of the doorway, moved as near to the corner as I dared and waited there for a moment, straining my ears. I had not been mistaken. Between the strokes it came again, quite clearly. It was a milkman.

The cart came trundling round from behind St. Mikulase, a blob of blue and white in the mist. I could hear the milkman exclaiming freely to his horse, boots ringing on the cobbles and bottles clanking, but I couldn't see him. The horse drew the cart a few yards into the square and stopped, shaking its head up and down.

The milkman came then, a big, red, beefy fellow in a dark blue overall and a white peaked cap. He replenished his wire basket at the cart, roaring endearments at the horse, and went off clanking across the square to serve the far side. Each time he returned to the horse he roared something that sounded like *"Whuyill! Whuyill!"* in response to which the horse slopped forward a few yards and stopped again.

I thought, *Oh, Jesus Christ,* and withdrew again into the doorway to practice a few silent *whuyills* to myself. The milkman was working round from the right; the Thunovska was on my left. I watched him for ten minutes until the cart had drawn level with my corner, and then with mindless action stepped out from the doorway, gesticulating.

The milkman looked at me.

I beckoned frantically.

Head forward in inquiry, he walked over with his empty basket. "What is it, comrade?"

He was sweating slightly; a smell of horses; an open, country face; a deep bass voice that awoke echoes from the early-morning buildings. I wondered if it was arousing any interest on the corner of the Thunovska. It was certainly arousing the interest

186

of the horse, which had begun to look across in the most pointed way.

I whispered, "Quick, quick," in panic. "In here a minute."

He followed me wonderingly into the doorway. "What's the trouble, comrade? What is it?"

"You go to the British Embassy?"

"*Yoh, yoh,* the Embassy. Why do you want to know?"

"It's this," I said. "Look at this."

Just at the last moment it was painfully hard to do it, the big sweating face so innocent.

"A hammer, comrade—what of it?"

I hit him on the head with it, hard. He seemed to put out his hand and lean on me just as I did it. The wire basket crashed to the ground. He looked at me with eyes wide open in mystified inquiry and puffed and fell down.

I unbuttoned his overall, shaking with panic, and tore it getting it off him and on to me. I put on his peaked cap, picked up the wire basket and walked out of the doorway, out of the street, out into the Malostranske. I felt as if I were walking out to my execution. I was trembling violently in every limb.

The horse, which had not turned its head away since the milkman had walked over, regarded me curiously. I said, *"Whu-yill!"* It came out in a strangled bleat. The horse merely stared. *Oh, damn and blast you, bloody well whuyill,* I urged it, putting out my hand to pat the large, dangerous head.

The horse bit me. It was not a sharp bite, more in the nature of a nip by a pair of nutcrackers, but painful. I stepped back and swore in its ear, softly but with great obscenity. I felt myself under acute observation. I had not dared turn round to the Thunovska. I doubted if they could have seen clearly in the mist my contretemps with the knowing animal. But the horse had not moved.

I went back to the cart and filled the basket with milk and cartons of sour cream, and turned blindly to walk to my goal.

I seemed to be walking for about two hours, on cotton wool, with my legs turned all to jelly. There were just two of them, one at each corner, buttoned-up and pinched in the gray mist.

I said, *"Dobry den,"* gruffly, peaked cap slanted over my eyes. *"Dobry den."*

"More rain again, I shouldn't wonder."

"Shouldn't wonder."

I was past. Unbelievably, I was past!

I walked up the Thunovska with my legs nearly collapsing under me. I turned in at the Embassy opening. The Union Jack, limp in the damp gray morning . . . a courtyard . . . steps . . .

There were big double doors, ornamental knockers, a bell push. I pressed it and heard the mad jangling inside somewhere. I was choked almost now, wits all away, nothing but the thumping of my heart, toes curled up hard inside my shoes.

There was no answer to the bell. I rang again, again, kept my finger on it. I didn't dare slam the knockers, had no idea at all what to do. The S.N.B. men would grow suspicious soon. The milkman would come to shortly. I'd not hit him all that hard.

I stepped back from the door. Away to the left of the courtyard was another door: CONSULATE. There was also an archway. Maybe somewhere at the back, in some domestic bits of the building, retainers would be stirring. I couldn't waste time investigating the possibilities of the archway. I thought, *Oh, God, I've had it,* and pressed, pressed the bell again. *Open up, get up, wake up, damn you!*

"You! Milkman! What are you doing?"

I turned. One of the buttoned-up men was standing at the entrance to the courtyard. My throat seemed to seize up. I opened my mouth speechlessly.

"Leave your milk and come away."

I said, "They told me—they told me to call."

"Put it down and leave."

"They want cream. The housekeeper said to call with sour cream. There's a reception."

He regarded me sourly. He seemed nonplused. He did not venture into the courtyard, but remained there watching me.

I turned in panic, grasped the knockers and began slamming furiously. The noise echoed thunderously in the courtyard. No answer.

"Right. Leave it now then. Come down here. I want to talk to you."

I didn't answer him. I turned blindly to thump the door, the knockers, the bell, lost now, no hope at all now, the end close in sight, in such a panic I could scarcely see or breathe. A commotion began in the street. A yell. The milkman. Another yell, another voice, shouting. Steps running. The S.N.B. man watching me turned away, exchanged a few sharp words and called, "Hi! You! Come here. Come here at once!" He had taken something out of his pocket. A pistol. There was no cover on the doorstep; nothing at all but the stone pediment, the big immovable doors.

I was so completely terrorized that all processes of thought seemed at that moment to stop. I remember that I bent and took a bottle of milk out of the basket. I don't know what I intended to do with this bottle—throw it at him, perhaps, defend myself in some way. I had not stopped pounding on the door, but I had given up my heart. Now, as the other man turned into the courtyard, there was a shuffling within the house, the clank of bolts.

I don't know, looking back, if the S.N.B. men would have dared to shoot me on the steps of the Embassy. Certainly I would not have gone with them otherwise. Perhaps, as they walked slowly up the courtyard in the misty morning, the two buttoned-up men were aware of this, were trying, in their chilled and worried state, to see some way out of the dilemma. In fact, the agony of decision never came.

While they were still several yards from the steps, one of the doors opened. I fell into the shadowy darkness, bumping into and knocking over the aged, black-clad crone who had opened it; not stopping, indeed, till one foot encountered a bucket of warm water and the other a bar of soap and my ill-used backside came to rest, jarred, numb but indubitably secure, twenty-five feet inside British territory. The bottle of milk, quite undamaged, was still in my hand.

chapter 13

"Hello. Feeling a bit more rested now?"

"Yes, thanks."

"You're looking rather more human. I'd like another session with you."

"Of course. Sit down."

He had already sat down. He was a tall, pale man called Roddinghead with a bulging, childlike forehead and small reptilian eyes. He had taken no pains to hide the fact that I had been causing him much trouble. I felt able to bear this. I was in bed in a small room in the Embassy. I had had two lots of sedative and two lots of sleep. I was feeling slightly mad with joy and relief.

Roddinghead said curtly, "It's that bit of paper. I've just had another cable from London telling me to get my finger out. I'll have to know a lot more about it."

"I'm afraid I've told you all I know."

"It isn't enough. Try closing your eyes again."

I closed my eyes.

"Now then, how big is it?"

"About the size of a packet of twenty cigarettes. Maybe a bit narrower."

"Very thin rice paper, you said."

"Yes."

"And curling at the edges."

"That's right."

"I want you to tell *me*. See it clearly. What's on the top?"

"The thing about Aldermaston. Banshee and Third-Stage, I think."

"Right. Now the bottom."

"I'm sorry. I really didn't look at it."

"Well, have a look at it now."

I gritted my teeth. It was the fourth time we had examined this lunatic cigarette-packet-sized bit of paper. I suppose it was part of some half-forgotten course. I could hear Roddinghead irritably tapping his pencil on his notebook.

"I'm afraid I can't remember."

"Try running your eye over it quickly. Anything stand out?"

"This isn't going to work, you know. I only saw the thing for a couple of seconds."

He made a savage note in his book. "All right. Now this old nanny, Hana Simkova. You say you're absolutely certain you never mentioned her to the girl?"

"I'm positive I didn't."

"Couldn't have dropped a reference when you were under the weather, say?"

"No. It never cropped up at all."

"So you reckon she must have got it from this fellow Cunliffe?"

"Yes."

"Who got it from whoever was watching you?"

"Well, he must have. I never told him myself."

"Right. Who else knew this nanny?"

"That's very hard to say. I've been thinking about it. There's her brother, of course—the Mr. Nimek I told you about."

"Yes, yes. They've taken him in for a going-over. . . . I'm glad you're amused by all this," he said malevolently. "I can assure you nobody else is."

"I'm sorry," I said, trying hard to control my delight at this marvelous thing that was happening to the Little Swine. "I was trying to think who else could know of Baba. Both my mother and Mr. Gabriel have quite a large circle of émigré friends in England with whom they correspond frequently. Quite a lot of people could have known about her."

"I'd like a list of the names of these friends if you can remember them."

"I'll try."

"The point being, of course, that we want to find out who was watching you."

"I'd like to find that out myself."

191

He gave me another malevolent look with his reptilian eyes. "Not that anyone could care terribly about you. The idea is to pick up all the network."

"Yes. Right. I'll try and think what names I've heard mentioned."

"You say your mother gave you a letter to this Hana Simkova. She evidently didn't know she was dead."

"Evidently not."

"How do you account for the fact that Mr. Gabriel knew and she didn't?"

"He is very devoted to her. He keeps unpleasant news from her."

"I wish someone would do the same for me. Now, then, this man Pavelka . . ."

That was the fourth interrogation. There were many more.

I stayed at the British Embassy in Prague for ten weeks. I occupied a small room on the third floor. I was not the most welcome of guests. Apart from Roddinghead, whose exact function I never discovered, and two younger and rather more civil colleagues, I had no contact with the staff. Nobody quite knew what to do with me; the policy appeared to be to pretend that I didn't exist.

I was confined to my room. I received no letters and could write none. I listened to the wireless for hours on end. I read numerous books. In the evening I was escorted down the back stairs by Roddinghead or one of his colleagues to walk about in a small walled yard.

The summer passed. The days shortened. I had no complaints. It was better than running up and down alleys. And I had plenty of time to think. I thought about Maminka, and hoped that Imre was devising suitable explanations for my absence. The old booby himself, I thought, must be distracted half out of his mind at not hearing from me. I thought of Maura, and wondered sickly what she must be making of my silence.

I thought of the Little Swine and to what extent he had been involved in this mad and now half-forgotten nightmare of the third stage of the Banshee. And of Mrs. Nolan, and how long she would wait before clearing out my things and installing someone else in my room.

But mainly I thought of my future, such as it was. That it would not be spent with Pavelka was one thing at least that I had gathered from Roddinghead. Pavelka had not paid for my trips. He hadn't any money. He lived in a single room in Bayswater and, like myself, had been a dupe.

On the question of the Little Swine, Roddinghead was curiously evasive. Mr. Nimek was being "looked into." A "bit of research" was going on. One way or the other, it looked as if I was finished there, anyway.

So I thought of Bela and Canada. But after a few weeks I didn't even think of this. To live in a single room, waited on, one's immediate needs satisfied, neither prisoner nor free man is a curiously anesthetizing experience. I slept, woke, ate, listened, read, slept again. Over and over again, day after day. A dreamlike time. Dreamlike still in the memory.

After the third or fourth week, the interrogations tailed off. I saw Roddinghead less frequently. His manner toward me had ripened slightly. I thought they were no longer bothering him from London. The reptilian eyes ceased to regard me with loathing. They were wry, sardonic, affable even.

He was absent for a week or so toward the end of the summer, and reappeared one day bronzed, the bulging forehead peeling.

He said, "Hello. How's the prisoner of Zenda?"

"Fine, thanks. Been away?"

"Yes. To the Tatras. Managed to snatch a few days. Things are a bit slack now."

"They're a bit slack for me, too. Heard anything about me going yet?"

"No. Still a few ends to be tied up. Getting fed up with us, are you?"

"I'd like to go home."

"So would I, cock." He ambled about the room, picking up a book, a magazine.

"What's happening exactly?"

"Nothing much."

"Do you think they've forgotten about me?"

"I doubt it."

"Have they managed to pick up all the members of the—of

193

the espionage network?" Even at this distance it seemed a ludicrous thing to be discussing.

"I believe so. All they know about, anyway. I shan't be requiring your further thoughts on the subject."

"Was there anybody I didn't know about?"

"As to that," he said, reptilian eyes smiling, "we don't know quite how much you know, do we?"

"Do you mean they're keeping me here because they're still not sure of me?"

"Might be. Might not. I don't know. I don't care very much, either. You got yourself into this. Maybe you won't be in such a hurry next time. There's no future in it, cock, no future at all," he said, moving to the door.

I said quickly, "Just a minute." I'd hoped he was in the mood for a chat. He dropped things from time to time. "What about Cunliffe? Is he in the bag?"

"So I believe."

"And the person who was watching me?"

"No information. They don't keep sending me postcards, you know."

"How about Nimek?"

"Nimek?"

"The one I told you about who ran the little glass firm I used to work for. The brother of my old nanny."

"Oh, him. He's a funny fellow, Nimek. He still writes to his sister, you know."

"Still writes to Baba? But she's dead."

"Yes. So you said. Maybe nobody told him. Come to that," he said, opening the door, "maybe nobody told her, either. She was looking remarkably lifelike last week. We sent somebody round to see her."

I stared at the door as it closed behind him, thunderstruck.

The sting-in-the-tail rapidly became his specialty after that. Perhaps his job bored him. Maybe I helped to break the tedium. I can't remember all the discussions. I remember very clearly one other. I had been wondering in a bemused sort of way why I had been involved in the operation at all. I said to Roddinghead, "It was surely a bit of a Heath-Robinsonish way of passing valuable secrets."

"Yes, wasn't it."

"Couldn't they have put it through the diplomatic bag?"

"I don't know, old cock. Maybe it had to be a very independent operation. There's still quite a bit of it going on."

"Were they a bunch of amateurs?"

"That isn't my information."

"You mean Cunliffe was a regular spy?"

"That's what I mean. It wasn't his only name, you won't be surprised to hear."

"Would I have heard of him by any other name?"

"Oh, yes. You gave me one of them. It was on the list of émigrés."

"Which one was it?"

"Can't remember offhand. But he had quite a nice lot of addresses, too, one in Ireland. He'd lived there apparently for a long time once—had a wife and daughter with him there."

"Whereabouts in Ireland?"

"I've forgotten. He separated from his wife some years ago, and the daughter lives in London."

"Was she in it—in this plot, too, the daughter?"

"Oh, yes. Quite a family affair."

"I see."

"Don't worry," he said, smiling and reptilian at the door. "We've nobbled her, too. You'll really have to take up another profession. You don't get much of a run these days."

I didn't listen to the wireless that afternoon. I didn't read either. I sat looking out at the trees and the gray sky. I felt sad and sick. The last piece of the jigsaw had fallen into place. I saw exactly how it must have happened.

The leaves fell in the Embassy gardens. The wind rose. A light but incessant drizzle set in. I had to put the light on several mornings when I got up. One day after breakfast there was a knock at the door and Roddinghead came in. His two colleagues were with him. He had a scroll of paper in his hand.

He said coldly, "Mr. Whistler, I am directed to read you the following." He unrolled the paper and read it out, at speed. It was the Official Secrets Act, 1911. When he had finished he handed me the paper. "Please read it over for yourself."

"What is it? What's happening?"

"Go ahead and read it."

I read over the Act in a state of some nervousness. The three of them watched me. I handed it back to Roddinghead.

"Have you understood what you've read?"

"I think so."

"Stamp, please," Roddinghead said. One of them gave him a rubber stamp and an inked pad. He impressed it on the paper and produced a fountain pen. "Sign it."

"Why?"

"I'm telling you to. Go ahead."

I signed where he pointed. "Look, what the hell's happening? What's going on here?"

Roddinghead briskly rolled up the paper, and, his official business evidently then over, relaxed. "You're going home, cock," he said amiably.

"Home! When?"

"Today. In about a couple of hours, I should think."

"Today? But I—why didn't you let me know?"

"Sorry. Only got the wire a few minutes ago."

I was so stunned I could merely gape at him.

"They're sending a plane in from Germany for you. Cunliffe and his daughter are flying off from the other side."

It seemed that an exchange had been arranged; that Cunliffe's plane would fly east as mine flew west, both aircraft leaving together.

"Sorry I couldn't give you a little more warning that it was coming off. Still, you didn't bring much luggage, did you? Just the single bottle of milk, as I recall."

"You mean I'll be free?"

"Within limits. The limits being as defined in the paper you've just signed. You're bloody lucky. You could have got a few years for what you've been up to. Evidently nothing is to be said about it. By you or anyone else. No heroic little dining-out stories. No sensational adventures in the newspapers. And I'm bound to point out that the Act means exactly what it says on that point. You so much as whisper a word to anyone, with or without *mens rea*—i.e., guilty intent—and you'll find yourself inside. O.K.?"

I said O.K.

196

I left before lunch. An Embassy car drove me to the airport, Roddinghead sitting beside me in the back. We waited in the car until the plane landed, and then drove out to where it stood on the apron. There were several buttoned-up characters standing around as I walked up the aircraft steps with Roddinghead. He looked straight ahead. He had said practically nothing to me in the car.

In the aircraft he held out his hand. "Well, cheerio, then, cock."

"Cheerio."

"I hope we made your stay a pleasant one."

I felt too bloodless for wisecracks. I said, "Thank you. Thank you very much for everything."

"Don't come back."

He went.

The plane took off almost immediately. Four hours later I was in London.

When you have imagined a homecoming for so long and in circumstances so diverse and apparently hopeless, the real thing tends to be something of an anticlimax. I got off the Tube at Gloucester Road and walked slowly to Fitzwalter Square in a mood of profound melancholy. It was six o'clock, a chill and darkening afternoon. The wind scurried leaves along the pavements. I felt like one of them myself, blown by any wind that came along.

From the airport a car had taken me to an office in Queen Anne's Gate. A man whose name I never learned had inquired if I had understood the provisions of the Official Secrets Act. I said I had. I had signed an undertaking to repay all moneys that had been laid out on my account. These appeared to have been for ten weeks' rent at Mrs. Nolan's, and seven weeks' lock-up at Ratface's. As the man said, this had been necessary to forestall inquiries. Everything had been taken care of in my absence; all interested parties had been informed that I was abroad on important business in which the government had a commercial interest, and that I had been asked not to correspond. He had then lent me a pound and wished me a very good afternoon.

197

I had had a cup of tea and an Osborne biscuit at Queen Anne's Gate. This was the only food I had consumed since breakfast. I was not so much hungry as devitalized. An enormous number of things had happened to me since I had walked these streets last. I felt I should have returned exhilarated, bouncing with joy, everything changed in some large and mysterious way. Nothing had changed. The gray buildings were as they had always been. The buses trundled drably along. The people walked by intent on their business. The wind whipped the leaves. I had been away and now I had come back. The summer was gone. I was three months older.

As I came to number seventy-four I got out my latchkey— miraculously retained through all my changes of clothing—and opened the door. I don't know what I expected to happen. Nothing did.

The hall was in darkness, the wireless on in Mrs. Nolan's lair. I stood there for a moment, listening and taking in the familiar odors. I didn't think I could bear to face her. I closed the door quietly behind me and walked slowly up the stairs.

On the third floor I opened my door and switched on the light. Everything in its accustomed place, neat, tidy, dusted. I might never have left it. Beside the plant pot on the plush tablecloth, however, was a large pile of letters. I flipped over them. Library reminders, football pools, circulars, two letters from my mother, three from Maura. . . . I didn't look any further. I took off the mac presented to me at the Embassy and sat down on the divan and lit a cigarette, looking round.

All this was far from being in the spirit of the returning traveler. I thought what I needed was a sleep. I stubbed out the cigarette presently and flaked out on the divan and went off almost immediately.

I must have slept for three hours. It was quite dark when I came to. I knew where I was before I opened my eyes, and lay there for a few moments feeling the sudden warm rush of relief and satisfaction flowing over me. The old batteries were charging up again, I thought. I was home, anyway.

I went down to Bournemouth next morning. Mrs. Nolan had been in a considerable twitter when I had poked my head round her door the previous evening. She had been sitting toasting her legs at the first fire of the autumn, but had bustled about in high excitement getting me something to eat and priming me on all that had gone.

It seemed that an exquisite man from the government had called to tell her about me, what an important job I was doing, and the arrangements I had made for paying the rent. My young lady had phoned very often at the beginning, but not for some weeks now. Mr. Gabriel had been phoning regularly from Bournemouth. And another foreign gentleman had been phoning too, a Mr. Nimek, and very angry he had been.

All this, together with the familiar food and the well-remembered brown-boot-polish tea, had proved highly revivifying. Imperceptibly, as she shaded in the ten missing weeks, I had felt a curious internal reconstitution taking place, as though ribs and organs were being replaced after a period of disuse.

I didn't ring up Bournemouth. I wasn't sure what I wanted to say. I thought I'd better think of that on the way down, and immediately after breakfast went round to the enterprise of Ratface Rickett to claim my car. It was a new and refined version of the Ratface I had known, a most mannerly little Ratface, who gave me a kindly salutation and actually shoved in four gallons without cash or cavil before waving me off the premises. By eleven o'clock I was halfway there.

At this time yesterday, I thought, slowing down through Winchester, I was sitting by the window on the third floor of the Embassy in Prague. Just twenty-four hours before I had been a prisoner in the middle of Europe, staring out at bare branches and gray skies. It seemed unbelievable. The whole episode was unbelievable: the night on the Vaclavske Namesti, the hours in the arms of the perfidious giantess of Barrandov, the alleys, the furniture store, the boiler room. No longer even a nightmare; too remote and impersonal for a nightmare; something I had read somewhere at some time and had remembered, names and all: Vlasta, Svoboda, Borsky, Vlcek, Galushka, Josef, fornicating Frantisek, Roddinghead.

Of them all only Roddinghead, detached and derisive, lingered as a flesh-and-blood reality. Only Roddinghead could inspire belief that these other phantoms had actually ever existed;

that they still existed, going about their business far away in gray and steepled Prague.

No future in it, cock, Roddinghead had said. No future indeed. Not even a very meaningful or profitable past. My only legacy of three dangerous and demented months was a bill for rent and a certain facility with a blunt instrument. Someone had steered me into all this. Someone should pay for it, I thought, swinging on to the A35. But I doubted if anybody would.

The old booby was examining a sheet of stamps when I went into his room. The glass fell out of his eye and his mouth dropped open with shock.

"Nicolas! Nicolas, my boy! Oh, thank God! It is wonderful to see you."

"Hello, Uncle. How've you been?"

"She has been worrying dreadfully. I just haven't known what to tell her. Have you been to see her yet?"

"I've just arrived. I thought I'd better have a word with you first. How is she?"

"Let me look at you, my boy." He stood up, shaking a bit. It was none too warm in the room. He had a muffler on and a cardigan underneath the alpaca jacket. He looked distinctly older, folds of skin hanging from his face and his eyes a bit glazed. His breath was whistling out with its accustomed vigor, however. "Oh, thank God you are here. Since the man from the Foreign Office came her head has been full of nothing else. She worries me from morning to night. She is a remarkable woman, your mother, when she gets a single idea in her head."

I smiled back with exasperated affection. Some people have a permanent claim on one's affections, whatever they do, however they behave. It was impossible to think of him merely as a man, subject to the same pressures and temptations of other men. He was neuter, a huge, flabby, permanent old booby with a single preoccupation.

He sat down again, shaking, and pulled the muffler tighter round his neck. "She asked him," he said, "she asked him how long you would be in Prague. I didn't know where to put myself."

"What did he say?"

"He was astounded. He asked why she should think you were

in Prague. So of course—you know your mother—she told him. She told him you had gone to start up the family business again. She told him your entire history from a baby. I couldn't make out what was happening. I didn't understand this business with the government. I didn't know what to think, Nicolas. And she sees I am worried," he said, tapping a finger against his forehead intensely. "She has a wonderful intuition, your mother. All the time she asks questions. She makes herself ill. She doesn't give me a moment's peace. And I'm ill myself, Nicolas. I am not a healthy man. But enough," he said. "Enough about me. Tell me what's been happening to you. Tell me everything."

I had meant to do this. I had meant to tell him each single and minute detail of it, the beatings-up, the running up and down alleys, the constant terror; the whole of the three awful months. I had been thinking about it as I parked the car and walked into the hotel and up to his room. I had been thinking of the expression on his face when he knew that I knew. I had thought of it a lot since that afternoon on the third floor of the Embassy in Prague. Now that it came to the point I couldn't do it.

I said instead, "Why did you do it, Uncle?"

"What, Nicolas? What do you mean?"

"Why did you spy on me for this man Cunliffe? Why did you send me out there?"

"I send you? Cunliffe?" He looked at me wildly. "I don't know what you say, Nicolas. I don't understand you."

"You'd better try. I don't know what you called him. I mean the man who asked you for all the details of me. The one you telephoned when I left Bournemouth last time. The one who made up the story about Uncle Bela dying."

The room went perfectly still. The hairs at his nose stopped waving for a moment. Then they began again, very fast. He breathed heavily. He leaned forward. "I should like you to understand, Nicolas," he said, and cleared his throat, breathing noisily—"I should like you to understand, my boy, that all was intended for the best. I love you. You are like my own son to me. Not only for the sake of your dear mother. Do you think I could do a bad thing to you?"

"Why did you?"

"Why did I? It's a bad thing? It's not better than working for Nimek?"

I opened my mouth, but he held out his hand, breathing loudly. "Sometimes, Nicolas, it is necessary to give a little push. I wasn't happy at your progress with Nimek. I could see there would be nothing with him. I had to consider the effect on your mother. She wants you to be a success."

I goggled at him. It was hard to know where the hell to start. I said, "Do you know why I went out there? Do you mean to say you've got no idea what I was supposed to do?"

"I didn't want to know. I didn't ask. It was enough that you were working for Mr. Pavelka!"

He told me about it then. How Cunliffe had written to him saying he was looking for a smart young man to be an assistant to one of his clients. How he had gone up to see him and learned the client was Pavelka.

"Pavelka! You wouldn't have remembered Pavelka from the olden days. He was a big man, colossal! It would have been your father's dearest wish that Mr. Pavelka would take an interest in you."

Cunliffe had told him the job was confidential; that Pavelka had grown a little eccentric and wished to investigate my capabilities in his own way, and that I must know nothing about it. So Imre had told Cunliffe everything about me; about my expectations from Bela; about how I worked and how I lived; that I earned very little and spent that little on the car. . . .

I said, "Did you know he was going to make up the story about Uncle Bela dying?"

He looked at the floor, breathing noisily. He said, "That I couldn't understand. I tell you frankly, Nicolas, I was uneasy. But he told me Mr. Pavelka positively insisted. He said he wanted to see how you would react to the news. Nicolas, I am no great businessman! I don't pretend I have made a success of my life. Pavelka, to me, is a colossus. If I understood how his mind works maybe I would be as successful as Pavelka."

"Haven't you met him?"

"Only once, in Prague, many years ago."

"You didn't meet him here in London?"

"No, no," he said, smiling. "Pavelka isn't interested in me. Pavelka is still a very big man. I thought I was acting for the best for you, Nicolas. If he wanted that kind of peculiar investigation, I didn't want to stand in your way. I was worried only for your mother. I knew you would want to run down and tell her this news about Bela. I would have to put you off. I didn't feel good about that. What was I to do? Tell me, Nicolas. Tell me if you think I did wrong."

"I don't know, Uncle," I said, gazing helplessly at the old booby. "I don't know about anything. Didn't he tell you he meant to send me to Prague?"

"No," he said uneasily. He didn't look at me.

"But you knew it. You guessed it."

He said in Czech, "No, no, it wasn't so." He was breathing like an express train.

"What made you tell him Baba was dead, then?"

He didn't answer, clenching and unclenching his hands.

"Why did you tell *me* she was dead?"

He said, "Nicolas . . ." and stopped. The heavy folds of flesh on his face began suddenly to shake. The puckered, mottled flesh round his eyes screwed up. He was crying. I said with shock and horror, "Oh, no, Uncle. Uncle, please don't. I'm sorry. I'm terribly sorry. Please stop it. It isn't anything."

He bent forward so that I shouldn't see his face. I put my arm round his shoulders. They shook tumultuously. He got out his handkerchief and buried his face in it. His shuddering neck was fat, creased and badly in need of a haircut; and so bloody pathetic I practically joined him with the hanky. I felt full of shame and self-disgust.

He blew his nose presently and sat up, mopping his eyes. They were watery and discolored. I looked away. He said thickly, "I must tell you all, my boy."

"I don't want to know. I don't want to hear anything more about it. It's forgotten."

"It isn't forgotten. I can't forget it." He shook his big, stupid old head. "I am ashamed! I am ashamed before you, Nicolas! Of course I guessed it. Ah, I'm not such an old fool as that. He started asking me if you knew anyone in Prague, if anyone was there still. Oh, this was later after I'd had time to think about it. He asked me if you'd had a nanny or a governess who might still be there. Of course I remembered Hana. I didn't want any trouble for you or for her. I told him she was dead. He asked if she'd been married, if you knew her husband. I said you wouldn't remember him. . . .

"Of course, when your mother gave you the letter to Hana, I had to tell you the same thing. But I was already very nervous. I couldn't understand this business. I was beginning to wonder what they wanted you to do. I thought you'd found out and didn't want to speak to me again. You remember, I telephoned you. I asked if you were offended with me about anything."

"Yes, Uncle, I remember." I did remember, just at that moment. It seemed a lifetime ago.

"And I began to wonder if Pavelka was really involved, or if this man was just tricking me—he was always sly, that one, even in the old days. He used to be a lawyer. It really was for Pavelka?"

"Not really, Uncle. Pavelka was fooled too."

"He fooled Pavelka also?" he said, and sat nodding his head for a bit, comforted in a melancholy sort of way, and then looked at me and looked away again. "But still this is not all, Nicolas. It is still not the worst. There is the money."

"What money?"

"He gave me fifty pounds. He said it was an introduction fee if you proved suitable for the job. I spent it. I couldn't give it back again. We would have had to move out of here if he wanted it back again."

There wasn't anything to be said to this, and a rather miserable silence fell.

After a moment he burst out, "Nicolas, understand! For myself, I would sooner beg in the gutter! It is your dear mother I think about. She has no idea what things cost. She thinks her annuity covers everything. It doesn't even pay the hotel bill! I must buy her clothes, cigarettes, the little extras she likes. . . . I am not complaining, my boy. Don't think I complain. It is my whole pleasure to do these things for her. But lately, I don't know, business isn't so good. . . . I think I'm getting old. Too old," he said, nodding to the sheet of stamps he had dropped when I came in.

204

All this was, in its way, rather more hideous than all the primitive things that had been happening to me for the past three months. We sat staring at each other in dismal silence. Something came to mind, after a while. Throughout his recital, Imre had been calling Cunliffe by another name.

I said. "This man you went to see in London. What do you call him?"

"Vogler. It wasn't Vogler you saw?"

I said, wearily, that I supposed it was. Vogler; and Vogler on the list of half-remembered émigré names I had handed to Roddinghead. I said, "He called himself Cunliffe. He had an office in Francis Street and a secretary with glasses and her hair parted in the middle."

"*Yoh, yoh.* That is Anna, his daughter."

Bunface. Miss Vogler. Cunliffe's daughter. I had rumbled that one, too, that afternoon when Roddinghead had told me about it. It was nice to get it confirmed. It didn't seem to help the present situation a great deal.

Imre sighed presently. "Well, Nicolas, I have now told you all. You think badly of me?"

"No, Uncle."

"I am bitterly ashamed, my boy. I apologize to you."

"You don't need to feel ashamed. I understand."

"Maybe in the long run you won't feel so badly. After all, if the government is really interested, it can't be—"

"It isn't. That was just a lot of hokum too."

"Oh, I am sorry. I am sorry, Nicolas."

We sat again in turgid silence. After a while, sighing gustily, he said, "So one door closes, another opens. It isn't the end of the world. At least you can go to Canada with a clear mind."

I said, "Yes," returning to the familiar lunacy.

"After all, you're an intelligent boy. You can learn the business quickly. And you've got to admit the prospects with Bela are magnificent."

"Yes. If he'll do anything for me."

He was looking at me in an odd sort of way. "If he'll do anything for you! You mean you don't know? You haven't heard?"

"Heard what? What about?"

He was gazing at me in astonishment, the hairs of his nose waving in his powerful breath. I said, "What?" in a kind of squeak, practically leaping up and down in front of him. "What is it, Uncle? What are you trying to say? What in God's name is it I'm supposed to have heard?"

"About Bela," he said.

Typically, he'd left it to the last. Bela had written. He had written saying specifically that I was his heir. He had written to say that he had sent me a one-way ticket. He wanted me in the business right away.

"Naturally," Maminka said, "I told him you would have to consider it. After all, does he suppose you can drop all your important business to fly to him the minute he remembers his responsibilities? He was always thoughtless, even as a boy. I told him perhaps you wouldn't care for the business, perhaps you would wish to act merely as a kind of consultant. I told him . . ."

I said, "Yes, Maminka. If you could just please try to remember when you wrote him. If you could try to think again."

"My dear child, I've told you—a month, two months ago. What does it matter? Let me look at you again."

"And he hasn't replied?"

"But of course he wouldn't, at this time of the year. This is the time they are so busy. I know Bela."

I only hoped she was right. Her clear almond eyes were smiling gaily at me. A large number of undigested items had recently come my way. I said, "And Maura was here? Maura was actually here three times?"

"*Bobitchka,* I've already told you. You are like a little puppy dog. Try to stand still for a minute."

"And you can't remember when she was here last? Do you think it was when Bela's letter came? Was it when she heard about Bela?"

"Nicolas, I'm not a calendar. Imre might know. Maybe I would think better with a cigarette. Do you know that ogre has tried to stop me smoking for good! He says it is my throat. Oh, I understand very well his reasons! Darling boy," she said, catching my arm, "I implore you to stay still for a minute. You are

206

making me quite giddy. Here, come and sit with me. Now tell me everything from Prague. Whom did you see? Where did you go? Did Baba weep to see you again?"

I told her presently. It was a very detailed story, containing everything she wanted to hear. She sat and held my hands, her lovely eyes alive with recollection, exclaiming from time to time. It is always a pleasure to tell Maminka a story, and this one certainly had many merits. It didn't contravene the Official Secrets Act, 1911.

I went back that night after borrowing a quid from Imre. I had meant to ask for five but, remembering what he had told me, desisted. I had only twelve and six left from the other pound. I didn't know how I was going to manage. I thought God would provide. I thought Maura might, at a pinch. I felt slightly drunk.

I thought of Maura, speeding after my headlights through the dark New Forest. I was pretty sure why she'd stayed away from Bournemouth. Bela's letter; the big time. She hadn't wanted to push herself. She hadn't wished to give the appearance of getting her foot in the door. The young master might have other ideas now. If she had only known; that I had been through all this before. There was a lot Maura didn't know. There was a lot she was going to know. I shoved my foot down and fairly let rip.

Just before Lyndhurst the road bends sharply right. I took it at sixty and suddenly was ramming the brake pedal practically through the floor. A pony was standing in the middle of the road looking into the headlights. I don't know if I touched him. I skidded right, left, tires shrieking, tree trunks rearing into the beam both sides. Car going over, over . . . not quite. Steady. Stopped. Silence. Light beams staring calmly into shrubbery. I had stalled.

I got out after a moment, heart still in my throat. The car was slanted into the shrubbery, nose buried in a bush. The registration plate was bent. That seemed to be the only damage. I got back in and started and reversed slowly. She came out quite easily and I pulled into the side of the road and switched off again and lit a cigarette and watched my hand still shaking. I thought it was the sort of Charleyish move I could always

207

expect of myself: to come through the three dangerous and fantastic months in Prague and end by piling myself up against a tree in the New Forest. I started off again presently. I didn't go at more than forty after that.

I had left Bournemouth just after seven o'clock. It was a quarter to ten before I drew up outside her house.

She had been washing her hair. It hung straight and damply gleaming and pleasantly scented. She was in a dressing gown and had no make-up on and seemed so small and finely drawn, after some I had known, that I wanted nothing so much as simply to gaze at her. We were sitting on the floor in front of the gas fire, holding hands.

She said, "Oh, Nicolas, if only I'd known. If only you could have given me some hint."

"I couldn't. I shouldn't be telling you about it now. They could still put me in prison."

"And you only guessed when this man asked about your nanny?"

I nodded. Some slight amendments had been needed to the official version. Vlasta had undergone a change of sex. "Yes. I knew I had never mentioned Baba. And later on, of course, when I heard that Baba was not in fact dead I realized where the information must have come from. It could only have come from Imre, because he was the only person who said Baba was dead."

She was silent for a long time. I withdrew one hand and put my arm round her and kissed her neck. It smelled of shampoo.

She said, "You're quite sure about us, are you?"

"Never surer of anything in my life."

"And you want to go to Canada right away?"

"Don't you want me to?"

"Because I've been thinking." Her eyes were blinking rapidly and intelligently at the gas fire. "I want to go with you. We could get married first. I mean, if you're really sure you want to. If you're absolutely certain of it. We could get a special license."

I looked at her and felt the faintest pang. She was a wonderful girl, a splendid girl in so many ways. If she didn't just have this thing about working everything out. Her eyes flickered at me and I realized I had been too long in answering.

I said, "Why, Maura, that's *just* what I want. That's a marvelous thing." And it probably was.

"It would only take a few days. And there are lots of things you need to clear up first—your car and other bits and pieces. And the Little Swine—we must have a clear understanding about your shares. He'll have to buy you out. Oh, Nicolas," she said, taking my head in her two hands and kissing me gently on the lips. "You're a lovely old idiot. I should have been looking after you long ago, do you know that?"

And again she was probably right.

"If only you'd told me about all this business. If only you could have dropped a word right at the beginning."

"Well. It's over now, and there's nothing you could have done about it. And anyway," I said, a bit irritably, "I got away with it. That's something in the circumstances."

"Oh, Nicolas, of course it is. You've been tremendously clever and terribly brave, and I love you. But you ought to have been a bit more careful about that man Cunliffe. You could have looked him up in the Law List right away."

"Why should I have looked him up in the Law List?"

"Well, why not? He didn't have anything about being a solicitor on his notepaper. And he was telling you about this legacy. I'd have looked him up. I'd have looked him up right away. It's the first thing I would have done. And then none of this need have happened."

And she probably would; and it probably needn't, I thought with a sudden grave and lowering feeling in my vitals.

"Oh, Nicolas, I've upset you."

"No, you haven't, silly."

"Yes, I have. And I didn't mean to. And I bet I wouldn't have looked up the list, that's only a thing you think of afterwards. Oh, Nicolas, you silly old silly, I do love you, and I wanted to make up to you for everything." She was kissing me in a certain kind of way between her words, and presently my spirits recovered. And she did make up for it.

It was after one when I left. I tiptoed down the stairs and out into the dark square in some confusion of mind; excited, perturbed, not knowing, as they say, whether I was on my knee or my elbow.

I drove home slowly and put the covers on the car and went in and up the three flights and switched the light on. The letters were lying as I had left them on the plush tablecloth. I went through them again, standing there in my raincoat. It was there, of course; a franked envelope I had mistaken for a circular.

My dear Nicolas,
Excuse the short note. I am busy and not well. Do not tell this to your mother. I have been thinking for some time to make a trip to England and to get an idea of you. This is not possible. I have a slight paralysis of the right side. I repeat, do not tell this to your mother. I want you, Nicolas, to come out to see me right away. I enclose you your ticket. You will understand me.

Your loving uncle,
Bela

It was dated August 23, five weeks ago. The ticket was inside.

I took off my raincoat. I went and brushed my teeth in the bathroom and undressed and switched off the light. Mrs. Nolan had drawn the curtains. I knew I wouldn't sleep for a bit, and I didn't want to lie in the dark. So I opened the curtains and got into bed and lay there with my arms behind my head, looking out at the night sky.

I had been shuttling about a bit lately. I wasn't sure that I knew myself. Too many things happening, a surplus of experience still to be absorbed. I thought maybe none of it had happened. Maybe it was a dream and I would shortly awake to face another day in the service of the Little Swine. But I knew it was not a dream. There was that inner disturbance, the sickness of events; a sensation of distances having been covered. It was not unpleasant. It was not particularly pleasant. I had been living it up, after a fashion.

An airplane drifted slowly across the window, winking like a firefly. Long ranges of cloud stood coldly corrugated in the moonlight. The sky was still now; not racing as on that other night, when the iron king had leapt with his iron horse in the moonlight.

None of it had been necessary, Maura had said. None of it need have happened. I didn't know about that. The pony in the New Forest need not have happened. It had happened. A part of oneself went out to meet the event. A part of oneself remained involved with it; one was diminished by it. It took time to recover what had been lost.

The airplane vanished slowly off the edge of the pane. I thought there was rather more Thinking going on here than was strictly called for. Events were mainly incalculable, their significance always dubious. If experience taught anything, it was not to think too much, but to sharpen up the responses. It was a lesson I had learnt on the night that Wenceslas leaped in the moonlight. I thought I'd got it now. I thought my responses had sharpened up a bit, and closed my eyes and went to sleep, not dissatisfied.

THE PERENNIAL LIBRARY MYSTERY SERIES

John & Emery Bonett

A BANNER FOR PEGASUS   P 554, $2.40

DEAD LION   P 563, $2.40

Christianna Brand

GREEN FOR DANGER   P 551, $2.50

TOUR DE FORCE   P 572, $2.40

James Byrom

OR BE HE DEAD   P 585, $2.84

Marjorie Carleton

VANISHED   P 559, $2.40

George Harmon Coxe

MURDER WITH PICTURES   P 527, $2.25

Edmund Crispin

BURIED FOR PLEASURE   P 506, $2.50

Lionel Davidson

THE MENORAH MEN   P 592, $2.84

NIGHT OF WENCESLAS   P 595, $2.84

THE ROSE OF TIBET   P 593, $2.84

D. M. Devine

MY BROTHER'S KILLER   P 558, $2.40

Kenneth Fearing

THE BIG CLOCK   P 500, $1.95

Andrew Garve

THE ASHES OF LODA	P 430, $1.50
THE CUCKOO LINE AFFAIR	P 451, $1.95
A HERO FOR LEANDA	P 429, $1.50
MURDER THROUGH THE LOOKING GLASS	P 449, $1.95
NO TEARS FOR HILDA	P 441, $1.95
THE RIDDLE OF SAMSON	P 450, $1.95

Michael Gilbert

BLOOD AND JUDGMENT	P 446, $1.95
THE BODY OF A GIRL	P 459, $1.95
THE DANGER WITHIN	P 448, $1.95
FEAR TO TREAD	P 458, $1.95

Joe Gores

HAMMETT	P 631, $2.84

C. W. Grafton

BEYOND A REASONABLE DOUBT	P 519, $1.95

Edward Grierson

THE SECOND MAN	P 528, $2.25

Cyril Hare

DEATH IS NO SPORTSMAN	P 555, $2.40
DEATH WALKS THE WOODS	P 556, $2.40
AN ENGLISH MURDER	P 455, $2.50
TENANT FOR DEATH	P 570, $2.84
TRAGEDY AT LAW	P 522, $2.25
UNTIMELY DEATH	P 514, $2.25
THE WIND BLOWS DEATH	P 589, $2.84
WITH A BARE BODKIN	P 523, $2.25

If you enjoyed this book you'll want to know about
THE PERENNIAL LIBRARY MYSTERY SERIES

Buy them at your local bookstore or use this coupon for ordering:

Qty	P number	Price
_____	_____	_____
_____	_____	_____
_____	_____	_____
_____	_____	_____
_____	_____	_____
_____	_____	_____
_____	_____	_____
_____	_____	_____
_____	_____	_____
_____	_____	_____
_____	_____	_____
_____	_____	_____
_____	_____	_____
_____	_____	_____
_____	_____	_____
_____	_____	_____

	postage and handling charge	$1.00
	_____ book(s) @ $0.25	_____
	TOTAL	[ ]

Prices contained in this coupon are Harper & Row invoice prices only.
They are subject to change without notice, and in no way reflect the prices at
which these books may be sold by other suppliers.

**HARPER & ROW, Mail Order Dept. #PMS, 10 East 53rd St., New
York, N.Y. 10022.**

Please send me the books I have checked above. I am enclosing $_____
which includes a postage and handling charge of $1.00 for the first book and
25¢ for each additional book. Send check or money order. No cash or
C.O.D.s please

Name_____

Address_____

City_____ State_____ Zip_____

Please allow 4 weeks for delivery. USA only. This offer expires 8/31/83
Please add applicable sales tax.